BLUE WO

BLUE CURSE

BRAD MAGNARELLA

Copyright © 2017 by Brad Magnarella

All rights reserved.

No part of this book may be reproduced in any form or by any electronic or mechanical means, including information storage and retrieval systems, without written permission from the author, except for the use of brief quotations in a book review.

ISBN-13: 978-198433-738-2

ISBN-10: 1-984-33738-6

Cover art by Ivan Sevic

Cover titling by Deranged Doctor Design

Wolf symbol by Orina Kafe

THE BLUE WOLF SERIES

Blue Curse
Blue Shadow
Blue Howl
Blue Venom

More coming!

———

For my brothers near and far

1

I watched the burqa-clad figure drift from one side of the dirt road to the other, coming nearer. She looked like a green specter through my night-vision goggles. A singing green specter. As she drew even with the compound two blocks from my position, I could hear the wavering notes rising above the clamor of the compound's generator.

"Nice pipes," I muttered.

Curling a finger over the trigger of my M4, I raised the rifle from the woman toward the rooftop of the cement building that stood above the compound's high walls.

A magnified guard appeared in my sight picture. He leaned over the north side of the rooftop, an AK-47 propped against his shoulder, then called to a second guard behind him. The two peered down on the woman, unescorted and apparently drunk, out in the middle of the night. In the suburb of the conservative Waristani city, that would draw anyone's attention.

Which was the whole point.

I centered the crosshairs on the nearer guard's head. "Mario in sight," I whispered into my headset.

"Roger that, Captain," Segundo, my team sergeant and second-in-command, answered. *"I have Luigi."*

"On three, two, one..."

Our M4s coughed a single round apiece, Segundo's from three blocks away. In sprays of glowing green mist, the guards we'd nicknamed Mario and Luigi dropped from sight.

"Move," I ordered, stepping from the corner of my building.

Four men in black camos and body armor followed me, weapons at the ready. We crossed the road and jogged the next block at a crouch, then proceeded single file along the compound's outer wall. The woman who had distracted the guards met us. She shed her burqa and became Sergeant Calvin Parker.

The lankiest member of Team 5, Parker was the only one who could have passed for a female. I nodded at my civil affairs officer to tell him good job. The young black man gave me a wry look as he ditched the burqa and readied his rifle and gear. He hadn't been thrilled about the role.

I gave the signal, and two of my men dropped off to establish perimeter security. On the other side of the compound two men from the split team were doing the same. Ten feet from the compound's north gate, my senior engineer moved to the front, pulling out C-4 charges to place on the hinges.

"Hot on the north," he said over his radio.

"Hot on the south," an engineer on the split team answered.

We crouched away, and both doors detonated. The hammering of the compound's generator helped cover the dry bangs, but we needed to move fast.

I took the lead, rushing low through the smoky doorway, three men following. We were in the compound's west outer courtyard. I spotted the two guards. They were beside a small outbuilding, fumbling their AK-47s into firing positions. We had interrupted their smoke break—one of many that aerial surveillance had shown us. Our rifles coughed. Each guard was hit at least twice before he collapsed to the ground. At the same time, suppressed shots echoed from the east courtyard. Not a single burst of answering gunfire so far.

Good. Execution is on point.

I led my team to the southern end of the courtyard where Segundo's team was mining the metal door to the inner courtyard. The engineers cleared the blast area. Another dry bang. Segundo and I shared the lead through the acrid smoke. We were eight strong now, two members remaining behind to secure the outer courtyard.

The main building rose ahead. Light slivered around the seams of a covered window on the third floor. I was cycling through the building's layout in my mind when the front door opened.

Segundo and I greeted the armed guard with a single shot apiece to his chest.

We stepped over his prone body and into the first floor. The rooftop generator that shuddered through the concrete building encased us in a wall of pounding, disguising the noise of our entry and movement. We had cut power to the sector an hour earlier for just that purpose.

I spotted the staircase to the second floor at the far end

of a corridor, doorways opening off it. I circled a pair of fingers to remind my team of the two guards still on the floor. They appeared from a back room a moment later, armed but unaware the building had been breached. We dropped them and cleared the remaining rooms. One man remained behind while the rest of us filed up the stairs.

Two guards saw us coming onto the second floor. Our suppressed gunfire cut their alarmed cries short. A third guard poked his head from a doorway. I squeezed my trigger before he could duck back to safety. Through my night-vision, the corridor glowed green with spattered blood.

All twelve guards were now accounted for. But had their shouts penetrated the din of the generator? Only one way to find out. I signaled for two of my men to stay behind to check the rest of the floor while I led Segundo and Parker to the top level.

From the shadow of the stairwell we peered onto a narrow corridor with two closed doors. Light glowed beneath the one on the right. Beyond, I could hear the shouts of men arguing. Segundo grinned broadly. They had no idea an American Special Ops unit was at their doorstep.

After clearing the other room, we stacked on the door. I signaled for Segundo and Parker to cover my breach. Flipping the night-vision goggles from my eyes, I seized the handle and threw the door open.

For a moment, the six men sitting around the lamp-lit room on rugs didn't notice me. Several were arguing, the sleeves of their loose shirts and gowns shaking as they pointed accusing fingers at one another, eyes blazing above their shouting mouths. I recognized all of the men, but at the moment, I only cared about the one I had singled out with a red laser dot on his chest.

Plump with a purple vest and trim gray goatee, Zarbat was trying to restore order. He glanced up at me distractedly, then away. I could almost see the image of a massive armed man registering in his brain. His eyes worked their way back to me. One by one, the other men followed the aim of his ashen face. The shouting fell to murmurs, then died.

Zarbat peered past me, as though expecting his guards to come to his defense. Instead, he saw Segundo and Parker, the three of us holding enough firepower to liquefy the room. The men understood this. They cast nervous glances around, none of them moving or saying a word. Glass tea cups rattled on saucers, and the plywood over the window shook as the generator hammered on.

At last Zarbat licked his thick lips and tried to smile. "Jason Wolfe," he called in his refined voice. "I didn't realize you were coming. Have a seat. Here is the tea you like." He reached for a pot in the middle of the gathering.

"It's not that kind of visit," I grunted.

"Oh?" He withdrew his hand and swallowed dryly. "Well, then. What brings you here?"

Six months before, when my team had been assigned to work with him, Zarbat had been one man. No army, no weapons, and little to no credibility with the ethnic tribe of his birth. Now he had all three—in spades. The last because we'd credited him with the overthrow of the Mujahideen in southern Waristan when, in fact, he had been safe at our base in nearby Afghanistan. We'd flown him in at the tail end of the battle to pose with an assault rifle and the militia we had trained. Zarbat never fired a shot nor was he ever shot at. His

U.S. education and influence among a handful of Washington decision-makers had served him well. Until he got greedy.

"The gentleman to your left brings us," I said.

I knew from our intelligence that Elam, one of the leaders of the Mujahideen insurgency, didn't understand English.

"Ah, yes," Zarbat replied. "We were just discussing the terms of his surrender."

I shook my head. "You and the representatives of the other four tribes were to meet in the capital this weekend to elect a government. Instead, you and Elam have been plotting their assassinations so the country would descend into chaos and you could present yourself as the only stabilizing figure. The U.S. would have no choice but to name you interim leader. Your first move would be to grant amnesty to the Mujahideen fighters, more than tripling the size of your armed forces. From there, you would assume complete power, all while assuring the U.S. you remained a loyal ally."

Some U.S. leaders would have been willing to live with that, if only to see a conclusion to the war. In the end, more hawkish voices had prevailed.

Zarbat's face flushed. "That's preposterous."

"We've been monitoring your communications for the last month."

Zarbat peered past me, as though looking once more for his guards.

"We also know you doubled your security for tonight's meeting, instructing them to kill anyone who tried to enter. 'Even the Americans?' they asked. 'Even the Americans,' you answered."

"Jason," he said, tilting his head companionably. "I do not doubt the power of your intelligence services, but you were my advisor. You know me. Does that sound at all like something I would do?"

It did, in fact. I had never trusted Zarbat.

But instead of saying that, I turned to Segundo. "Take Elam into custody."

"With pleasure," he said, his Colombian-born machismo coming through.

I covered the room while Segundo lifted the Mujahideen leader roughly to his feet, patted him down, and then placed him in flex cuffs. Elam protested in bursts of Pashto as Segundo dragged him from the room.

"This will all get sorted out," Zarbat said calmly, refilling his tea cup. "You will see."

I looked at Parker, who besides being our civil affairs officer was also our interpreter. "Ask him," I said.

Parker turned to the young man seated to Zarbat's right —his second in command—and posed the question in Pashto: *"Are you ready to lead?"*

Despite his small build, the young man had the bearing of a prince. His penetrating brown eyes moved from Parker to me. "Yes," he said in accented English.

"What's this?" Zarbat said, alarm entering his voice for the first time. "You're replacing me?"

"Uncle Sam thanks you for your service," I said.

My M4 coughed twice. The shots slammed Zarbat against the wall, the tea he'd just poured splashing across his lap. My superiors hadn't considered him an intelligence asset. The Mujahideen leader would prove more valuable in that department.

I lowered the rifle as Zarbat's body slumped to a rest and motioned the young man, Mehtar, over.

He stood, adjusted his turban, and stepped toward us. While the three seated men—local officials—wrung their hands and murmured worriedly, Mehtar remained stoic. Though he had no ties to the U.S., he was a natural leader and, from my estimation of having worked with him, someone we could trust.

I angled my mouth toward Parker. "Tell him that the declaration will be that Zarbat was killed by a Mujahideen leader, who is now in custody. He will use the tragedy to rally support around himself. The U.S. will provide him with whatever resources he needs. A security detail is arriving as we speak, and an advisor will be along shortly. Top officials will meet with him in the capital this weekend."

When Parker completed the translation, Mehtar took my hand. For an uncomfortable moment, I thought he was going to kiss it. Instead, he bowed low and said, "This is great honor for me." He then turned to the seated men and spoke rapidly.

"He's having them prepare Zarbat's body for a procession tomorrow," Parker explained.

I nodded—we'd promoted the right man—and checked my watch. Sixteen minutes since touch down. Not bad. I spoke into my headset: "Mission complete. Prepare to roll out."

As we filed from the house and into the courtyard, Parker hustled up beside me.

"I still think the burqa was unnecessary, sir," he shouted above the noise of the generator. "But I am going to miss you."

I snorted out a laugh, then stopped as the reality of his words sunk in. I had just completed my fifty-second and final Special Ops mission. After ten years of service, the last four consisting of solid deployments, I was going home to Daniela.

For the first time that night, my heart began to speed up.

2

Colonel Don Stanick received my report before we touched down at the main operating base two hours later. I found him reading it on his laptop as I stepped into his office. "That traitorous son of a bitch," he muttered, his hard eyes moving across the screen. "Good riddance."

"There should be no surprises under Mehtar, sir," I said. "Besides being a capable leader, he's solidly in our camp."

"Plus he saw what happens to those who turn against us."

I had talked with Mehtar through Parker enough to pick up his admiration for all things American: from superhero movies to our judicial system, for which he showed an impressive understanding. We would never need to demonstrate hard power with someone who was already in the thrall of our soft power. But it wasn't my place to disagree with a superior officer's assessment.

"Intelligence will handle him from here," he said.

"Yes, sir."

Colonel Stanick raised his eyes from his screen and straightened. At almost sixty, he was tall and sturdy with iron-gray hair and a face of severe lines. Though he was three links up the chain from me, he was a soldier's colonel, preferring to hear from the men themselves about conditions in the field.

"I've spoken with Central Command. Your transfer orders should come in the next couple of days. I'm sorry as hell to lose you, Wolfe. You're the best I've ever worked with, and I've been doing this a long time. My only consolation is knowing you'll be training the next generation of soldiers."

He was referring to the commandment position being set up for me at the training battalion near my hometown in Texas.

"It's been an honor serving you," I said sincerely. Colonel Stanick wore several hats, and he was in the U.S. for meetings as much as he was in country, but he always took care of us.

"If there's ever anything you need, you let me know," he said. "I mean that."

"I appreciate that, sir."

"Now go and get some rest. You've earned it."

We stood and shook hands. I left, making my way from his office to our concrete barracks. When I stepped inside, I found half the guys sacked out and the other half reclined on their cots, laptops propped on bellies and knees while they gamed, watched videos, or in Parker's case, brushed up on his Pashto.

"Good work tonight," I said.

Segundo looked up from his glowing screen. "No keg and dancing girls, sir?"

"They were shipped to Pakistan by mistake. If you want them, you'll have to go over and sign for 'em."

"Or we could send Parker in his dress."

The other team members who were awake broke into laughter. Parker threw his pillow at Segundo. "Hey, that *dress* is a big part of what got us through tonight's mission casualty free."

"See there?" I said to him. "I knew you'd come around."

As others joined in the ribbing, I thought about how much I was going to miss these guys. I'd spent two years with the now-senior sergeants and at least a year with the juniors. Long enough to know they put the *special* in special ops. Segundo still needed to rein in his bulldog instincts a bit, but he was going to make a solid captain one day. I envied him in a lot of ways. Hell, I envied them all. But I had a life to get back to. Or more accurately, a life to start.

I checked my watch.

"Excuse me, gentlemen," I said and strode to my room.

I sealed the door behind me, took a seat at my desk, and logged on to my laptop. One of the perks of being team captain was having a private room, even if it was partitioned off with cheap plywood.

I accessed the secure video-conferencing app and clicked the topmost name in my directory. As the line rang, I centered the camera on myself, running a hand over my sun-bleached brown hair, then the dark two-day growth that covered my jaw. My eyes, which Daniela called "arctic blue," peered back from a face browned and toughened by the country's harsh climate.

I had stripped down to my tan shirt and was conscious now of how filthy it looked on the screen. Few and far between, these video conferences were special occasions. I peeled off the shirt, and was reaching back into my closet for a clean one when the line connected.

"Hey, baby!" came my fiancée's voice. "Ooh, are you trying to make me crazy?"

I turned back to my laptop, where Daniela's face now filled the screen. I paused to take her in: the smiling lips, the soft cheeks, the brown eyes that always seemed to gleam with some inner joy. An occupational therapist who worked with special-needs kids, she was a saint, and I was damned lucky. We'd met two years before, in a bar of all places. I was on leave and in need of some booze and a dark corner after learning about the combat death of a good friend. Daniela had needed the same after being told one of her patients, a five-year-old girl with spina bifida, had died during an operation. She saw my grief before I saw hers and asked to join me. We talked from noon that Saturday until two the next morning.

"Sorry for the show," I said, my chest and abdominal muscles flexing as I pulled on the clean shirt. "Hey, did you do something to your hair?"

"This?" she asked, and tucked a loose honey-blond strand behind an ear. "Yeah, I tied it in a sloppy bun so it wouldn't drop into the pasta sauce."

I imagined the smell of her homemade sauce filling the kitchen, imagined myself coming up behind her, slipping my hands around her waist, stooping to kiss the soft, clean nape of her neck. I couldn't believe that would all be happening as early as the following week.

"Well, you look amazing," I said.

Blushing, she stuck her tongue out at me, then turned serious. "How's everything going?"

I gave her my pat answer. "Right as Waristani rain."

"No, really, Jason. You're staying safe? I heard about that chopper that went down."

"That wasn't our guys. Listen, hon, you've got nothing to worry about. With the conflict winding down, the missions lately have been pretty routine."

Dani gave me her admonishing look. "Would you tell me if they weren't?"

She had me there and she knew it. When I hesitated, her frown steepened.

"Well, hold on," I said with a chuckle. "There's more."

She raised a skeptical eyebrow.

"You didn't hear this from me, but..." I lowered my voice and looked around even though I'd been cleared to share the news. "...there's a good chance someone's getting his transfer orders this week."

Daniela let out a squeal that froze the screen on her wide eyes and open mouth. I quickly hit the screen capture. She'd kill me, but that was going into the scrapbook she'd made for us.

"Are you serious?" she asked when the feed resumed.

"One hundred percent."

"And you'll be done?"

"Finished. No more deployments."

"I can't believe..." Her lips trembled as tears spilled from the corners of her eyes.

Daniela was the most empathetic person I'd ever known, but she also had a rock-solid core. Though my deployments were tough on her, I could have counted the number of times I'd seen her cry on one hand. I wanted so badly to be able to reach forward and thumb her tears away, to pull her into my arms. Instead, I said, "So how does a summer wedding sound?"

She released a wet burst of laughter. "That sounds perfect, baby." Reaching off screen, she returned with a napkin and pressed it to her eyes. "I'm sorry, I just can't believe it's really happening."

"Me neither."

"I've been looking at houses," she said, pausing to sniffle. "There's a ton of vacancies on the market. I found this beautiful five-bedroom near my parents' place. It will need a little work, but—"

"Whoa, there," I said, showing my hands. "Five bedrooms? How many kids are you planning on having?"

"Didn't we agree to four?"

"I'm pretty sure I said three. Which is a lot of little monsters as it is."

"What?" Dani teased, her lips pursing out. "The big, tough soldier can't handle one more little monster?"

I smiled. "We'll talk about it when I get there."

"Good." She bit her lower lip. "That'll give me time to come up with all sorts of naughty ways to convince you."

The overhead light crackled and browned while the laptop screen flickered. "I'm on electrical power, Dani, and it looks like we're about to lose the connection again. Listen, I'll be in touch as soon as I have some exact dates."

"Please do," she said, turning serious again.

"And there's no more missions, so don't worry. I'll see you very, very soon."

"Be extra safe, Jason. I love you so much." She kissed her left palm, right below the engagement ring, and was reaching to place it against her camera when the lights died and the laptop went offline.

"Love you too, Dani."

3

The message to see Colonel Stanick arrived while I was eating in the chow hall the next morning. I worked a piece of hash brown out of my teeth as I crossed the base, wondering if my transfer orders had come through. If so, Daniela was going to be over the moon.

I thought of the captured image of her face from the night before. When the power had been restored, I'd printed it off and tacked it on the wall next to the head of my bed. It made me smile when I was getting dressed this morning, thinking about how I'd be seeing that face in the Houston airport shortly. But the moment I crossed the threshold into Stanick's office, I could tell by his sober demeanor that this was not about my transfer.

"Have a seat, Captain." He gestured to one of two folding metal chairs that faced his desk. Files and reports were arrayed in front of him, one of them having to do with efforts to curtail the country's illegal poppy-growing trade.

"Thank you, sir," I said, sitting down. "What's going on?"

"There's been an important development."

"Oh, yeah?"

"China isn't thrilled with our influence on the incoming government here, but they're anxious to stop the influx of refugees across their border. Their aid camps topped one million Waristanis last month. As a result, China has agreed to grant us temporary use of the Wari Corridor as a supply route to help stabilize the eastern part of the country."

"China cooperating? That is a development."

"Central Command wants a team to check out the valley on the Waristani side, specifically a pinch point inhabited by a little-known tribe. We've received intelligence suggesting they might be sympathetic to the Mujahideen, which would put any supply route in danger."

I nodded, knowing where this was headed.

"Either way, CENTCOM wants to establish cooperation with them, which will mean finding out what they want: tools, building materials, humanitarian aid. Whatever's needed to drive a wedge between them and the Mujahideen. Look, Jason, I explained that your team had just come off a level-one mission, but with the meeting of the grand council coming up, the remaining teams are all committed. And CENTCOM insists this is urgent. They're concerned the Chinese will get cold feet and yank their offer. They want to get materials moving along the route as soon as humanly possible."

My heart pitched a little for Daniela, but until I was officially transferred this was my job. "I understand, sir. Give me the mission specs, and I'll have the men prepped and ready."

"There's something else," he said. "The pinch point is in

Wakhjir Province, which is Centurion's jurisdiction. Meaning they have oversight on this. They want to send a man along with you."

Though my face remained stoic, I dropped an inner F-bomb. Following the financial crash, and with the U.S. economy still in the gutter, budgets at the major departments had been slashed. Defense was no exception, despite that we were in the middle of what some were calling "The Never-Ending War," pursuing the Mujahideen and terrorist factions from one Central Asian country to the next. That meant contracting out half the war to Centurion United, the U.S.'s largest private military corporation. And that bothered the hell out of me.

The soldiers who fought for Centurion weren't here to sacrifice for country. They were mercenaries, here to profit. Plus, they knew nothing about unconventional warfare, which was our game.

"We'll have operational control, though, right?" I asked.

Stanick nodded. "Centurion is mostly interested in seeing if there are any terrorist targets in the area."

Of course, I thought bitterly. Centurion earned a commission for every high-value target they eliminated—and there were several among the scattered Mujahideen.

"Just as long as their agenda doesn't intrude on the mission," I said.

"I'm sorry this is being dumped on you, Wolfe, but it should be a quick in and out. Nothing Team 5 can't handle. A pair of Pave Lows will arrive at 1800 to transport you to a Centurion base further north. From there, you'll infil on Black Hawks at night. The Centurion rep will meet you at Sigma Base. His name is Baine Maddox."

Baine. I already didn't like him. But as long as we had operational control...

"We'll be ready, sir."

Back in our barracks, Segundo, Parker, and I huddled over the map I'd spread across our planning table.

"This is where we're being dropped," I said, tapping a point on a dry riverbed about two miles south and east of our target. "That little box is an old Soviet outpost that we'll use as a base of operation." I traced a finger up the twisting riverbed to the valley CENTCOM intended as a supply route. The satellite map showed terracing, which indicated farming, and a complex of buildings. "That's where the Kabadi tribe is located. It's small, only a few hundred people or so, but it's in a prime location to create problems along the supply route."

"What do we know about them?" Segundo asked, his vein-lined muscles rearranging themselves over his stocky torso as he sat back and crossed his arms. We all lifted weights, but Segundo was obsessive. He wore his shirts two sizes too small to showcase the fruits of his efforts.

"So far, only that they might be sympathetic to the Mujahideen," I replied.

"I was actually able to get a little research in," Parker said, adjusting his glasses. "The Kabadi are extremely isolated. They've been in that valley since the time of Alexander the Great, if not before. We're talking thousands of years. It's a harsh region, the summers scorching, the winters brutal. How they've persisted for so long is beyond me, but they're mostly self sufficient, primarily through farming and sheep herding. They—"

"What can we expect?" I cut in. Parker was one of the smartest people I knew, but he still needed to learn how to trim information down to the essentials.

"Well, given the isolation, their customs and beliefs are likely to seem strange. Their religion is a form of shamanism, and the men dye their beards blue. They speak a dialect of Wakhi, which is actually what I was using last night to communicate with Mehtar. He speaks Pashto, but he's originally from Wakhjir Province, and there are certain tonal nuances that—"

"Good, so it's a language you're familiar with."

"Yeah ... if what they're speaking sounds anything *like* Wakhi. It goes back to their isolation."

"You'll figure something out," I said, trusting he would.

Calvin Parker had been loaned to us from another team two years before when our then-interpreter was sent home with a lung infection. Only twenty-two at the time, Parker had been our youngest member. Add to that his gangly build, and I was skeptical. But after witnessing Parker's proficiency in local languages and cultures—he had one of the country's most notorious warlords crying with laughter over a crude joke—I lobbied to make his inclusion in Team 5 permanent. He hadn't disappointed, becoming a close friend in the process. We'd even managed to put a little muscle on him.

Across the barracks, the rest of the team members were organizing guns, ammo, and an assortment of equipment and supplies into piles for packing. The team medic, Mauli, a native Hawaiian built like a sumo wrestler, was sitting off to my right, double-checking an arrangement of medical stock that hopefully none of us would need.

There had been no complaints when I announced the last-minute mission, and I felt lucky to be leading Team 5 one final time.

"What's this, sir?" Parker asked.

I looked back down at the map where he was pointing. Across the corridor from our target and set back among a series of peaks was another complex. "The resort of some wealthy poppy grower, according to Stanick. It stands empty most of the year. Not our concern."

"Think the weirdo tribe will give us a fight?" Segundo asked hopefully.

"No telling," I said. "We'll approach it like we did the Kamdesh mission last year, only with Centurion providing air support."

Segundo scowled.

"Yeah, I know, but it's their province," I said. "And we're going to need someone overhead. Even if the tribe doesn't give us trouble, there are rumors of Mujahideen hideouts in the area."

After an hour of additional planning with Segundo, I returned to my room to finish packing. Lifting my emergency pack from my foot locker, I placed it on my bed and unzipped it. So named in the event things went sideways and we had to abandon our heavier gear, my emergency pack held a two-liter Camelbak, a couple of MREs, and a small medical kit, among other essentials. Some of the men slipped in personal mementos or good-luck charms. Not being superstitious or especially sentimental, I'd never done either.

Now I found myself looking at the printout of Daniela's

surprised face. For operational security, we were forbidden from calling home before upcoming missions, so she had no idea I was heading out again—despite what I'd assured her. As I unfastened the picture and smiled down at it, I could hear her stern voice telling me to be careful.

"It's just one more mission, baby," I said. "I'll be fine."

I started to tack her photo back up, but instead folded it into a square and tucked it into my pack.

———

Just before 1800 hours, two large Pave Low helicopters touched down on the landing strip and dropped their ramps. Hefting our hundred-pound rucksacks, and bearing an additional fifty pounds of body armor and gear, we split into two groups of six and lumbered into the cargo holds. Our mission was officially underway.

I spent the hour-long ride reviewing the plan. The info on the region and tribe was thin, but we'd been handed thinner. I needed to make sure every contingency was covered. In my four years as captain, I'd yet to lose a man. Most of us had been hit by bullets or shrapnel at one time or another—my senior weapons sergeant had even taken a rifle butt to the nuts—but we had a record of zero KIAs.

I wasn't going to blow that streak.

My stomach dipped as the Pave Low descended and set down heavily. The ramp had barely dropped when a team of Centurion soldiers trotted into the cargo hold to begin unloading.

I disembarked and walked around to where the pilot was climbing down from the cockpit. A fellow Texan, Warrant Officer Pete Southall had been in Central Asia for ten years and was as dependable as they came—which I couldn't say for every pilot who had flown us. More than once we'd been left hanging in sketchy territory. Twice by Centurion pilots. I also happened to know that Pete had a good two-way line with the officers who cleared rescue flights.

"Got a sec?" I called beneath the dying rotors.

Pete removed his flight helmet. "What's up, Wolfe?"

I clasped his outstretched hand. "First, thanks for the lift."

"Yeah, sorry we're not carrying you all the way in, bro. This being your last mission and everything."

"That's actually what I wanted to talk about. It's been hit and miss with Centurion in the past." Pete rolled his eyes in understanding. "If we find ourselves stranded up there, could I give you a call?"

"I'll beat your ass if you don't."

"Thanks, Pete." I clapped his arm.

"Hey," he called as I started to leave. "Be careful, bro. Some strange shit up that way."

I turned back toward him. "Oh yeah?"

"A number of years back, we had a guy flying an Apache on a solo mission. Swears he was chased by something."

I nodded. That would have been about the time China was getting testy about its border. "Probably an Mi-8," I said.

"Naw, man." Pete looked around as though to make sure no one could overhear us. "He said it wasn't another vehicle but this big fucking white thing with a long neck and wings like a bat. Bigger than his helo. He'd deviated off course over the Hindu Kush, and this thing came after him.

Knocked him into a spin before he was able to get the hell out of there."

I liked Pete, but I didn't have time for this. "I'll spread the word," I said dryly.

But Pete's face remained serious. "Hey, I thought it was bullshit too till I got a look at his helo. Three big gashes across the side door, like claw marks." He held up a hooked hand. "Swear to God. And our guy was for real messed up after that. Couldn't fly. The very idea of going back up would set his hands shaking. The military DXed his ass on a Section 8 and sent him home."

I nodded. Protracted warfare did that to some people. "Thanks again, Pete."

"Just be alert, bro," he called after me. "Lot of dark corners out there."

I went in search of Segundo to fill him in on our backup plan and found him on the edge of the landing strip.

"Get a load of this place," my team sergeant muttered. "Shangri-fucking-La."

The base beside the landing strip could have been a small college campus, with its red-brick buildings, white sidewalks, and an athletic field surrounded by a regulation-sized track. It made the kinds of bases we were used to operating out of seem like refugee camps.

"Probably looks good on a recruiting pamphlet," I said.

Segundo snorted. "Not to me, it wouldn't. One week in this joint and I'd be softer than a sergeant major with erectile dysfunction."

"Captain Wolfe," someone called.

I turned to find a man who looked about twenty-five walking past our stacked rucksacks where the rest of my team had assembled. He approached with a hop in his step that bounced his sweep of blond hair and rustled his shiny black flight suit. On the left side of the suit's chest, the Centurion logo of a Roman shield gleamed silver in the airstrip's lights.

"Baine?" I asked.

A gleaming smile spread over his plastic face. "The one and only. Welcome to Sigma Base." He pumped my hand a little too enthusiastically, as though trying to force friendship through the gesture, then did the same with Segundo, who looked at him askance.

I took the moment to size Baine up. He was on the short side, and what I'd first mistaken for a muscular build was actually the load-bearing vest he was wearing underneath his suit. Stripped of those and his boots, he was no more than five foot, six and a buck sixty.

"When can we expect the Black Hawks?" I asked, peering around.

"They're en route. Oh, and we've got another man coming. Boss's orders. We're going to need to find him a spot." He hooked a thumb over his shoulder at a large, dull-looking soldier with a shaved head. He was standing about twenty feet back, not meeting our eyes as we looked him over. He carried an AK-47 style gun with a fat grenade launcher mounted underneath the barrel."

Segundo looked at me wide-eyed as though to say, *Can you believe this?*

"Yeah, that's not gonna be possible," I said. "Our guy in charge of the load plan weighed and logged everything down to the ounce. We're maxed out. We even had to leave some gear behind. And what would we be talking? Another three-fifty, four-hundred pounds? No way."

"Seeing as how they're Centurion's helos, yes way," Baine said, his eyes hardening above his smile.

"Well then order another one," Segundo jumped in, his chest bowed. "You heard Captain Wolfe, we're maxed out. And there's no way in hell we're ditching a man."

"If you want our higher-ups to duke it out, fine," Baine said with a chuckle. "That's always entertaining, but it's also going to mean delaying the mission. And then you'll get a call telling you to lose a man." He tilted his head as though to suggest we were all trapped in the same bullshit bureaucracy. "C'mon, you know how these things go."

I clenched my jaw. "Mind giving us a minute?"

Baine stepped back, his eyes already gleaming with victory. "Take all the time you need."

I turned to Segundo, who was glaring after him. "Little prick," he muttered. "Waits until the last minute to tell us."

"It sucks, but he's right. CENTCOM kisses their ass every time."

Segundo sighed. "So who are we going to have to break the bad news to?"

I surveyed the men sitting and milling around the rucksacks. *Shit.* "You came up through communications, right?" When Segundo nodded, I said, "Then let's go with Melker. He's the junior commo sarge, which will still leave us with Hotwire and you. Sound okay?"

"No, but it's the least worst option. I can tell him."

The captain usually broke that kind of news, but it would be good practice for Segundo. As he trudged over to the team, Baine rejoined me. Having won, he was ready to bro up again.

"Hey, I hate to kick things off like that. I'm really stoked to be working with you guys. I've heard great things." I knew the type: a trust-fund brat who had signed up with Centurion for a chance to play soldier.

"Good, then let's be clear," I said. "Team 5 has operational control. We'll be executing the mission plan. No deviations." That was something I *would* scrap the mission over. There was no way in hell I would be taking orders from some Ken Doll-looking mercenary and his pet caveman.

"Absolutely," Baine said, nodding. "Olaf and I are just going to observe."

"And we'll be linked up to your pilots providing air?"

"Whatever you need dropped, they'll drop."

I looked at him for another moment. He met my gaze, his pale blue eyes unblinking. More important than my instinctive dislike for the man was whether or not I could trust him. I had a team depending on me. I glanced over at Olaf, who seemed to have moved closer in the last minute. He kept his large weapon clutched to his chest as if someone was going to try to rip it from his grip.

"Okay," I said, looking back down at Baine. "I'll walk you through the mission plan when we reach our target area. But I don't want any more last-second surprises. We clear?"

Baine laughed and slapped my shoulder. "You've been in country far too long. Relax, brother."

"I'll take that as a yes," I growled.

Far away, the deep thumping of rotors sounded, heralding the arrival of the Black Hawks. I wheeled from Baine to check in with the team. The sight of Melker hanging his head jabbed me in the gut. The decision was necessary to complete the mission, but barely two hours in, and I already didn't like the direction it was headed.

4

Rotary fire thundered from the left gunner's mounted M134 as the Black Hawk in which I sat climbed and banked steeply right. Machine gun bursts rattled from the other Black Hawks. I gripped my M4 and looked over the mountainous landscape, trying to see what we were shooting at.

"What's happening?" I asked into my headset.

"Shep 1 took some small arms fire," the crew leader responded as the explosive bursts ended. "We're out of range now."

"Any damage?" I asked.

"Negative, but we've called up the coordinates."

"What's our distance to the landing zone?"

"Just over ten klicks."

Which meant those rumors of fighters in the area were now verified. And really damned close to where we'd be staging. As the Black Hawks reorganized into a staggered formation, a dull boom sounded behind us, then another. Our escorts—armed drones thousands of feet above—were bombing the shooter's position. That was some reassurance.

Minutes later, our Black Hawk dropped straight down. Sand and grit gusted up as we touched ground. Olaf and I jumped out our side of the helo and, dragging our rucksacks, ran for several yards. We set our rucks down and dropped behind them onto our stomachs. A storm raged behind us as the remaining Black Hawks landed and then lifted off. Within minutes, everyone on the thirteen-man team was in a defensive perimeter around the landing site, the helos thumping back to base.

With my night-vision goggles flipped on, I scanned the craggy wall ahead of me, then peered up and down the boulder-strewn valley. Nothing stirred among the wash of green hues.

"Anyone see anything?"

When my team answered in the negative, I ordered them to move out.

I took point along with the engineers, alert for mines and ambushes, while the rest of the team followed in a two-by-two procession. We moved with weapons at the ready, our heavy rucksacks bending us forward. Baine had shed his flight suit and was wearing Centurion's patented ultra-light body armor and digital camos. Team 5's gear, in contrast, had changed little in the last twenty years. When Baine's sleek night-vision optics met mine, he grinned and gave me a thumbs-up.

Before long, the valley opened out and the former Soviet outpost appeared on a five-story hill to our left.

I dropped my rucksack and signaled for the team to stop. "Have them establish a perimeter around the hill," I told Segundo. "We'll check it out." I waved for the engineers to follow.

"Mind if I come?" Baine asked.

"I need you to get Hotwire linked up to your air support."

"We need to secure the bunker first," he said.

I ignored him and trudged up the hill. Situated at a bend in the valley, the old outpost provided a great vantage point in both directions. There were no signs of recent activity outside the stone building, and we cleared the three bare rooms inside quickly. While the engineers performed a second sweep for traps and old munitions, I stepped back outside to radio Segundo.

"Come up in pairs," I told him.

"You've already got two on the way," he radioed back. "These guys aren't listening."

At that moment Baine's and Olaf's heads came into view. The men were lugging their rucksacks up the hill. "Don't shoot!" Baine called with a laugh, the sound echoing down the valley.

I don't frigging believe this. "Is Hotwire linked up?" I asked, already knowing the answer.

"There's no rush," Baine said, arriving out of breath. "The drone operators reported the area clear when we landed, so I released them back to base." He handed his heavy sack off to Olaf, who hefted it toward the bunker, past the emerging engineers who gave him an all-clear sign.

"You sent them back to base?"

"Is there a problem?" Baine asked.

"Yeah. There is. We're in an unfamiliar area with hostiles nearby. We might be clear now, but if they observed our landing, they'll be en route. I want you to get those drones back overhead. If we're still clear after midnight, *then* you can release them. In the meantime, you're going to set Hotwire up so he can talk to the operators and coordinate our approach to the village tomorrow morning."

Baine remained grinning up at me. "Buddy, did I mention you need to rela—"

Something whooshed past and exploded into the side of the bunker. Olaf, who was just emerging, shouted and disappeared in a plume of smoke. I grabbed the front of Baine's vest and pulled him to the ground as debris and hot shrapnel rained over us. A metallic smell filled my lungs.

"The hell's happening?" he demanded.

"We're under attack! Get air support back here! Now!"

Another rocket-propelled grenade roared past as the valley erupted in gunfire. The explosion rang in my ears and more debris hailed around us. I checked on my engineers. They had hit the ground and were working their way toward their rucksacks for cover. Olaf hadn't been so lucky. Part of the bunker had collapsed over him. Through my night-vision, his protruding head and right arm glowed with blood.

I turned back toward the valley and, M4 in my grip, belly-crawled toward the edge of the flat hilltop. "How are you doing down there?" I asked Segundo through the radio.

"They're attacking from at least two positions," he answered. "We're pinned pretty good."

When I reached the edge, I could see Segundo and the others, bodies pressed flat behind their rucksacks, carbines cracking. On the opposite ridge gunfire flashed from two different spots about one hundred yards apart. Even without night vision equipment, the enemy could see my team members' silhouettes against the sandy riverbed, while ours were obscured by the bunker behind us.

Jamming a pair of foam plugs into my ears, I waved my engineers forward. With my M4 braced against the ground, I aimed at where the heavier fire was originating. Several figures moved in and out of my sight—Mujahideen. I squeezed off four shots, dropping two of them. When the engineers arrived on my left side, I pointed out the targets, and they began to engage them.

"How are we doing with air?" I asked Baine.

He was half-shouting, half-stammering into his radio. The same adrenaline that was enhancing my senses, helping me to focus, was unnerving the Centurion rep. Probably his first real action.

"I need an ETA!" I shouted.

"Tw-twenty minutes to arrival," he called back.

I relayed the information to Segundo as I sighted another combatant and took him down. My team sergeant swore in response. Not knowing how many hostiles we were facing, and with most of the team pinned, twenty minutes was an eternity. "The medium guns are down there," I reminded him, referring to the pair of M240 machine guns. "Can you reach them?"

"Doubt it," Segundo answered. "We'd have to be able to drag them to cover to set up, and the fire's still too heavy."

At that moment another RPG glowed into view. I threw myself to the right as the rocket ripped past, searing the side of my face. It detonated against the valley wall, the bunker shielding us from the shrapnel this time.

I followed the lingering vapor trail back across the valley. It terminated at a dark hole high on the opposite wall. A cave. It must have curved back because I couldn't see anyone through my sight picture now. I released a burst of fire to keep the shooter back.

The shooting from both points on the ridge continued. With air support, the combatants would have been eviscerated by now, dammit. We needed more firepower on them.

"Start sending the team up here two at a time," I told Segundo as I changed magazines. "Have them come around the backside of the hill. We'll lay down suppressive fire." I signaled to my engineers that they were responsible for the combatants on the left side of the ridge. I waved Baine forward. He crawled up reluctantly, still talking to his drone pilots, urging them to hurry.

I pointed toward the hostiles on the right. "We need to put pressure on that position."

Baine nodded and found them through the ACOG on his weapon. When two of my team below began to move, I gave the word and opened fire. Baine did in kind, sending streaks of light zipping across the valley. The dumb bastard was using tracer rounds—and he was wildly off the mark.

Answering fire began pinging the rocks around us.

I pounded his shoulder with a fist. "Switch your mag! No tracers! They're pinpointing us."

Swearing, Baine ejected his mag and began fumbling over his vest for another.

As the two members of my team made the backside of the hill, I dropped my sights to the cave again. A solitary figure glowed into view. I squeezed off two shots but missed. He ducked back out of sight.

The weapons sergeants—Dean and Dan—arrived on either side of us, and I ordered Segundo to send up two more of the team. With five capable shooters now, we were forcing both groups of fighters on the opposite ridge to take cover. I sent periodic bursts into the cave to discourage further RPG fire. When two more members of Team 5 arrived, I ordered the weapons sergeants onto the ridge in back of us to see if any fighters were approaching from behind.

"Can you get the guns up now?" I asked Segundo.

"It's going to be iffy. They're still hitting us in bursts."

I cycled through our options before settling on Olaf's weapon. The grenade launcher would be able to reach the cave. But when I looked back at the collapsed section of bunker, Olaf's mangled body was no longer there. Had one of our team members dragged him out?

Someone shouldered in between me and Baine. I glanced over, expecting to find a new member of Team 5, but it was Olaf. The left half of his head was caked in blood, and his elbow seemed to be holding on by the sinew, but he gripped his weapon gamely in both hands.

"Where do you need heavy fire?" he asked in an Eastern European accent, which wasn't surprising. Centurion recruited broadly, and foreign soldiers were often cheaper. But none of that mattered right now.

"Get back to cover," I said. "Our medic will be up to treat you."

"Where?" he repeated.

I sighed and pointed out the cave across the valley.

Olaf lowered his head to his sights. With a small grunt, he squeezed the trigger of his launcher. Seconds later, the dark hole lit up with a detonation. A scream echoed from inside the cave an instant before secondary explosions erupted: the RPG rounds. The hole filled with smoke and the dust of collapse.

"Where else?" he asked.

My weapons sergeants had reached the ridge behind us and were lighting up the opposite ridge. Sporadic gunfire answered. I didn't want the enemy to retreat and regroup. I wanted them eliminated. I gauged the distance to the fighters to be about two hundred yards.

"What's your launcher's range?" I shouted above the noise.

Olaf held up five fingers of his gloved right hand. *Five hundred yards? Must be a special make.* He lowered his face to his sights, but his injured arm was trembling now, affecting his aim.

"Do you mind?" I asked, reaching for the gun.

His hands clenched around it for a moment, but then he relented and shoved it toward me. I handed him my M4 and then took a moment to position the automatic grenade launcher and line up the sights. Calculating for the trajectory, I took aim above the leftmost group and fired four shots. Seconds later the grenades detonated with a series of bright flashes that sent bodies flying.

Damn, never seen power like that in a grenade round.

I aimed and fired above the other group. A second series of explosions lit up the night, and the enemy fire ceased. I scoped the ridge. "How's it look from your vantage?" I asked my weapons sergeants.

"No movement," Dean, my senior, responded. "I think we got 'em all."

"There's a drone on station," Baine shouted triumphantly.

"Better late than never," I muttered. "What are they seeing?"

"About a dozen dead and dying fighters."

"Tell him not to go anywhere." I stood and removed my earplugs as the rest of Team 5 arrived on the hill. "How is everyone?"

"No casualties if you don't count the rucks," Segundo responded, bringing up the rear. "Up here?"

"Just one," I said, cocking my head toward Olaf, who remained on his stomach. "Mauli? Could you take a look at him?"

"I am fine." Olaf stood, clamping his injured elbow. "It will be good by morning."

I'd seen this before. In the adrenaline-pounding heat of battle, a soldier often had no immediate sense of how badly he was wounded. "Mauli's going to check you out anyway."

"Yeah, let's find you a room inside," my medic said. He took Olaf by his other arm and led him toward the bunker. That Olaf could walk under his own power impressed me. He'd been in the immediate blast radius of an RPG and buried under a stone wall. Regardless, he was in good hands with Mauli. Our medic would stabilize him until we could get him out.

I turned to the rest of the team. "All right. I want the engineers to get working on restoring the bunker wall. Baine, you're going to put Hotwire in contact with your pilots. He's taking over air."

The Centurion rep didn't grin or talk back this time. Instead he stared around with shocked eyes.

"I want everyone else bringing up the rucks and gear. Get the guns set up there and there." I pointed at locations with zones of fire that covered any approach to our position. "Even with recon overhead, we're going with fifty percent security tonight."

As the team got to work, my number two came

over to talk to me. "You think the fighters were connected to that village we're visiting tomorrow?" Segundo asked.

"No telling. But based on how long the Kabadi have been here, any alliance is probably reluctant, maybe even being forced on them. We'll know more when we meet with their leaders tomorrow."

"What are we going to do about Blondie?" Segundo asked.

Baine was seated on the ground with Hotwire now, their laptops and radios spread in front of them. Baine was going over the ciphers. "He's unfit in just about every way," I said in a lowered voice. "I'd leave him behind if I could, but we're going to need Centurion's drones tomorrow, and he seems like the type who would sabotage our support out of spite."

Segundo nodded in agreement. "At least we don't have to worry about his buddy."

"Olaf is actually the competent one, but yeah. The fewer mercenaries tomorrow, the better. Baine's only getting the bare mission essentials. I want you to keep him in the back, out of the way. I also want you holding his ammo. He doesn't handle pressure well, and he could fuck this up royally."

"One babysitter coming up," Segundo said.

I picked up my rucksack and clapped his shoulder. "If it's any consolation, I don't see this going beyond tomorrow. Once we're back at base, Stanick has promised the team a solid week of R and R."

"While *you* slip out the back door, you bastard."

"The team will be in good hands." I paused the appropriate beat. "I think."

Segundo waved his middle finger at me as I grinned and walked toward the bunker.

Across the ridge where the dead and dying combatants lay, a wolf's howl went up.

Sounds like someone's getting a late dinner, I thought grimly.

5

I emerged from the bunker the following morning to find the valley shrouded in cold mist. Most of the team was outside, cleaning their weapons and doing final prep. I summoned the others still in the bunker and then walked over to Baine. "Can I talk to you for a minute?" I said, making quick eye contact with Segundo.

Baine looked up from his meal ration with bleary, red-rimmed eyes. Even though I'd kept him off the security rotation, I doubted he'd slept. I had heard him tossing and turning in his sleeping bag most of the night. He set his MRE down and followed me to the other side of the bunker, where Segundo joined us.

"You can keep your weapon," I told Baine, "but Segundo is going to carry your ammo."

"Afraid I'm going to shoot myself in the foot?"

I ignored the bitter remark. "He'll give you whatever you need *should* you need it."

Baine looked from me to the ammo pouch Segundo held open. "I'm not under your command."

"No, but I have operational authority. Besides endangering us by calling off air support last night, you were a liability in battle. It would be entirely within my authority —and good sense—to scrap the mission and request a different rep." I paused to let that sink in. Something told me he would do anything to avoid the shame of being swapped out. "I'm still willing to let you come along as an observer, but on the condition you lose the ammo."

He clenched his jaw but began pulling mags from his vest and dropping them into the pouch. Removing the mag from his SCAR last, he held it up. "I'm going to report this," he promised. "It's a violation of the Public-Private Defense Agreement."

"Whatever," Segundo muttered, prying the mag from his grasp.

I ejected the round from Baine's chamber, which he had conveniently forgotten, and returned to the head of the ten-member team. Mauli would be staying behind to tend to Olaf. An armed drone would remain overhead to provide security. I was preparing to give the order for final check when Olaf appeared from the bunker, fully outfitted and carrying his weapon.

"I go too," he said.

I shook my head. "You're in no condition."

Mauli appeared close on his heels and sidled his big body past him to approach me. "Sir? I wouldn't believe it if I hadn't seen it myself," he said in a lowered voice. "But he's practically healed."

"That's not possible. His left arm was barely attached last night."

"No kidding," Mauli said. "Thought I was going to have

to amputate, but by this morning, the tissue had grown back. And his shrapnel wounds are just scabs, some of them already flaking off."

Handing off my M4 to Mauli, I walked over to Olaf and pushed up his left sleeve. A clean bandage wrapped his elbow. Gripping his wrist, I told him to flex his arm while I resisted. I expected Olaf to grimace and tremble with the painful effort, but it was all I could do to arrest his motion. I checked his other arm to make sure I had tested the correct one.

"I go," he repeated.

I wondered if the apparent miracle had something to do with Centurion's bioengineering division. Sigma Base had declined to medevac Olaf last night, instead requesting periodic updates on his condition.

I turned to Baine. "What in the hell is going on?"

Baine's lips split into a grin as he gave an exaggerated shrug.

Yeah, keep your company secrets, you little shit. Blowing out a sigh, I signaled to Segundo that he would also be responsible for Olaf. I didn't feel the same need to confiscate his ammo. Whatever Olaf's background, he was steady.

Ten minutes later we descended from the outpost and turned up the valley. Hotwire had arranged for the one drone to remain above the bunker while two more escorted us and one reconned ahead. The word from the sky was that the way was clear. After a mile, we crested a section where the valley had fallen in on both sides and we found ourselves looking down on a lush Eden.

The village was set in the center of a green bowl, peaks

rising protectively on three sides. Meadows with herds of shaggy gray sheep extended all the way to the Wari river, while level upon level of terraced farmland and orchards scaled the valley's sides. Small mud huts dotted the landscape, seeming to converge on a large compound that I recognized from the satellite map. The compound had looked big on paper, but like the rest of the valley, appeared more impressive in person.

I signaled for the men to keep moving. "How's it looking from above?" I asked Hotwire as we waded into the knee-high pasture grass, the nearest sheep hustling out of our path.

"Like a ghost town," he answered. "No one's out."

As I scanned the ground, something caught my eye. I stopped and knelt. Half buried in the soil was a chunk of metal. I dug it out and brushed it off, then held it up. A large mushroomed bullet, which meant heavy weapons. I scanned the huts and compound again.

"There's another one back here," Segundo called.

"Permission to speak, sirs?" Baine asked sarcastically.

"Go ahead," I said.

He pulled a laminated gridded map from a pocket in his cargo pants and spread it out. I noticed his digital camos had changed from the gray desert colors to the green of the grass he knelt in. "I would have pointed this out last night," he said, "but no one seemed interested in anything I had to say. Centurion's satellite technology gives us the highest resolution imagery of the area."

"So?" Segundo said.

"So, I might have an explanation for the bullets."

I walked over to him and looked over his shoulder at

the map. The bird's eye view of the village was closer up and much more detailed than ours.

"See that?" Baine said, pointing to a pair of large lumps on top of one of the buildings that made up the compound. "Those are canvas covers. Our friends are hiding something up there. Judging by the size of the rounds, I'd say a pair of anti-aircraft guns. Probably Soviet era."

I looked toward the compound but couldn't see the rooftop from our angle. I raised my gaze further to the clearing skies. What had they been shooting at? I scanned the ground again. Several feet away, I pried up a translucent plate. Pale, and glittery when tilted, it looked like mica, but the crusty plate was rounded on three sides, like a fish scale, and I couldn't break it in half.

Pete's words from yesterday returned. *A number of years back we had a guy flying an Apache on a solo mission. Swears he was chased by something.*

Though the account seemed slightly less ridiculous now, I wasn't ready to buy in. I tossed the plate aside and turned to Hotwire. "Ask a pilot to keep an eye on those weapons. If the covers come off them, I want to know."

As Hotwire sent up the request, Baine refolded his map and smiled smugly.

"Is there anything else you're holding back?" I asked.

"No," Baine replied coyly. "That was all."

I looked at him another moment, then gave the order to continue moving. We left the pasture and followed a network of trails past the huts. Chickens pecked beneath lines draped with traditional clothing, but the villagers themselves had cleared out, probably spooked by last night's battle up the valley.

"Shouldn't we be kicking down doors?" Baine asked.

Yeah, what better way to get a populace on your side, I thought.

As we approached the compound's main gate, I eyed the formidable stone walls. I waved to Parker, my interpreter, and he clattered up under the weight of his body armor and rifle. Behind us the rest of the team assembled into concentric layers of security, covering our sides and back. I moved my M4 to one hand and knocked on the tall wooden door.

Baine snorted. "Yeah, like they're just going to open..."

His words trailed off as something clunked on the other side of the door: a crossbeam being lifted from a latch. A moment later the door opened a crack and a young woman's green eyes peered from the shadows.

Parker stepped forward and spoke our planned introduction in Wakhi:

"Forgive our intrusion. We represent the United States of America on a friendly mission. This is Captain Wolfe, the leader of the team, and I am Sergeant Parker, team interpreter. We request a meeting with your tribal leaders to inform them of a project in the area. We would also like to learn of any help your village may need."

The woman watched him, eyes keen and unblinking. She was young, but the sun and wind had already begun to weather her skin and draw faint crow's feet at the corners of her eyes. When Parker finished, the woman looked from him to me. I started to smile through my beard, then stopped. A halo of green light seemed to surround her, almost as if I was viewing her through night-vision goggles.

"Daroed," she said.

"She's inviting us inside," Parker told me.

"Does she have a name?"

Parker exchanged a few words with her, then said, "Nafid."

I nodded in greeting as I led the men through the door and into a courtyard. Nafid was short and slender. Over a neat tailored gown she wore an embroidered green vest. A thick scarf wrapped her dark hair, while a large wolf's tooth dangled against her chest from a leather strap. Her bold gaze lingered on mine before she turned and disappeared into a narrow passageway on the courtyard's far side.

We followed her, turning this way and that, until we arrived in another stone courtyard where a group of old men in sandals and traditional robes sat on rugs, smoking pipes and sipping tea. When Nafid hailed them, they grunted and gestured for us to join them.

"Just Parker and me," I told the team.

While Segundo organized the remaining members into a security perimeter, Parker and I crossed the sunny courtyard and sat on a pair of rugs where the old men had made room for us. "These are the tribal leaders," Parker explained. "What Nafid is calling 'The Old Ones.'" The men continued to grunt as steaming tea was poured into ceramic cups and passed to us.

"Begin by asking if the Mujahideen have been in the area."

Parker posed the question to the men, but it was Nafid who answered.

"She says no."

"Have they had any trouble from outsiders?"

"She says no to that as well."

"Is there anything we can help them with?" I said. "Building materials, medical supplies, protection?"

Following a short exchange, Parker said, "She insists they're fine."

"Explain to them the proposal for the supply route through the Wari Corridor. Tell them it will be temporary and that it is meant to stabilize the area, which will also improve their security."

As I waited for Parker to translate, I looked around at the men. They showed no reaction to the message. If anything, they seemed more interested in their tea. I wondered if they even understood what was being said, because once more it was Nafid who answered.

"She says the village has no problem with the supply route."

That was the guarantee CENTCOM was looking for, but something felt off. I'd met with enough tribal leaders to know that the men around us weren't in charge. Neither was Nafid, who was too young. The real power center lay elsewhere. But why hide it? And if they weren't having any trouble, what was up with the big guns on the rooftops? They'd been shooting at *someone*.

"If it pleases our host, we would like a tour of the compound," I said.

The woman's eyes had already begun to harden before Parker started translating. She waited until he finished before saying something to the old men, who grunted among themselves. Necklaces and bracelets, all featuring wolves' teeth, rattled softly as they spoke.

"What are they saying?" I whispered.

Parker shrugged. "Whatever it is, it's not Wakhi."

At last Nafid turned abruptly back to us and spoke.

"She's going to show us," Parker said, then added in a whisper, "but she doesn't sound happy about it."

As Nafid led us from the courtyard, I pulled Segundo to one side so we were out of earshot of Baine and Olaf. "She told us what we wanted to hear," I said, "and she's agreed to show us around the compound, but something feels sketchy. Keep your eyes peeled."

Segundo nodded as the rest of the team fell in behind me. As we were led deeper into the compound, the Kabadi people began to appear. They watched from doorways with pinched and weathered faces while wide-eyed children peered from behind their legs. The adults were mostly women and the elderly, I noticed. Few men of fighting age were among them.

Nafid spoke in clipped Wakhi as we walked, which Parker translated.

"Food storage." He pointed to a granary off to our right. "Weaving," he said as we passed an open room where rudimentary looms and large spools stood in rows.

I noticed Nafid was avoiding the compound's central building, where the suspected anti-aircraft guns were positioned. When we passed its main door, I stopped.

"What's in here?" I asked.

"She's calling it a place for the sick," Parker said.

I arched an eyebrow. Given the number of villagers, the tall building with two wings was much too big for an infirmary. Parker shrugged as though to say, *We both know she's lying, but what can we do?* Whatever the village was hiding was inside. And if that included Mujahideen fighters, then coalition lives would be in danger when the supply route opened.

"Tell her we have a medic on our team. We can help."

After a short conversation, Parker said, "She insists that no help is needed."

I gave Segundo the sign that we were dividing into split teams. Then, pretending not to have understood the translation, I smiled and pulled the door open. Nafid said something and tried to cut ahead of me, but Parker stepped up beside me, effectively blocking her. While Segundo's team remained on security, my team filed through the doorway.

"Stop!" Nafid called.

6

I hesitated at her surprising use of English, but the Kabadi woman's next burst of words was in Wakhi. Inside, a staircase illuminated by smoke-blackened lamps rose steeply. With my M4 trained ahead, I began to climb. A layer of soot clung to the walls, but halfway up the soot broke apart into primitive drawings of wolfish shapes, the flickering lights bringing them to life. Parker was right: isolation had made these people strange.

"Where are the sick?" I asked.

Parker posed the question to Nafid as she caught up to us. She shouted something up the staircase—a warning?—before answering Parker.

"She says they're ahead on the left, but that we shouldn't disturb them."

There was something she didn't want us to see, which likely meant the village was harboring fighters. I'd been down this road before. Whether the village was doing so voluntarily or under threat didn't matter. Coalition lives were in danger, and it was my duty to neutralize that danger.

The staircase arrived at a T-intersection with a door straight ahead. Nafid gestured left. After another ten yards, the corridor turned sharply to the right. Sweat dripped off my nose, and for the first time I realized how humid it had become compared to the bone-dry atmosphere outside. It was starting to smell too, like crowded bodies—or penned animals.

Up ahead, a woman with a white headdress peered from a doorway. I aimed my M4 but saw she was unarmed. Nafid spoke to Parker, then rushed ahead, calling after the woman, who ducked away.

"She'll let us in," Parker said, "but she's asking us to wait outside for a minute."

I turned to my split team. Baine had ended up among them somehow, but there was too much going on to deal with him right now. "We're either walking into an ambush," I whispered, "or an attempt to hide enemy fighters. I'll take point. I want the rest of you to cover the room in sectors. You see someone aim a weapon, you take them out. Dan, you stay outside with Baine to guard our rear."

Nafid reappeared and motioned for us to enter.

I approached the doorway and took a quick look inside. Half expecting to be met by combatants and gunfire, I was surprised to find rows of what looked like sleeping pallets. Bundled bodies lay on top of them while a half dozen women in white headscarves stood among them.

I checked the room's blind corners, then stepped through the doorway. The smell I'd picked up in the corridor grew stronger. My men followed, carbines covering every angle of the open room. The women watched us nervously, not moving.

I stepped forward, my gaze ranging over the fifty or so pallets. Their occupants were wrapped in blankets, scarves covering their faces. I searched for the black turbans of the Mujahideen, but saw none.

"Are they all men?" I asked.

"Yes," Parker confirmed from Nafid.

"What's wrong with them?"

After speaking with Nafid again, Parker said, "They're sick."

"That's a lie," a voice whispered at my shoulder. "Those are enemy fighters."

I looked over to find that Baine had entered the room despite my order. "Get your ass back in the corridor," I said. He glared up at me, his lips a tense line, but he retreated from the room.

"What's their illness?" I pressed.

"She claims they're recovering, they just need their rest," Parker said.

She's not answering the question. "Mauli, can you check out that one there?" I nodded at the closest pallet.

As our medic stepped forward, one of the women moved in front of him, but Nafid said something to her, and she backed away. Arriving at the pallet, Mauli set his M4 down and took out his medical bag. "Explain that I'm going to check his vital signs: blood pressure, pulse, temperature."

When Parker translated, Nafid didn't respond. Her attention, along with the other women, was on the bundled man. Mauli removed a blood-pressure cuff, stethoscope, and thermometer from his bag, then began to unwrap the long scarf that hid the man's face. He stopped suddenly.

"What's wrong?" I asked.

"Come take a look," he said.

The women murmured as I approached the pallet. When I arrived, Mauli pulled the scarf the rest of the way from the man's face. I stared for a moment, trying to make sense of what I was seeing. The blue hair was consistent with what Parker had told us about the men staining their beards. But the thick growth covered the man's entire face, including his forehead. And was his jaw protruding? The man blinked up at us with jaundiced yellow eyes before squinting away from the light.

"The hell?" I muttered.

"Hypertrichosis," Mauli said, slipping his thermometer between the man's dark lips. I caught the edge of a large canine before his lips closed back over the metal end. "It's a rare genetic condition where hair grows over the entire face. Harmless, but probably embarrassing for them."

"Are all the men here like this?" I asked Nafid.

Parker carried out the translation and replied, "Yes."

I pointed to two of my team members. "Pick one apiece and check them out."

The women whispered nervously as my men approached two different pallets and began unwrapping the men's faces. "We've got another Harry," one of them called uncomfortably. The other reported the same. Meaning we had likely gotten to the bottom of the secrecy.

"All right," I said, waving the men back.

Mauli removed the blood-pressure cuff from his man's arm. "His temperature and heart rate are high; otherwise, he sounds healthy. I can leave some aspirin and recommend more hydration."

I shook my head. "No, let's leave them alone."

The women fixed the displaced scarves over the men's faces as we retreated from the room. Nafid joined us in the corridor. I would apologize for our intrusion outside. Right now I just wanted to get out of the building.

At the top of the staircase, a storm of barking echoed from the corridor ahead. The savage clamoring was accompanied by what sounded like claws scratching metal. I craned my neck. Was there a kennel in here?

I jerked as Nafid dug her fingers into my arm and unleashed an explosion of Wakhi.

"She's demanding we leave now," Parker said nervously. "And I'm thinking that's a really good idea."

I was turning to do just that when a cry sounded from behind the closed door opposite the stairs. With my men providing cover, I forced the door open. Nafid hung on my arm, trying to restrain me. I dragged her with me into a room dimmed by smoke. Ahead, fires burned from a pair of pyres. Between the pyres a hooded woman knelt in front of a shrine crowded with urns and strange stick configurations. She was wailing up at something on the wall. Only when I'd progressed far enough inside could I make out what it was: a rotting wolf's head.

"What in God's name?" Parker muttered behind me.

Nafid was yanking my arm now, but the old woman sounded as though she were in mortal pain. The thought that she was being kept here as some sort of sacrifice roiled my stomach.

The floor became uneven underfoot. Looking down, I saw I was stepping on bones. Human, animal, I couldn't tell, but they had been arranged into designs and symbols that covered much of the floor. In the thick, smoky atmosphere my heart began to beat harder and I was having trouble breathing. I turned to Parker.

"Ask the woman if she's okay," I said.

Parker coughed into his shoulder, then shouted the question in Wakhi.

The woman stopped wailing and whipped her head around. She tilted her head back as though sniffing the air, then drew her hood away. Wispy white hair framed an ancient face that had purpled and wrinkled like a fig. She had no eyes. In their place were sunken pockets of pink flesh. They puckered wetly as though trying to fix on us. I cut my gaze to the mounted wolf's head. A swollen tongue lolled over the huge teeth of its sagging lower jaw.

When I dropped my gaze back to the old woman, tendrils of light seemed to twist around her like smoke from a cauldron. Fitting, given that the woman looked like a witch from a fairy tale. A very disturbing fairy tale. And eyeless or not, she seemed to be staring straight into me, as though weighing my soul.

Something told me she was the village's power center.

Sweeping her hands toward us, she spoke in a shrill tongue.

"It's that dialect I can't understand," Parker said. "But I think the message is clear enough. She wants us gone."

As Nafid ran up to calm the woman, I saw she was fine. We'd apparently interrupted a spiritual ceremony that involved crying in pain. I signaled to my men that we were leaving.

It wasn't until we were down the stairs and outside, mountain air chilling my sweat-drenched body, that I drew a deep breath. Clean air filled my lungs, pushing out the stench of the building.

"Everything all right?" Segundo asked, looking from me to the rest of my split team.

"Just a lot of strangeness," I said. "They're not harboring fighters. We'll leave them a sat phone and show them how to use it. They can contact us if the Mujahideen give them trouble." But I had a gut feeling the Mujahideen wouldn't give them trouble and that the reason they'd been left alone all these centuries had to do with whatever the hell we'd just seen.

"We need to take them out," Baine panted.

"Why? So you can collect a commission?"

"You read the intelligence," he said. "They may be sympathetic to the Mujahideen. And most of the men of fighting age are in that building. They're not sick, they're being hidden. Would you rather wait until they're shooting at us to do something?"

"And you wonder why we confiscated your ammo," Segundo muttered.

Baine scowled and said something to Olaf, who grunted noncommittally. When Nafid emerged from the building, I turned to Parker.

"Tell her we're sorry. We didn't mean to intrude. We were just concerned for the safety of our fellow soldiers. Thank her and the village for allowing the passage of supplies through the Wari corridor." As Parker translated, I unshouldered my pack and removed the satellite phone and some battery packs. "Can you go over these with her? Explain that they can use the phone to contact us?"

Speaking Wakhi, Parker showed Nafid the phone. She looked over it suspiciously, but now that we were out of the building, the tension across her face appeared to be releasing.

I checked our surroundings, then walked over to Hotwire. "How's it looking from the skies?"

"All clear, according to the drone operators."

"Good. Radio a situation report to CENTCOM that the Kabadi intend to cooperate and that there are no apparent threats from their quarters. Then arrange for our transport out of here."

"Yes, sir."

I'd learned to trust my gut over the years, and right now my gut was saying *get out*. When Parker finished explaining the phone to Nafid, I signaled to Team 5 that it was time to move. Nafid escorted us back to the compound's main gate, remaining by the door as we filed out. When I turned, her intense green eyes fixed on mine. "Thank you," she said in her accented English.

I nodded back, then turned to Parker. "Something you taught her?"

Before he could answer, Olaf pushed past Nafid and trotted to catch up to us.

Suspicion prickled through me. "Where did you go?"

"Bathroom," he replied.

"In a toilet, I hope," Segundo said.

I considered tearing Olaf a new one for wandering off without telling me or Segundo, but what was the point? Our association was about to end. He paired up with Baine as we cut through the village and entered the pasture.

At the top of the collapse that separated the lush valley from the dry river bed ahead, I took a final look back. One of the strangest missions I'd ever led, but one without casualties, if I didn't count Olaf. And he appeared to have recovered fully from his injuries. Like I said, strange. I'd process it all when the team and I were safely back at base.

As we descended the collapse, gravel and grit replacing the dark soil beneath our boots, I heard Baine key his radio.

"The target's marked," he said in a low voice. "You're cleared hot."

Cleared hot? I wheeled around. *Did he just order a bomb drop?*

When our eyes met, Baine smiled. I strode toward him. "What in the hell did you just do?"

"Your job," he said defiantly.

I looked at Olaf. The infrared sticks that had been jutting from his pocket that morning were gone. I remembered how Baine had muttered something to Olaf after I'd denied his appeal to take out the hospital. *Bathroom, my ass,* I thought. *He had Olaf climb onto the roof and mark the wing.*

"Hotwire," I said, "call off the strike."

He nodded and spoke quickly into his radio, then frowned. "I'm being blocked. They can't hear me."

"Call off the strike," I said to Baine.

"Too late, Captain." He smirked. "Bombs away."

I scrambled to the top of the collapse, arriving at the same moment the laser-guided bomb consumed a section of the compound in a booming plume of smoke. As the rest of the team hit the ground, I remained standing. The young men on the pallets, the women tending to them. Gone.

The bedrock shuddered, and a wave of heat and pressure hit my face. Secondary explosions began to pop off.

"Hear that?" Baine said, coming up beside me. "Those are munitions. Not as innocent as you thought, huh?"

I turned and with my entire two-hundred-fifty-pound frame smashed the butt of my M4 into his face. Baine dropped like a sack of dirt, blood spouting from his broken nose and mouth.

"Every village in Waristan has munitions, you asshole," I said coldly.

When I stepped toward him to deal more punishment, Olaf aimed his weapon at me. The rest of Team 5 responded by turning their M4s on him. "Don't even fucking think about it," Segundo growled.

Olaf ignored him and spoke directly to me. "Leave him alone. I take."

He grabbed the strap on the back of his groggy companion's body armor and began dragging him down the collapse. The team looked at me for direction. "They're going to need rescue and medical help," I said of the Kabadi, breaking into a run back toward the compound.

The rest of my team followed.

7

"Muzzles down," I ordered. "I don't want our return to be mistaken for a follow-up attack."

Ahead, smoke and screams rose above the compound wall. We arrived to find the gate open, children and the elderly streaming out. Several were dust-coated and bleeding. One child stopped to stare at us, blood trickling from his right ear, before an old woman seized his wrist and pulled him after her. We filed past them and ran toward the large building.

Dense, metallic smoke stung my eyes and burned my lungs. Through the haze, I could see where the building's hospital wing had once stood, now sheared away and pulverized into a crater. The able-bodied women and men of the village had already begun climbing down, pulling away stones and digging into the blasted wreckage in an attempt to reach anyone still alive. They cried back and forth to one another, coordinating their efforts.

"Mauli and Dean," I said. "Begin triaging any wounded you see. Segundo, I want your split team helping the rescue effort outside. Parker will remain with you to interpret. The rest of us will see if we can extract anyone from inside."

I led three men through the building's blown door and up the stairs. The blast had knocked lanterns from their hooks, and oil fires trickled past us, but the main building was surprisingly intact, as though held together by magic. At the top of the steps, I snapped on my weapon-mounted tactical light and shone it down the dust-filled corridor that had led to the infirmary. After ten or so feet, the corridor ended in a collapse.

Behind us, the barking from earlier continued, though more feverishly now.

"Start excavating, but watch the ceiling," I said, eyeing the timber beams. "I'm going to see if there's anyone back this way."

I hustled down the opposite corridor, my flashlight beam slashing across the walls with the strange wolf art. When the corridor took a sharp left, the barking became so loud that it hurt my ears. I soon spotted the source of the sound: a shaking wooden door banded with metal slats. A thick crossbeam sat in a latch, locking the door from the outside.

As I neared the door, the barking and shaking stopped. Several powerful noses snuffed along the top of the eight-foot-tall frame. I pressed on, but the corridor only turned left again and ended at another collapse.

I called and then listened, but couldn't hear anything above the barking, which had started up again. I turned around, approaching the door from the other direction. Now I noticed a greenish current moving across the metal bands, seeming to stiffen every time the door shook. Was some sort of energy field reinforcing the door? If so, what in the hell was powering it?

Fresh shouting broke out, pulling my thoughts from the question. My men were in trouble. I raced past the rattling door, rounded the corner with my M4, and stopped cold.

The old witch had emerged from her shrine room, ragged robes dragging across the floor. Green tendrils of light lashed around her as she spoke in a shrill voice. I crept forward and shone my light past her. My men were no longer in the collapsed corridor. Groans sounded from down the stairwell. I peered around the corner and aimed my tactical light down the steps. My men lay at the bottom in a heap as though they'd been thrown.

"You guys all right?" I called.

At the sound of my voice, the old woman whipped her wrinkled face toward me, her eye sockets puckering and relaxing like tiny fists. She sniffed the air, then broke into a toothless grin.

"Something hit us," my junior weapons sergeant answered groggily.

"Yeah, felt like another bomb went off," one of my engineers put in.

The witch scuffed toward me on the leathery soles of her feet, the tendrils of light seeming to feel their way forward. I didn't know who or what she was, but something told me she was the reason my men were in a heap. I trained my M4 on her chest and started to sidestep around her.

"Get outside," I called down to my men. "Now!"

They complied as I continued to move around the witch. Her face followed me, black gums showing through her insane smile. I was almost to the steps when her right hand shot forward and grasped my lead wrist. Her grip was as solid as a metal cuff. I tried to twist away but couldn't. A sudden lethargy had overcome me. I felt like my limbs were strapped with hundred-pound weights. I fought to keep my rifle trained on her.

Leaning forward, she spoke into my face. *"Sarbozi kavi."*

Whatever she'd said evoked a giggle, making the small wooden cube that hung from her neck shake. The beasts continued to bark. The witch angled her face past me, as though listening to them. Coming to some decision, she nodded and trained her face back on mine.

"Ozad ba." She giggled and nodded some more. *"Ozad baaa..."*

The breath that broke against my face might as well have come from the rotten wolf head mounted in her shrine room, it was that putrid. But I remained rooted to the spot, unable to move. What the hell was she doing to me?

"Gurgi Kabud?" she asked.

"Can't understand you," I slurred.

"Ha ha, Gurgi Kabud," she repeated, apparently answering the question for me. The tendrils of light surrounding her seemed to arrange themselves into a monstrous wolf shape, similar to those adorning the walls. I noticed that my M4 was no longer aimed at her. It had fallen against my chest, hanging on its sling. It felt too heavy to hold now. The witch pulled me closer, as though I weighed nothing.

"Let me go," I demanded, but could hardly bolster the words. My voice was weak, not my own. It belonged to a frightened child, and I couldn't deny that I was the most scared I'd been since I was twelve.

She grinned broadly and lifted a gnarled hand to my face. A horny thumbnail caressed my cheek, the contact sending a chill through me. Suddenly her face clenched into a horrid grimace, tears squeezing from the flesh of her eye sockets. Fierce heat seared my cheek as her thumbnail cut into me and began carving the skin with sharp strokes. I strained to pull away.

"Gurgi Kabud," she said decisively, and released me.

I stood for a moment, my cheek on fire. The witch wavered in front of me like a nightmarish mirage, and then my legs folded. I collapsed down the staircase. My helmet and body armor absorbed a lot of the impact, but I arrived at the bottom battered, my rifle digging into my side.

I recovered my weapon quickly, shook my head clear, and aimed up the staircase. The witch was gone.

Pushing myself to my feet, I stumbled outside into bright light and confusion. Beyond the smoke and rescuers racing back and forth, I found my men standing in a huddle away from the demolished wing.

"What's going on?" I asked them. "Why aren't you helping?"

Dean, my senior weapons sergeant, nodded at where Nafid was shouting at Parker, Segundo standing beside him. When I walked over, Segundo gave me an aggrieved look.

"Parker's been trying to explain that the bombing was a mistake, that we're here to help, but she's ordering us to leave. She keeps repeating, 'You don't know what you've done, you don't know what you've done.'"

"Parker," I said, "tell her—"

But before I could finish, Nafid spun on me and began beating my chest with her fists. The fear and lethargy that had overcome me in the witch's presence dissipated, and I gripped her forearms forcefully.

"Listen, we didn't order the bombing," I said, Parker translating quickly. "That was a mistake. A horrible mistake, and I am so sorry. But let's think about the ones we can help right now. We can bring in rescuers and medical supplies. We can evac the seriously injured. Tell us what we can do."

She stopped struggling long enough to glare at me. "You have done enough," she said, the accented words sharp and venomous. "Leave now if you and your men want to live."

I released her, and she stormed back toward the demolition.

"That sounded a lot like English," Segundo said. "And was that a threat?"

"It doesn't matter, we're clearing out," I said. "We can't force ourselves on them."

And Nafid was right, we had already done enough. I'd known Baine and Olaf were mercenaries. I should have kept a closer eye on them, goddammit. I turned and walked toward the gate. The rest of the team followed.

Outside the smoking compound we moved into a single file and trudged back toward our valley, the cries of the injured and grieving slowly fading off behind us.

―――

I looked from where we had set up the 240s the night before down to the valley floor. A circle of blasted sand showed me exactly where the helicopter had landed and picked up Baine and Olaf as well as our machine guns.

Son of a bitch.

"Our rucksacks are gone too," Hotwire said, emerging from the building.

Make that an effing son of a bitch, I thought. The rucks held most of our computers and commo equipment, not to mention our spare food, water, and ammo.

"Think Centurion has any more helos coming for *us*?" Parker asked timidly.

"No, we're gonna be on our own," I said, remembering Baine's smug, defiant face the instant before my rifle stock smashed home. There was no way he was sending help. "Hotwire, see who you can get on the radio. Start with Stanick. Give him a full update on our situation. If he can't get us anything today, try Pete. We'll have to rely on what's left in our packs and vests in the meantime."

"Anyone need medical attention?" Mauli asked.

I answered in the negative along with the rest of the team.

"Hold on, sir, what happened here?" Mauli asked, gesturing toward my cheek.

I brushed the crumbs of dried blood from the burning wound. "An old woman scratched me."

"Well let's get some antibiotic in you." He reached into his medical bag and pulled out a syringe. "No telling what's in her fingernails, and you don't want that getting infected."

Now that he mentioned it, my face felt flushed with fever and I had the beginnings of a goring headache. *Didn't think an infection could spread that quickly,* I thought as I pushed up my right sleeve. Mauli scrubbed a spot behind my bicep with an alcohol wipe and plunged the needle in.

"There," he said, depressing the plunger and withdrawing the needle.

One moment I was thinking about how pale everything looked and in the next I was in Mauli's arms, my big medic struggling to hold me upright. The tingling sensation of recovering consciousness filled my head.

"Whoa there, Captain. Why don't we get you inside and lying down?"

I noticed the rest of the team watching us. I had never so much as caught a cold during a mission much less fainted. "I'm fine," I said, patting his arms. "Just a head rush. Segundo, can I talk to you?"

Mauli's brow bent in concern. "You might need some fluids."

"I said I'm fine."

I left Mauli's side and led my number two to the far side of the bunker, out of earshot of the rest of the team. My head was still swimmy, and my legs weren't all there, but I disguised both by leaning an arm against the wall. Now wasn't the time to show weakness.

"How bad's our situation?" Segundo asked.

"That depends on how long it takes to get a ride. Who knows what Baine is telling his superiors right now, but you can bet it's not good."

"When I get my hands on that little shit..." Segundo muttered.

"Which means we can forget about Centurion's help," I continued. "That leaves the other services, most of which are going to be committed to the capital. If Stanick can't find us something, Pete might be able to work some magic. But I think we should prepare the men to spend another night out here."

"Without air support or heavy weapons?" Segundo asked, scanning the opposite ridge. "Fuck."

"Yeah, we'll have to assume there are still fighters in the area, but we have another eight hours of daylight. We'll bolster our defenses, scout out retreat routes and rally points." My face felt like it was on fire, and I could hear my heart pounding in my ears. I wiped my drenched brow with a forearm. "Tonight we'll run security at fifty percent and deal with whatever we have to deal with."

"Captain?" Hotwire called.

When I turned, the image of him sitting on the ground wavered. He had screwed in the long antenna on his radio and was working the knobs with one hand while holding a headphone to his ear with the other. "Stanick is headed to D.C. for a meeting, but I spoke to the deputy commander. He doesn't think he can get us anything until early tomorrow. I'm trying Pete, but no luck so far."

Segundo swore under his breath.

"Keep trying," I mumbled, right before the gravely ground slammed into the side of my face.

8

In my feverish sleep, I was twelve again, on the bank of Mission Creek with my best friend, Billy. It was Labor Day, the final day of summer break. We'd gotten up early, packed four peanut butter and jelly sandwiches apiece, and hiked the two miles with our fishing poles to our favorite spot, splitting for a container of night crawlers and a big bottle of Pepsi on the way. Now we sat against a pair of shady tree trunks, slowly reeling our lines through the muddy water.

"If I could quit school and fish for a living, I'd do it in a second," Billy said.

"Yeah, school sucks," I agreed. "And I heard seventh grade sucks worse than sixth."

I hadn't heard that, but it felt good to say. My family lived in the country in a house my dad had built. He owned a machine that split wood, which he sold by the truckload along with pine straw. Between that and his construction projects, we did fine. I figured I'd carry on the work when I grew up, so what did I need earth science and pre-algebra for?

Billy took a swig from the Pepsi bottle. "There's good squirrel hunting in those woods back behind the school, though."

"Maybe we can hit it on the weekends."

"Weekends? I'm talking about after school."

I was about to tell him that I didn't think we could bring our shotguns to school when a branch snapped behind us. I turned my head expecting to see a deer—the woods were full of them—instead, three teenaged boys were wading toward us through the brush. They wore denim jackets even though the morning was warming quickly and would hit ninety by noon. The shoulders of their jackets were littered with leaves, suggesting they'd slept out here, maybe just woken up. I'd never seen them before, but I knew right off they were trouble.

"Well, looky here," the lead one said. He was thin with a scruffy blond beard and a dirty John Deere hat that was too big for his head. "If it ain't Tom Sawyer and Huck Finn."

I peered over at Billy, then squinted back at John Deere. The boys on either side of him were built like linebackers, but they looked sick, their faces pasty and dull, dark rings around their eyes. A coldness seemed to encompass all three of them, making my throat tighten with fear.

"You boys catching anything?" John Deere asked.

"Not yet," Billy said in a tone of annoyance.

"Well, maybe you're not doing it right," John Deere said. "You ever try bleeding the waters? Good way to lure fish in. Might even attract some sharks." The other boys chuckled. John Deere only grinned, his eyes seeming to glint from the shadow beneath his green bill.

"We know how to fish," Billy said. "And there aren't sharks in fresh water."

Because of his size, Billy could usually get away with being defiant. But these guys were bigger—and there were three of them. I stayed quiet, hoping the less said, the less reason they'd have to hang around.

John Deere stared at Billy, his mouth straightening. "Is that right?" he asked thinly. The boy to his right whispered something to him that seemed to restore John Deere's charm. "Say…" He coughed into a fist. "Our car broke down, and we could use some help. You boys wouldn't have a few bucks you could spare so we can fix our ride and get outta here?"

"We didn't bring any money," Billy said.

But that was a lie, and John Deere knew it. He was looking at our foam container of night crawlers, "$2.50" written in black ink across the plastic lid. I thought about pulling out the two bucks and change I could feel sitting in the bottom of my pocket, but instead I gripped my pole tighter in both hands.

"Didn't bring any money," John repeated. "So you must've stolen that."

Billy followed his gaze to the container. Seeing he'd been caught, he muttered, "What's it to you? You want money, go earn it yourself."

"What did you say?" John demanded.

"He told you to get a job," the boy to his right said, laughing dully. His front teeth were brown, one of them chipped in half. The other boy laughed too. This time John didn't even grin.

"Bring him over here," he ordered.

Billy dropped his pole, but by the time he scrambled to

his feet, the two boys had him by either arm. He swore and tried to stomp their feet, but they only laughed and lifted him into the air. I stayed sitting, icy fists clamped around my pole, insides frozen through.

The boys carried him struggling to John Deere, whose lips had turned up at the corners again. This time a pair of canines flashed, their tips filed to perfect points. He stuck both hands into Billy's front pockets, his left hand emerging with three five dollar bills, money Billy had earned helping his dad deliver hay bales.

"Give it back, you son of a bitch!" Billy shouted.

John pocketed the bills. "You see? Being charitable ain't so hard."

Cheeks red with rage, Billy unleashed a spray of spit into John's face.

Oh crap, I thought. *Oh crap, oh crap, oh crap.*

John calmly lifted the front of his T-shirt and patted his face dry. His stomach was lean and white with a strange network of veins. When he lowered his shirt again, his shaded eyes looked dead. "I'm a nice guy," he said in a dangerous monotone. "I really am. It's just every time I turn around, someone else is giving me shit."

He pulled something from his jacket pocket, but I couldn't see what.

"Sort of hard to be nice when everyone's giving you shit, you know?" he said.

When he stepped forward a switchblade popped from his fist, the metal dirtied with dried blood.

Terror detonating through my body, I forced myself to stand. "He didn't mean it." But the words couldn't seem to get past my throat. No one heard me. I tried to swallow, but my saliva had turned to paste. "Stop. He didn't mean it," I said with more force but the same result.

"So, fuck you too," John said, and plunged the blade into my friend's neck.

The shock kicked me from the dream/memory and into a stifling space. I was lying on the ground, a sleeping pad beneath me. My shirt was soaked through with sweat. I couldn't seem to open my eyes, but I could hear voices outside.

"...needs to be kept in isolation until he can be medevacked," Mauli was saying. "I'm the only one who goes in or out of that room."

"They're still telling me no rides till 0700 tomorrow morning," Hotwire said.

"He gonna be all right till then?" Parker asked.

"I'm doing everything I can to bring his fever down," Mauli said, "but he's cooking. And his heart rate's through the roof. I'm pushing IV fluids fast as I can, but his body's not responding."

I was vaguely aware of the needle in the crook of my elbow.

Segundo swore. "Centurion has a fleet of helos that could be here in under an hour. Try them again."

"They're not responding," Hotwire said, "and I need to save battery."

Segundo swore again as I plunged back into sleep.

The witch's puckered eye sockets were clenching and relaxing in front of me.

"*Gurgi Kabud,*" she sang through her black lips. "*Ha, ha, Gurgi Kabud.*"

Shadows stalked over the walls, assuming the forms of wolves, their eyes flashing yellow. Men with sharpened canines and blue hair on their faces filed past. The barks of beasts thundered around us.

"Too late, Captain," I heard Baine saying. "Bombs away."

Bombs away, bombs away, bombs away…

The witch reached forward, her thumbnail biting into my cheek. "*Gurgi Kabud,*" she whispered. My punishment for raining death and destruction on her children. For not protecting them.

As she carved her nail into my skin, her face changed, morphing into the rotting wolf head. The head grew until it loomed over me. I tried to back away but was frozen in place. The wolf's lower jaw dropped open, wrapping me in its feral breath. Above and below its swollen tongue, a set of razor-sharp teeth glinted in the growing darkness. The air turned impossibly humid.

It's swallowing me, I realized in horror.

And then the dream began again…

———

Darkness beyond my lids.

I was on my sleeping pad, head hammering, body burning up. I could hear deep breathing and the rustle of sleeping bags in an adjoining room. Outside the Soviet bunker, I recognized the cadence of Segundo's boots, the crunch of gravel like bones. Everything seemed so frigging loud.

"Can I have a word?" I heard Mauli saying to him.

"How's he doing?" Segundo asked in a lowered voice.

"He's incoherent, calling for someone named Billy and then babbling some foreign-sounding nonsense. I'm doing everything I can, but his vitals are still through the roof. And his head's starting to swell. That probably means meningitis."

"Is that bad?" Segundo asked.

Mauli blew out his breath. "We don't get him airlifted to a hospital, and he won't last the night."

Billy lay in a fetal position on the ground. The boys had taken turns drinking the blood from his neck before stalking off, mouths smeared red. They hadn't said a word to me. Hadn't even glanced my way when they left. I could hear brush snapping beneath their distant footfalls.

"Billy?" I said, finding my voice finally.

I had watched the whole horrifying show as if from a great distance, not speaking, not moving, willing myself to blend into the trees at my back. Now I dropped my fishing pole and stepped toward him. His face was white—too white—the splash of red freckles across his cheeks an alien constellation. My eyes fell to where he'd been stabbed.

Blood trickled from a pale, puckered gash a couple of inches above his collarbone. I would be told later the blade had severed his jugular vein.

"It's bad, isn't it?" Billy croaked.

I swallowed dryly and nodded as a cicada chorus rose to a feverish pitch around us. "What do I do?" I whispered.

"Go get my dad," he said.

I ran the two miles back to town, horror-stricken for my friend but at the same time relieved that it wasn't me back there on the ground, stabbed and drained.

The shame of harboring that relief, of not having done anything to prevent what happened, of allowing my friend to die in the woods that day, would haunt me for years—through high school, military training, every special ops deployment. In a strange way, I felt like an accomplice. A feeling made worse by the fact the teenagers were never caught.

In my feverish sleep, I tried to change that. Instead of racing toward town to get Billy's dad, I veered in the direction of the killers. They'd had a good head start, but I was tracking their smell, which might as well have been splashed over the brush in red paint.

In my running dreams I usually felt like I was trudging through mud, but now everything was a rushing blur.

Before long, I picked up an exchange of voices. I couldn't understand what they were saying, the words fast and foreign-sounding, but I had them. My lips stretched from my teeth. I was only vaguely aware that I was running on all fours, muscles pumping over my shoulders and flanks. I was too transfixed by the hunt. And the boys had no idea I was coming for them.

I skidded around a large tree and found them crouched behind a boulder, their backs to me.

But the scene had changed to nighttime, the woods becoming a high, wind-swept desert. And instead of denim and John Deere hats, the three were wearing dark, olive-colored clothes and black turbans. They chattered back and forth in Pashto, the language of the Mujahideen, AK-47s protruding from their grips.

I'd been coiling to pounce, but now I stopped cold.

I'm not dreaming anymore, I realized in horror. *This is real.*

9

I pawed for my pistol, but it wasn't at my waist. I was wearing only my camo pants, tan undershirt, and what looked like a dark thermal top underneath. Though my shirt was damp, I wasn't cold. Instead, the lingering fire of the hunt burned through me. I felt clear-headed, strong. But I was also defenseless and out in the open—regardless of how in the hell I'd ended up here.

One of the men turned, his eyes starting wide. He released a horrified shriek.

I sprang forward without thinking, my hand forming a hook. My fingernails ripped through tissue and cartilage. A spray of hot blood hit me across the cheek. Before the men beside him could get their weapons in position, I slammed one of their heads against the boulder hard enough to feel his skull crack, then buried my face into the other one's throat.

Terrified cries sounded beneath my thrashing, tearing jaws.

A burst of radio chatter broke the spell. I stood back,

dark blood dripping from my hands, the slick, coppery taste filling my mouth. The men lay in a mangled mess at my feet, like the floor of a butcher shop. I looked at my arms. What I'd mistaken for a dark thermal top was matted hair.

The hell?

The hand I ran along my arm was huge, the fingers tipped with razor-sharp claws. I turned the hand over and looked at a palm layered in dark padded flesh. I touched the hand to my face and felt over a jutting, hair-covered jaw. *A snout?* My nose, which was picking up a riot of smells—blood, metal, desert scrub—seemed to have fused into the blunt muzzle. I felt over both ears now. They'd shifted higher onto my head and were pointed like an animal's. I opened my jaw and ran my tongue over a serration of sharp teeth and massive canines.

This doesn't make any fucking sense.

I was standing in a hunch, my arms and legs seeming to have stretched out while thickening with new layers of muscle. My bare feet were long, the toes bent like claws. I felt powerful and agile, like I could run forever.

More radio chatter.

I reached down and lifted the radio from the gore. I didn't understand the words, but I knew they were coming from another Mujahideen fighter. I peered around, the night clear and vibrant in my vision. I could see for miles. I was on the ridge opposite the Soviet bunker. My men were on the hillock around the bunker, calling my name, spreading into a search. But I couldn't think about that or whatever was happening to me right now. I had to think like a captain.

The men I had mauled were a scout team. They had

been spying on our position, which meant a larger force was nearby. Without heavy weapons or air support, Team 5 was vulnerable—unless I acted.

I scanned the valleys and hills that spread from the dry river valley. We had examined the map of the area the night before, identifying the most likely routes the Mujahideen would take if they were coming up from the south.

My gaze settled on a narrow valley running roughly parallel to ours. When the wind shifted and came up over the rim, I smelled the pungent odor of the men. I caught a whiff of their weapons too—a combination of oily metal and gunpowder. Knowing we were a small unit, they wouldn't expect a rear assault.

I slung two of the AKs over my left shoulder and looted the men of their spare banana mags, stuffing them into my pants pockets. Despite that my hands were altered, I had a powerful prehensile grip as well as dexterous fingers.

I was turning to leave when I spotted the metal tube of a loaded rocket launcher on the ground beside the boulder. I picked it up by the strap and pulled it over my right shoulder. Fully armed, I ran low to the ground, remaining behind cover as I circled the fighters' position. My new body seemed to posses its own muscle memory, moving with efficiency and strength. Despite my fifty-pound load, I climbed in and out of craggy ravines with ease.

When I reached the floor of the narrow valley, I could hear the enemy fighters. Their voices were coming from a honeycomb of caves about two hundred yards up the valley. Three fighters formed a small security perimeter around the caves, while a spotter stood on the ridge above them, using a night scope to scan the terrain toward our valley. When he spoke into a radio, I recognized the high voice as belonging to the man who had been trying to contact the scouts.

He's going to know something's wrong soon.

Picking out a cluster of boulders across the valley, I pressed the weapons to my sides so they wouldn't clatter and made a run for it. I crossed the hundred-yard distance in seconds and concealed myself. No shots. No shouts of alarm. The fighters hadn't seen me.

But I could see them. Nighttime glimmered like a light dusk in my enhanced vision. Heat auras radiated around their bodies. I counted about twenty-five of them. The smaller unit the Mujahideen had dispatched the night before had been meant to gauge our force size and strength. Tonight's attack would be larger and better coordinated. And with my team isolated and outgunned, not to mention distracted by my disappearance, the Mujahideen would have an advantage.

The spotter radioed back and forth with a commander in the caves now. The urgency suggested they were preparing to move. Lifting the rocket launcher to my right shoulder, I checked behind me and then lined up the sights on the cave where the commander was shouting orders. A handful of fighters clustered around him, several kneeling in prayer.

Time to take out the leadership and create some chaos.

I squeezed the trigger, my muscles absorbing the concussive recoil. In a jet of vapor, the missile hit its target, obliterating the commander and his men in a burst of smoke and fire. Flames shot into the adjoining caves and blew dust into the valley in giant plumes. Survivors scrambled for their lives while secondary explosions boomed and the men on security looked wildly about.

Check and check.

I ditched the launcher, raised one of the AK-47s, and picked off the perimeter security with short bursts. By the time I raised the weapon to the spotter, he was out of sight. I'd find him in a minute. In a chattering stream, I emptied the mag's remaining rounds on the fleeing survivors. Switching AKs, I sprayed the caves, changing out the mags until nothing moved beyond the dust. I emerged from my concealment and stalked toward the caves.

Feeble moans crawled through an air thick with smoke, sand, and gunpowder. I took aim at the sounds and silenced them with single shots. I then slung the AK around my back and climbed past the caves on hands and feet. Nothing moved now. The annihilation was total.

At the place where the spotter had been standing, I found his night scope and radio in the dirt.

Good, probably fled before reporting the attack.

I sniffed around until I picked up a scent sharp with adrenaline and fear. It trailed toward a mound of boulders off to my right. I could hear the spotter's breathing, cycling in and out in a rapid whisper that sounded like praying.

I bounded up the boulders until I was looking down on him. The young fighter couldn't have been more than fifteen, his face smooth except for a threadbare mustache. He gripped a pistol in his right hand and a string of wooden beads in the other. He had no idea I was right above him. I dropped, tearing the pistol from his grip. He cried out in terror. Aiming the pistol at his head, I backed up so the kid could get an eyeful.

"G-Gurgi Kabud," he stammered. "*Gurgi Kabud!*"

They were the same words the old witch had spoken. The boy threw himself prostrate on the ground and began to babble. Though I couldn't understand him, I got the message. He was begging for his life. A feral urge to tear him apart clawed up inside me, but I forced it back down.

"*Go home,*" I said in broken Pashto, my voice deep and guttural. "*Go back to your village.*"

His right ear had been burned, I saw, held to a flame until it was a lumpy mass of flesh—a common Mujahideen punishment. He had probably been recruited when he was just old enough to hold a rifle. He was as much a victim as those the Mujahideen had tortured and murdered.

"*Go!*" I repeated, jabbing a taloned finger south.

The boy nodded quickly and scrambled to his sandaled feet.

In the next instant, pain seared through my right shoulder. It took a second for the crack of the shot to register. As the pistol I'd been holding thudded to the ground, I spun to find a bloody Mujahideen fighter on his stomach, holding a shaky AK-47 at an awkward angle. He'd slipped from the carnage somehow, and in my struggle to spare the boy from whatever instincts had overtaken me, I hadn't heard him.

I streaked toward him as he tried to adjust his aim and finished him with a hammering blow that crushed his skull.

I wheeled back around, but the boy had already fled. My muscles tensed to give chase, a part of me already anticipating the hunt. But I willed what humanity I still possessed back to the fore.

He's a child, I reminded myself. *Conscripted against his will.*

I let him go.

By the time I returned to the ridge that looked across to the former Soviet bunker, eight members of Team 5 were crossing toward me. Having heard the shooting and explosions, they assumed I'd been spotted. They were racing over to engage the enemy before I was captured or killed.

I considered shouting down to them, but I crouched out of sight instead. The priority needed to be tomorrow's airlift and getting the team safely out. My condition was of secondary concern and would only distract from that objective. I stole another look. The entire team was coming except for Parker and Mauli, who were standing guard at the bunker, and Dan, the junior weapons sergeant, who was covering the advance group from the opposite ridge.

I needed to reach Mauli. As team medic, he could assess me, tell me what was going on. I ran along the ridge, remaining out of sight of the team, until I reached a bend in the dry river valley. I crossed there and scrambled partway up to the opposite ridge where Dan couldn't spot me from above. I moved swiftly, the pain in my right shoulder diminishing until I could hardly tell it was there.

I reached our hill as the eight-man advance group was climbing to the opposite ridge. I approached Mauli from behind. His M4 was in firing position as he tracked the group with a pair of night-vision goggles. Hunkering behind a clutch of dried brush, I whispered, "Mauli, it's your captain."

He spun toward me. "Wolfe?"

"Shh. Go inside and bring me an emergency blanket."

"What's going on, sir? Are you all right?" He craned his thick neck for a better view.

"Bring me an emergency blanket," I repeated in my that's-an-order voice. "And tell no one I'm here."

He disappeared into the bunker and reappeared a moment later with one of the foil-like blankets.

"Toss it over."

When he did, I draped the blanket over my head and shoulders, clutching it at my neck to form a deep hood. With my face concealed, I emerged from the brush in a low crouch to disguise my height.

"What's going on?" he repeated.

"Turn around and lead me back to my room. Do it," I said when he hesitated.

Even though I was acting out of character, he complied. I waited until his back was to me before following. I ducked into the bunker behind him, passed through the large room where the men had created a makeshift barracks, and entered a smaller back room where the torn sleeping bag, ripped-out IV lines, and burst saline bag told the story of my departure.

"Wait," I said as Mauli removed his night-vision goggles and reached for a battery-powered lantern hanging from the wall. "Radio the team and tell them I've returned. They're to come back to base immediately but no one is to see me except for you. I'm back under quarantine."

While he relayed this to Segundo, I closed the door behind us.

"They're on their way back," he said. "But, geez, what happened, man? One minute you're lying here at death's door, and in the next you're taking off like a man possessed."

That must have been when the transformation began, I thought. "I'm hoping you can tell me." I turned the lantern on now and dropped the emergency blanket from my head.

When Mauli saw my face, he pressed himself flat against the wall behind him. "Oh, fuck no."

"I look like the men on the pallets, don't I?"

Mauli stopped staring long enough to dig into his medical bag and, with a trembling hand, pass me a small mirror. I took a breath, then raised it in front of me. The men on the pallets had looked human with animal features. The face staring back at me was pure animal—especially with the Mujahideen fighters' blood matting the blue hair around my nose and mouth. I examined my face from several angles before handing the mirror back to Mauli.

"You look like a... a..."

"A wolf," I finished for him. "Could I have contracted—"

"Hypertrichosis? That's not an infection, it's a genetic condition. Whatever this is, it's not hypertrichosis. Hell, it's not anything I've ever seen. We need to get you to a hospital. I can give you a basic exam, but it's going to take experts to diagnose and treat you." He was starting to babble.

I pulled my right sleeve up over my shoulder, the blue hair knotted and stiff with blood. "You can start with my shoulder. In addition to turning into this, I took a bullet earlier."

"So all that AK fire we heard was directed at you?"

"Actually, most of it was directed at them. They've been neutralized."

Having something to do seemed to steady Mauli slightly, and he donned a pair of latex gloves. When I sank to my haunches, we were almost the same height. I tensed as he began probing the wound, but all I could feel was the pressure of his fingers. "There's scarring," he said, "but nothing fresh." His fingers moved to the front of my shoulder. "And here's where the bullet exited, but again, just scar tissue."

"Are you saying it already healed?"

"Yeah." He stared in disbelief. "First Olaf's arm, now this." He donned his stethoscope and listened as he moved the metal disk around my chest. "Your heart's still going a mile a minute. How do you feel?"

I thought for a moment. I was stronger, faster, and with the knowledge the bullet wound had already healed, damn near invincible. But it was all wrong. "I feel like my brain's been scooped out and dropped into an animal's body," I replied. "An animal with reflexes on a hair trigger that can react without thinking. An animal that's really fucking lethal."

"And this has never happened to you before?" He showed his hands when I narrowed my eyes at him. "Hey, I had to ask—and don't look at me that way. I feel like you're gonna take a bite out of me."

"Are there any conditions, any at all, that could explain this?"

Instead of answering, Mauli leaned forward, eyes squinting at my face.

"What?" I said.

He pulled a pair of scissors from his bag and began snipping the hair over my right cheek. "When we got back here earlier today, your face was bloody where that old woman scratched you. I gave you the antibiotic, but after you passed out, I cleaned and disinfected the wound. I expected to find a nasty gouge, but there was a design or something." He lowered the scissors and brushed the hair away with his fingers. "Yeah, it's still there."

"Can I see?"

He handed the mirror to me again and I held it up. He was right. There was a complex arrangement of gashes—almost like a Chinese symbol, but cruder. A circle around an inverted triangle around what looked like a crescent moon. And unlike the gunshot wound, it hadn't healed. I could see subcutaneous layers of flesh, and the spot still burned.

"I started feeling like crap right after she did that," I said, touching the wound with the pad of a finger. "Is there any way she gave me something? An infection or...?" My voice trailed off.

Mauli raised his eyebrows. "Or what?"

I was thinking about the green tendrils of light that had been moving around her like tentacles. I remembered how she'd flung my men down the staircase and then subdued me with little more than a hand around my wrist. And all without eyes. I didn't really believe in witches, but...

"A curse," I said grudgingly.

"Hey, I don't know about any of that stuff."

I described both of my encounters with the witch, pacing the room as I did so. Whatever animal intelligence possessed my body it was starting to feel hot and restless, shut in. Mauli might have felt it too, because he backed into a corner.

"Here's the thing," Mauli said, his voice accelerating into a babble again. "*I* don't know about any of that stuff, but I have this aunt who swears it's all true. She lives in Staten Island, New York, writes me all the time. She used to have an apartment in the Lower East Side, but the place went to pot after the Crash. She claimed ghouls were coming up from the subway lines and scavenging the streets. Got so bad, the mayor called in some wizard dude to help exterminate them."

Despite being the one to bring up the supernatural, I cocked a skeptical eyebrow.

"I know how that sounds, but this isn't coming from the National Enquirer. My aunt was sending me clippings from the *New York Gazette*, the city's main paper. This was all going on last summer. Goblins in Central Park, vampires in the Financial District. Crazy shit."

"I did hear about that. Some sort of political stunt for the mayor's reelection."

"Hey, you were the one that asked," Mauli countered. He seemed to will himself calmer as he peeled off his latex gloves. "All I'm saying is that if any of that stuff is true, then maybe a curse isn't out of the question."

"I might have some information on that," Parker said, stepping through the door.

10

I grabbed the emergency blanket when I heard Parker's voice, but was too slow pulling it over my head. My interpreter stood in the doorway, eyes large behind his glasses as he stared at me. At last, he blinked twice.

"Hello, Captain," he said quietly.

"You were under orders to remain outside," I grunted, dropping the blanket.

"I'm sorry, sir. I came in to get a battery for my night-vision goggles, and I heard you talking."

"How much did you overhear?"

"Um, pretty much all of it."

I turned to Mauli. "Do you think this is contagious?" When Mauli shrugged, I waved for Parker to come the rest of the way into the room. He hesitated, then complied on stiff legs. I listened for any other eavesdroppers before closing the door behind him. "You were saying you might have some information."

Parker sidled over to Mauli. "Yes, sir."

"All right, you need to relax. I know how I look, but it's still me."

But *was* it still me? I remembered the bloodlust I'd felt when I was ready to hunt down the child soldier.

Parker nodded and inhaled deeply, but when he exhaled, he remained ramrod straight. "I heard what you were telling Mauli about the witch, and it jibed with some of what I came across during my research into the Kabadi yesterday. As I said, there wasn't a lot on them. They inhabit this isolated corner of Waristan, and Waristan has seemed content to let them have it."

As I often did, I circled a hand for him to get to the point—only now my hand was giant and featured lethal talons that glinted in the lantern light. Parker swallowed and nodded quickly.

"Well, Waristan has also seen wave after wave of invaders, so I started digging into some of their accounts. The armies of Alexander the Great avoided the Wari Corridor after an attempted incursion in 300 B.C. Ditto the armies of Genghis Khan a thousand years later. No records as to why, though, not until the Anglo-Waristan Wars in the eighteen hundreds, when England invaded the country three times. I came across the journal of an English Army captain who was responsible for Wakhjir Province during the second Anglo-Waristan War. He described contact with the Kabadi in an attempt to take control of the Wari Corridor. Following the encounter, his entire unit came down with a strange illness. 'My men became racked with muscular pain,' he wrote. 'They writhed and babbled and began throwing up copious quantities of blood.' Wolves attacked their encampment that night, dragging off several soldiers. Blue wolves," Parker added, looking pointedly at me.

"The English retreated from the valley shortly after," he continued. "Something very similar happened to the Soviets. In fact, the soldiers who built this outpost were wiped out by dysentery and wolf attacks. Their replacements abandoned their post after two nights, insisting the valley was cursed."

"So bad things happen to those who try to impose their will on the Wari Corridor," I said in summation.

I thought about yesterday's bombing and my encounter with the old woman. *Had* she cursed me? It was the craziest damned thing I'd ever considered, but there was nothing sane about what was happening.

For the first time, I allowed myself to think about Daniela. I turned my hands over, examining the black-padded palms, then the backs: bulging knuckles the size of walnuts, lethal talons. When Mauli carried me inside earlier that day, he'd removed my pack, tactical vest, holster, and boots and set them in the corner. I stalked over to them now and began pulling on the vest.

"Um, sir?" Mauli asked. "What are you doing?"

"I don't know much about curses, but it stands to reason that the person who puts one on you can take it back off, right?" I made adjustments to the ballistic plates so the vest would fit over my enlarged chest. Though I could heal from bullet wounds to the extremities, I didn't want to test a shot through the heart.

"So you're just going to go down there and ask the witch to take it off?" Parker asked.

"Pretty much." I racked the slide on my sidearm to

make sure the first round was in the chamber, then stuck the pistol back in my hip holster.

"Should I radio Segundo?" Parker asked.

I shook my head. "This is a solo mission. If I'm not back by 0700, you make sure you and the team are on those birds and you take off without me. That's an order. I'll radio for a separate ride."

"But you'll need an interpreter," Parker pressed.

"I'll use Nafid. You heard her. She speaks English."

"I don't like the idea of you going back there alone," he said.

Mauli swallowed. "I'm with Parker on this one."

"That doesn't change anything. What I'm doing falls outside the mission parameters. There's no way in hell I'm going to put the rest of the team at risk." I dug into my pack until I found the balaclava and pulled it over my head. The mask was too small, smashing my protuberant ears flat and barely fitting over my muzzle, but it did the job of concealing my face. I considered my boots, but there was no way my feet would fit inside them now.

"We don't leave fellow soldiers," Parker said, reciting a mantra that had been drilled into us during training.

"We do this time. What happened to my rifle?" I asked Mauli.

"It's in the other room," he said, stepping out to retrieve it.

"Grab the strap too," I called.

When he returned and handed them to me, I could hear the rest of the team trudging up the base of the hill toward the bunker. *Crap.* I needed to get past them without being seen; otherwise, I'd have to explain what was happening, which was going to be hard enough—Mauli and Parker still looked shell-shocked. Then I'd have to discourage them from coming with me, which was going to be next to impossible.

I clipped the strap to my M4, slung it across my back, then turned to Parker and Mauli. "We're going out together, but I want you two to head off the team. They don't need to know about this," I said, gesturing to my face, "so I don't want you mentioning it. Tell Segundo that I returned to the village to discuss compensation for the victims. Depending on how long I'm there, I may require a separate lift, but the rest of the team is to leave when the birds arrive. You're not to tell him or the team anything else we've discussed here. Understood?"

"He'll want to talk to you," Parker said.

"My radio will be off to conserve battery power. Now let's go."

Mauli and Parker led the way reluctantly. When we arrived outside, I split toward the deep shadows of the valley wall while they continued straight ahead. I took off, my claws digging into the rocky ground, muscles propelling me forward in powerful bounds. The animal in me rejoiced at the freedom.

By the time I heard Parker talking to Segundo, I was dropping into the valley hundreds of yards away and breaking into a full sprint toward the village.

———

The building Baine had bombed continued to smoke. A suffusion of lantern light shone above the compound wall, illuminating the rescue effort, which had been going on more than twelve hours now.

I descended to all fours, which enabled me to run faster, and sped through the pasture and village. At the gate to the compound, I found the door locked again. Though I now possessed the strength to smash through the wood, I leapt instead, grabbing the top of the wall, slinging myself over, and landing inside the compound.

My M4 remained on its strap as I walked toward the damaged building, where scores of villagers continued to labor. A large portion of the debris was in piles now, beams separated from heaps of rubble and dirt. More than twenty dead lay in a line to one side of the crater, their bodies covered by blankets. Women knelt beside them, weeping and chanting prayers.

With a hard swallow, I turned from the bodies and scanned the crowds for Nafid.

"Gurgi Kabud," a woman whispered as she passed me, fear shining in her dark eyes. Whispers and murmurs proliferated, spreading in a wave as more and more of the villagers took notice of me. The sound soon reached rescuers perched around the smoking ruins. They stopped working, tools limp at their sides, as they stared at me.

"What are you doing here?" a sharp voice said.

I turned to find Nafid glaring up at me. She was the only one who did not appear cowed by my presence.

"We need to talk," I said.

"No talk. I told you to leave."

"Which I was preparing to do until your witch did this." I yanked off the balaclava, revealing my lupine face.

Nafid's green eyes stared into mine, unflinching. Then she looked me over, her gaze eventually arriving at the trimmed spot on my right cheek where the old woman had etched the symbol. I could see it meant something to her by her compressing lips. "It is a mistake," she spat.

"Good, then tell your witch to change me back."

"It is not possible," she said as she spun and strode away.

Villagers scurried from my path as I caught up to Nafid. "Why not?" I demanded, seizing her arm.

"Let me go."

"Not until you start talking. What did your witch change me into? Why are you saying she can't change me back?"

She rounded on me sharply. "What? Did you think there would not be consequences? Look around you, soldier. Look at the ruin and death you have brought. You take from us, but we cannot take from you?"

"If this is about vengeance," I said between my teeth. "You've got the wrong person."

She looked past me. "Two of my nephews were killed this morning. Boys I helped raise. Honorable men."

I followed her gaze to the covered bodies, then glanced around. Since arriving in the compound, my senses had remained alert to an attack, but the villagers were simply watching. Some touched the wolf tooth pendants that hung from their necks. My jaw clenched as I imagined Baine sitting in a climate-controlled office somewhere, filling out his kill report.

You're gonna pay for this, you son of a bitch, I thought.

When I turned back to Nafid, I realized I was still squeezing her arm. I let my giant hand fall away.

"I can't pretend to know your pain right now," I said, "but I can promise you that I will not stop fighting until the person who ordered the attack is punished. In the meantime, we will give you just compensation plus whatever else you need. But you must change me back."

"That is not for me to decide."

"Then take me to your witch."

"The woman you call a 'witch' is my great-grandmother. And that is not for Baba to decide either."

"She's the one who did this, and you know it."

Nafid shook her head. "She conjures at the will of Gurgi Buzurg, and he has spoken."

"Who's Gurgi Buzurg?"

"He is the Great Wolf."

I remembered the monstrous, rotting wolf head mounted above the old woman's shrine. A strange charge detonated from my core, seeming to heighten all of my animal senses at once.

"If your great-grandmother is in touch with him, then have her tell him to remove the curse."

Nafid flinched back as though I'd slapped her. "A curse? You believe you have been cursed?"

"What would you call it?" I shot back.

"Buzurg has chosen you to be the *Gurgi Kabud*."

That word again. "And what the hell is that supposed to be?"

"With the death of our warriors, he has named you Blue Wolf. You are the Principal Protector now, second only to the Great Wolf himself." She spoke in a kind of reverence. But then seeming to remember herself, her lips thinned along with her voice. "Like I said, a mistake."

"Protector against what?"

At that moment, a cry went up among the villagers and they began to scatter in various directions. Nafid's eyes shot up to the mountains to the north. Below the snow-capped peaks, three white figures had appeared, their wings stroking the night sky in great flaps, long tails shifting side to side. A horrid screech echoed through the valley. Only when I realized how far away the white figures were did I understand their enormous size.

"What are those?"

"Dandonho," Nafid said, backing away from them. "The white dragons."

11

"The white dragons?" I repeated.

In a flash, I remembered Pete's account of the pilot who had been chased by something large and white over the Hindu Kush, something that had torn through his Apache's plate-metal body like it was tinfoil. I also remembered the giant bullets littering the pasture and the translucent plate I'd lifted from the soil.

A dragon scale?

I had wondered what these people needed anti-aircraft guns for. That would be one explanation. I stared at the approaching creatures, their forms growing ever larger, their screeches more penetrating.

The villagers fled into the compound's several buildings, some already beginning to reemerge onto rooftops. They bore AK-47s—weapons they must have acquired during the Soviet occupation. A few of the weapons appeared to go back even further, possibly to the Anglo-Waristan wars. But the weapons were few and far between—thanks to Baine, who, judging from the secondary blasts earlier, had destroyed a chunk of their arsenal.

Nafid shouted above the approaching screeches. "You can hurt their eyes if they are unprotected. Otherwise, you must attack their necks. The scales are dense, but pressure can cut off the blood to their heads. Beware their words!"

Before I could press her for more info, she took off running toward the partially-demolished building that housed her great-grandmother's shrine. Alone in the courtyard, I readied my M4 and crouched behind a corner of a building.

The three creatures had swooped down the south face of the mountains and were flapping over the foothills toward the Wari River. They approached in a V formation: an enormous point flanked by two smaller dragons—smaller, of course, being a very relative term. None of them were less than twenty-five feet in length. Moonlight shone through their leathery wings and glistened from their scales. When they crossed the river, I could see fog pluming from their mouths.

Guns began to crack and thump from the rooftops.

This is crazy, I thought as I sighted the lead dragon. It was a duller white than the other two. Scales covered its head in an ornate mosaic that peaked at a spined crest. Black eyes scanned the landscape, its mouth slanting up on both sides of a hatchet-shaped face. Remembering Nafid's parting words, I took aim at the dragon's right eye.

This is fucking crazy.

I squeezed off four shots. Sparks glinted from what must have been transparent plating over its eyes.

Squinting, the dragon pinned its wings to its body and dove lower. The other two dragons followed, their slender forms slipping through the air as easily as eels through water. And then they were fifty feet overhead, bellies glistening white. The air chilled by several degrees, and a foul, reptilian smell washed over us. The villagers fired another volley of shots. Pieces of scale fell, but they were like flakes of dead skin. The tougher protection lay underneath.

I released three bursts from my own weapon, then ran to a corner of another building for a better angle. Beyond the compound the two smaller dragons split from the lead and coasted over the village's huts, flying low. Their throats began to convulse like cats gagging up hairballs. A moment later white plumes jetted from their mouths. The plumes swept over the fields and orchards like crop dusters, turning them frosty and brittle.

They're freezing them, I realized.

Limbs cracked and trees toppled. A piercing laugh—one belonging to a male—emerged from the lead dragon who had turned and was aiming for the compound. With several powerful flaps, he was over us again, this time low enough to reach the tops of the buildings.

Foreign words emerged from his mouth of spine-shaped teeth, the dragon's tone cruel and taunting. Villagers fired final shots before throwing themselves flat.

The dragon lowered his head and grabbed a man by his legs. I heard the wet crunch of flesh being skewered, but the man didn't relent. He battered the dragon's snout with the butt of his rifle as his robes turned crimson and stiffened with ice. I took aim at the dragon's eye again—a dangerous shot with the man so close to the target, but it was that or nothing.

My animal heart beat hard and fast in my chest, but the effect was strangely settling. The shot hit dead center, but it only flashed off the dragon's eye protection, even at close range.

Dammit.

The dragon gave the man a light toss, sending him end over end, before catching him in his mouth and gulping him down. His tail lashed, and the top half of a building crumbled on impact. Something told me that the lead dragon was toying with a village that had just lost its warrior class. He and his junior dragons could level this place in minutes.

What had Nafid said? Attack their necks?

I spotted the tallest standing building and sprinted toward it. Inside, I found the stairs and climbed them in a blur, soon emerging onto a rooftop where four villagers, two men and two women, were crouched with their weapons in firing positions. To the north, the large dragon was circling back, but in a long, lazy arc. To the south, one of the dragons was unleashing more frost over the helpless sheep while the second was cutting back toward the compound, its course about a hundred feet to my left. Shots began popping from the rooftops.

Need to draw the dragon in somehow.

I recognized an old man on the rooftop. He'd been at our first meeting in the courtyard. I shook his shoulder to get his attention.

"*Gurgi Kabud!*" he said, his face crinkling into a smile of recognition.

By pointing and miming, I managed to communicate that the villagers on the other rooftops needed to stop shooting and get down while the five of us intensified our attack. The old man, who had never stopped smiling, bobbed his head. With surprisingly powerful lungs, he shouted the instructions to the rest of the compound, then stood and shot at the approaching dragon with gusto.

I unleashed a burst of gunfire that stitched the dragon's side with sparks. As I'd hoped, it wheeled toward us and pinned its ears back. I signaled for the others on my rooftop to get down, while I climbed onto the raised containment wall and fired another burst.

The dragon lowered its head, its widening mouth a malevolent smile.

I waited until the last moment before jumping. By the time the dragon's teeth gnashed empty air, I was hooking my claws between the thick ridge of scales that ran down the back of its neck and clamping my legs around its throat: movements guided by an intelligence not my own.

The dragon reared skyward, its wings writhing as it tried to dislodge me. I'd done some bull riding in my teens, but this was taking it to another level.

I worked my arms around the dragon's neck until all four limbs were squeezing the thick cords that pulsed beneath the scales of its throat. The dragon bucked while a hollow sound built in its chest. The starry sky spiraling above us disappeared as frost plumed from the dragon's mouth. My hair stiffened into icy bristles. Gritting my teeth against the bone-deep chill, I squeezed harder.

Strange reptilian muscles squirmed beneath my clench as the dragon fought against me to free its blood flow. It wasn't going to happen.

The dragon staggered mid flight as its wings missed a beat. We stopped climbing and began to fall in a disorganized spiral. The dragon's wings missed more beats, speeding our descent. We were north of the compound, almost to the river. I caught glimpses of the large dragon circling back on the compound in his lazy arc and the smaller one still attacking sheep farther south. Not realizing their teammate's distress, neither dragon was coming to help.

Maybe realizing this, my dragon tried to steer itself toward them, but it couldn't summon enough lift. Its belly scraped over boulders, climbed slightly, then fell again. I leapt off and bounded on hands and feet with our momentum as the dragon tumbled and clattered over the boulder-strewn moraine to my left.

It came to a rest on its side, one wing angled skyward, the other crumpled underneath it. I rounded on the unconscious creature. The clear protective plates that covered its eyes were half cocked now, exposing the all-black orbs underneath. I pulled my sidearm and fired twice into each eye at pointblank range. A mucousy liquid bubbled and oozed from the entrance wounds as the eyes slowly stove in. Seconds later, the dragon's chest deflated.

One down, two to go.

I turned back toward the compound as the large dragon flew over it a third time. He bellowed another taunt before seizing several more villagers and leveling another building with his talons and tail. I broke into a sprint, closing the five-hundred-yard distance in half a minute. I climbed the wall, then scrabbled to the top of a building, this time not bothering with the stairs.

But by the time I arrived onto the rooftop, the dragon was beyond the compound and embarking on another lazy arc. I sighted the smaller dragon with my M4 as it continued to blow sheep into icy statues and swallow them whole. I fired several shots at its head. If I could lure it in and take it down like I'd done the last one, we could concentrate our attack on the leader.

With my third shot, my hearing picked up a distinct crack. The dragon whipped its long neck around and glared at the compound. The moonlight glinted over a network of fissures in the plate covering its left eye. My shot had damaged it. Expecting the dragon to flee, I was surprised—and encouraged—by its angry roar. With a series of powerful wing strokes, it stormed toward us.

"Its left eye!" I shouted to the villagers, pointing to my own eye as an example. "Aim for the left eye!"

The villagers may not have understood the words, but they got the message. The translation volleyed around the compound in shouts, and the villagers unloaded at the fast-approaching dragon. Sparks flashed from the left side of its face. I took several more shots with my M4, but from a poor angle.

Beneath the moon, the dragon's shadow was passing over the outer wall when one of the villager's shots hit home. The protective plate shattered and spilled from its eye. The dragon unleashed a pained roar as it careened off course. It crashed into a building and tumbled to the courtyard beneath me. Struggling to right itself, the dragon's wings buffeted the air with foul gusts.

But before it could regain its footing, glowing green threads spread over the dragon, ensnaring it.

I looked around until I saw Nafid crossing the courtyard with a staff that blazed with green light. Had it been even a week earlier, I would have thought I was seeing things. But I had been cursed by a witch, turned into a wolf, and was now battling dragons. Believing that Nafid was manifesting the threads of light no longer required a stretch of the imagination.

She shouted something at the dragon, and it sounded personal. When the dragon growled back, its lower jaw snagged in the tightening threads and wrenched open.

Nafid appeared to have things under control, but all of the commotion had attracted the large dragon, who was sharpening his turn back toward us and accelerating with strong strokes of his wings.

"Stand clear," I shouted to Nafid.

She paused in her advance and looked up at me. I pulled a grenade from a vest pouch and held it up. Seeming to understand, she retreated. I flicked off the thumb safety, pulled the pin, and tossed the grenade down into the dragon's pinned-open mouth. I watched long enough for the grenade to rattle around its gullet before crouching away.

The detonation was loud and wet. When I looked again, the dragon's head was blood drenched and misshapen, the scales either bulging or blown off. Its body slumped into Nafid's green webbing as its chest deflated.

I lifted my face to the final dragon. He was over the village now, the gusts from his wings uprooting trees and blowing roofs from huts. White fire burned in the pits of his eyes.

"Can you ensnare him with another web?" I shouted down to Nafid.

With a jerk of her arm, the dead dragon flopped to the courtyard as the threads of light flashed back into her staff. I watched the incoming dragon. Bullets sparked over his eyes as the villagers' shots found their marks. But his protective plating was more developed than those of the junior dragons. With a roar, the enormous creature swept in.

Nafid shouted something, and another glowing green web shot from the staff and across the dragon's path. He glided over it deftly. Clear of the web, his throat began to convulse in booming grunts.

Knowing what was coming, I crouched behind the retaining wall as the icy blast from the dragon's mouth plumed over our rooftop, covering it in crystals. My hair, recently thawed following my ride on the junior dragon, stiffened into icicles again, but my body was unharmed. The old man behind me wasn't so lucky. He cried out and seized his leg as though he'd been shot.

I ran over to him as the shadow of the dragon passed. Wiping the frost from the man's ice-stiff ankle, I checked the pulse. Nothing. His entire lower limb was frozen through.

I removed the man's twine belt and cinched it tightly above his knee to prevent clotted blood in his crystallized vessels from reaching his heart. I then signaled for the other three on the rooftop to take him somewhere warm. He would lose the leg, but he could still be saved.

I straightened and looked around. Steam rose from the frost-streaked compound like smoke. I spotted several villagers who had suffered direct hits, their crouching bodies statues of ice. Two more buildings lay in ruins.

Another few passes like that, and we're all dead.

The thought had hardly formed when the dragon turned sharply.

"Be ready," Nafid called to me from the courtyard.

I looked down in time to see her dart behind a building. As the dragon approached, green starbursts exploded in front of him. The dragon evaded each one, but I realized Nafid wasn't trying to hit him. She was steering him toward me.

The dragon pinned his wings as he ducked beneath an especially bright burst, talons dragging furrows through the courtyard, before surging up again—right beneath me.

I jumped down and landed hard, tumbling partway down the dragon's back before thrusting my claws into an arrangement of scales above his left shoulder blade. Head lowered to the freezing wind, I began scaling his neck toward the leathery section where the angle of his lower jaw met his throat.

With his dense layers of crusty scales, the dragon didn't seem to notice me. Clear of the green bursts now, his throat began to convulse. Villagers scattered from his path.

In anticipation of another ice blast, I sped up, the talons on my hands and feet knifing into the crevices between his scales, my muscles bulging against the relentless forces of wind and motion. I was almost to the dragon's upper throat when he stopped and cocked his head to one side.

Must have felt me.

I held on tight, but instead of trying to buck me off, the dragon climbed from the compound. Head still cocked, he said something that sounded like a question.

"Sorry, pal, don't speak your language," I grunted.

"An American," he said in a thick Asian accent. "And judging from your voice, I would guess from somewhere in the south? Texas?" He laughed. "What is a Texan doing among these beasts?"

I ignored him and shimmied higher.

"I admire your warrior spirit, but you have no idea what you are mixed up in. I know our attack must appear brutal and unprovoked, but *they* are the invaders, Texan. They seized our land, murdered our kin. We are only claiming what is rightfully ours." My thoughts began to blur pleasantly, like I'd just polished off a six pack. The dragon glided around the village in a smooth arc. "Here, let me set you down so I can finish my—glarg!"

Remembering Nafid's warning about his words, I had dropped to the underside of his neck and sunk my teeth high in his throat. A foul reptilian taste filled my mouth, but I had him where I wanted him. And now the dragon did thrash, neck whipping side to side, his short arms pounding my back. I bit down harder, the muscles over the hinges of my jaw bunching into small fists.

I wasn't penetrating the scales, but that didn't matter. The crushing pressure was pinching off the arteries that pumped blood to his brain. Eventually, he'd go down like the other one.

The dragon launched into a tight series of rolls. The muscles in my arms screamed as the forces tried to peel me from the dragon's neck. My arms held, but the same couldn't be said for my legs, which were suddenly dangling beneath me.

Before I could kick them up again, the dragon righted himself, and I plowed through something. Adobe bricks burst around me. Wrenched from the dragon, I slammed against the ground, scattering chickens as I tumbled for several yards and came to a dizzying stop.

A roaring inhalation of breath sounded, like wind through an encrusted flue, and the recovering dragon climbed with leathery slaps of his wings. Behind me, the hut that had broken my grip lay in ruins. I couldn't smell anyone inside, which was a relief. Most of the adults were fighting at the compound, and I'd caught scents of the children in a below-ground bunker.

I stood and checked myself. Nothing broken, and the pain was already receding from my healing contusions. But I had lost both my pistol and rifle, and the dragon was circling back.

His feral black eyes narrowed in on me as his grin steepened.

"Now I understand, Texan," he said, seeing me for the first time. "You've become the embodiment of their Guardian. Transformed by that crazy woman, no doubt." Hungry fascination gleamed in his eyes.

I waited until the last second before diving behind another hut. The dragon's wing broke through the roof, and his lashing tail destroyed two of the walls, but I had already darted behind a third hut.

"What a pity," the dragon continued, climbing until he could see me again, "a fine warrior like you. The spell the old woman cast was potent but corrosive. While it empowers your body, it steals from your mind. Tit for tat, as you Americans like to say. Even had you survived our encounter this night, within days you would have gone stark, raving mad."

The dragon dove toward me, his throat convulsing in deep grunts.

12

I darted from one hut to the next as the dragon's icy blast stormed past me, crystallizing the ground and freezing pigs and chickens in place. Frost billowed around in a disorienting white storm. Not realizing I had reached the end of the village, I stumbled from behind the last hut and into open pasture.

Behind me, the dragon laughed as his ice blast tapered off.

"Trust me, Texan, I'm sparing you from a fate worse than hell."

I felt him eyeing me through the dissipating frost, gauging the effects of his words on me. The words had registered, but I had filtered out their meaning and influence. All that mattered right now was figuring out how to get my jaw back around his throat.

But the dragon wasn't going to give me that chance. Remaining high overhead, his throat convulsed again. He meant to freeze me.

With animal quickness, I began cycling through my

options. My best short-term bet was another run through the village, though I wasn't sure how much longer my stamina would hold out. I needed to get to higher ground, up to the ridge maybe, and make a leap for him.

But before I could launch into my first step, a fiery whoosh sounded from the dry river valley. I watched in amazement as a pair of Hellfire missiles streaked overhead and struck the dragon in twin eruptions of flames. The dragon shrieked and reared back.

A deafening burst of cannon fire followed, throwing scales and sparks from the dragon's hide. The great beast began to flap backwards, his tail flipping side to side like he was a fish stranded a hundred feet above water.

The next burst of cannon fire ripped a tattering hole through the dragon's right wing, the force spinning him around. He began to flap drunkenly back toward the mountains. Two Apache's thundered overhead, chasing the dragon with more missiles and now a relentless stream of cannon fire.

On the far side of the river, the white dragon climbed toward the high peaks from where he had first appeared. The Apaches ripped off final attacks, then circled back.

"Thought you were going to a fight without us?" Segundo called from behind me.

I turned to find him and the rest of Team 5 standing at the top of the collapsed section of valley. As they jogged down the slope toward me, I dug into my pockets for the balaclava and pulled it over my head.

"Oh, c'mon," Segundo said when he arrived in front of me. "I want to see if your face is as ugly as Mauli says it is."

I glared over at my senior medic. "Is that right?"

"I wasn't going to mention anything," Mauli explained

quickly, "but when we heard shooting and Segundo started moving the team out, I figured I needed to warn everyone. I told them what happened."

"I helped a little," Parker confessed.

"What *was* all that shooting about?" Segundo asked. "And what the hell was that thing that flew away."

I sighed. "I think we've stepped into the middle of a battle between ancient enemies. And that flying thing was ... a dragon." I felt foolish saying the word, even as my men looked over my massive lupine form in awe and fear—everyone except Segundo, who made a show of taking it in stride.

"Bet he never tangled with a pair of Apaches," he snorted. "Listen, we finally got through to Pete, and he delivered. Man, did he deliver." I followed his glance toward the Apaches that were setting down in the pasture about a hundred yards away. With my animal vision, I could make out Pete through one of the windows. My fellow Texan managed both a look of amazement at having just engaged a dragon and satisfaction at having been right to believe they existed in the first place.

"There's two more birds coming in," Segundo continued. "Enough to lift us all out of here. Plus we've got an F-18 escort overhead. I've already arranged for your transfer to a hospital to get you checked out."

"You did good," I said, "but I'm not going with you."

"What? Why the hell not?"

I took off the balaclava. "I don't think this is something medicine can fix."

My men stared at me, whispered cusses escaping a few of them. As Spec Ops forces, we were trained to handle any and all shocks with professional poise, no matter how fucked up, but nothing could have prepared them for this. Segundo swallowed visibly but kept his macho composure. It was part of what I loved about the guy. "Well, Mauli was right about your face," he said, eyeing it warily.

"It's temporary," I growled.

He shuffled back before resetting his feet. "C'mon, man. You really think that old woman cursed you?"

With the symbol still burning inside the flesh of my right cheek, I thought about what Nafid had said about some entity called the Great Wolf naming me the Principal Protector. My thoughts then flashed to Daniela and my need to get home to her as Jason Wolfe—not Blue Wolf.

"Yeah, I do. And I'm not leaving here until she changes me back. Nafid has a sat phone, and I also have a radio in my pack. I'll call for a lift when everything's back to normal."

"We can't leave you here alone," Segundo said. "You know that."

"I've already had this conversation with Parker and Mauli, so unless you're taking me by force, it's a moot point. You're getting on those helos without me. And when you're back at base, I want you to have Colonel Stanick's deputy file a formal complaint against Baine. I'll follow up when I get back, make sure it's moving up the chain and not getting buried."

"Well, what the hell am I supposed to tell them about you?" Segundo said.

"The situation that happened yesterday with the bombing, over fifty villagers killed, requires engagement with the population to ensure we don't lose them to the enemy. I'm taking it upon myself to be that engagement. It doesn't require the whole team."

"And that's your story, and you're sticking to it," Segundo muttered.

"It's the truth. I'm just choosing to leave out certain details. I hope you will too." I was most concerned about those details finding their way back to Daniela. This was my problem, not hers.

I looked at each member of Team 5. They were scared shitless, but they were good men. Men I had trusted with my life in too many firefights to count, and men who had trusted me to lead them into those firefights. So when they nodded, I knew that what had happened to me would not leave our circle.

"Only a couple of problems that I can see, though," Segundo said. "First, you're not carrying any weapons." He thrust the stock end of his M4 toward me, then handed me his sidearm. He stepped aside so the weapons sergeants could place two large cases at my feet. "I had the helos bring in a heavy machine gun to replace what that little shithead stole. There's a fifty cal in that case and ammo belts in the other. You should be good if that dragon thing comes back."

Heavy fire power. That was what I had been missing. "Thanks."

"And how are you fixed for food?" Mauli interjected.

Now that he mentioned it, I was ravenous. I had four MREs left in my pack, but I could see myself going through the fifteen-hundred calorie meals in one sitting. The rest of the team must have noticed my hesitation because they began pulling MREs from their own packs and handing them to me. As I stowed them away, Segundo cleared his throat.

"The second problem is that we're not leaving you out

here alone." He held up a hand before I could reaffirm my decision. "I'm not talking about the whole team anymore. Protocol dictates that at least one other team member stay with you. The buddy system, remember? Plus it will seem less suspicious."

"I can't ask anyone to do this with me. It's outside the mission parameters."

"The situation that happened yesterday, over fifty killed, requires engagement to ensure we don't lose the population to the enemy," he recited back to me. "So with all due respect, sir, fuck your 'outside the mission parameters.' As the civil affairs officer and interpreter, Parker staying makes the most sense. I'll take the rest back to base."

He was right. My condition aside, we still had an obligation to rebuild and recompense the village and ensure they would allow us use of the corridor as a supply route. If anyone could help facilitate that, it was Parker.

I turned to him. "It's your choice."

"I'm staying with you, sir," he said resolutely.

"Then the rest of you better get going," I said. "I'll see everyone soon."

Still in shock, my team members uttered their goodbyes from a safe distance and began moving toward the Apaches as two more helos arrived. Lingering behind, Segundo gave me an admonishing look. "You might look like a giant flea bag, but you're still our captain. You get into trouble, you give us a call."

"I will. Take care of them. You're the primero now."

Segundo smirked at the joke, then trotted to catch up to what was now effectively his unit. As I watched them leave, I had the visceral sense I wouldn't see them again, at least as a team. I slung the M4 over a shoulder and hefted the giant cases that seemed to weigh little more than gym bags with my newfound strength. I turned from my departing team and toward the compound.

"You ready?" I asked Parker.

"Yes sir."

I returned to a familiar scene: Kabadi villagers cleaning up. The attack had been more destructive than I'd realized. In addition to the ruined buildings, several structures had suffered damage from wings and talons, and great fissures showed where the ice had rent cracks in the stone and dried mud. A dozen frozen bodies lay in the piece of courtyard recently occupied by the young men killed in yesterday's bombing.

"Did the dragon do all of this?" Parker asked.

"Dragons plural," I said. "There were three of them."

"Holy crap."

"Yeah, I've been saying that a lot lately. You're about to see one of them up close."

As we entered the large courtyard, I expected to find the dragon who had choked on a high-explosive grenade. I'd been wondering how the villagers planned to move the enormous creature—cutting it up seemed out, given its nearly indestructible hide—but the dragon was no longer laid out in the courtyard. When I looked around, I couldn't even see a blood trail.

"They were shifters," Nafid said. I turned to find her striding up behind us, her staff pinned beneath an arm as she wiped her hands with a scarf. "With their death their dragon bodies return to the Great Dragon."

"What are shifters?" I asked.

Unable to help himself, Parker jumped in. "In various myths and folklore, shifters are people who possess the ability to change into other forms—often accomplished through some kind of divine intervention or powerful magic. There are stories of them in many cultures."

"Your friend is correct," Nafid said. "In this case, they change into dragons. They are known here as *dhin-dhins*. Dragon shifters."

When I looked again at the spot where the junior dragon had eaten a grenade, I saw the covered body of what I had assumed to be one of the Kabadi. But when the wind lifted a side of the cover, I glimpsed a naked leg. The part of the cover over the head was dark with blood.

"The big dragon," I said. "Will he be back?"

"Not tonight," Nafid replied ominously. "Orzu must first recover."

I set down the cases with the machine gun and ammo. It didn't sound like we would need them right now. "Parker and I have medical training. What can we do to help the injured?"

"Thank you, but we have healers in the village."

"What about the man whose leg was frozen? He was on that rooftop."

"They will cure him."

After having witnessed Nafid's light show, I didn't doubt their skill. I noticed her watching me with the same intensity as before the dragon attack, but her green eyes were no longer hostile. I was reminded of a pair of soldiers who had come to Team 5 a few years back. They refused to speak to one another, something about a girl they'd met on leave. But following their first extended firefight, you couldn't pry them apart. Battle had a way of doing that.

"Then let us help you rebuild," I said.

"That is not why you came back. You want Buzurg to change you."

I thought of Daniela, who was expecting me home in a few days. "Yes."

She nodded and tucked the scarf into a fold in her gown. "Let us speak to him, then."

As she strode toward the bombed building with her wooden staff in hand, Parker and I looked at one another—was it really going to be this easy?—and then hustled to catch up to her.

I could only hope.

13

Parker and I followed Nafid into the building and up the staircase. The lanterns were still down, but Nafid's staff illuminated the way. When we reached the top of the stairs, she asked us to wait outside, swirling her staff to send up a glowing green ball of light that hovered above Parker's head. She then entered her great-grandmother's shrine, closing the door behind her.

Parker looked from the light to me in confusion. I held up a finger to preempt his questions and pointed to the door for him to listen and translate. The two women had already begun to speak, Nafid's voice sharp and hard, the old woman's high and wavering, almost like singing.

After a moment Parker shook his head and whispered, "They're still talking in that dialect I can't understand."

I frowned in frustration, but in a second I realized it didn't matter; my animal hearing was picking up nuances in their tones. Nafid seemed to be arguing, possibly on my behalf, while her great-grandmother was brushing her off. That went on for several minutes until Nafid said something in an especially sharp voice that rendered the old woman silent. When at last she replied, a sigh carried her words—and then she added something that sounded like a warning. Now it was Nafid's turn to go quiet.

The door opened, surprising both Parker and me. I hadn't heard Nafid's approach from the other side.

"Baba has agreed to a *da'vat*," she said.

"A *da'vat*?" I repeated. "What's that?"

"A ceremony for you to express your desires to Buzurg. But it will be your one chance, and she warns that Buzurg may be greatly insulted. Out of many, many warriors, he has chosen you."

"And if my wishes greatly insult him?"

The green light above us flickered, dimming Nafid's face. "The Great Wolf can be merciless."

Parker cleared his throat. "Sir, I'm not sure you should…"

"Show me what to do," I said to Nafid.

"You must remove everything and enter alone."

I looked down at my camo pants. "Everything?"

Nafid nodded, grave lines etching her brow.

"When in Rome…" I muttered, handing off my weapons and vest to Parker and then stripping off my shirt. I undid my camos last but peeked inside before dropping them. I had no idea what I looked like down there, but a long sweep of a hair appeared to cover my personal effects. I pushed the camos down and stepped out of them, which felt oddly freeing.

Nafid opened the door and moved to one side.

"Be careful," Parker called from behind me as I entered.

The door shut, and a darkness that my wolf vision couldn't penetrate closed around me. I sniffed the air, but the smells were too dense and conflicting. My ears pricked up as I listened.

"Baba?" I called.

Disoriented, I began walking toward what I thought were the old woman's breaths. But then her muttering voice sounded off to my right, and I turned to find her sitting cross-legged on the floor, facing a pit of embers that hadn't been there a moment before. The glow colored her white hair a dark orange, while the heat bent her wrinkled features like a mirage.

For an instant, my rational mind rebelled. Nothing about this made sense. I should have joined my team and been taken to a hospital. I looked behind me for the door. But something was still telling me the only way back to normalcy was forward, through this dark corner of the world, as Pete had called it, through the insanity. The old Jason Wolfe was waiting on the other side, as well as the love of my life, the very soon-to-be Daniela Wolfe.

I couldn't falter now.

With a steadying breath, I stepped forward. The old woman's face canted upward, her fleshy sockets meeting my eyes. With the same gnarled hand she'd used to carve the symbol into my cheek she pointed to a rug on the floor across the pit, then angled her face back down toward the embers.

As I sat, the rest of the room remained pitch black. It felt like we were floating in a giant void without walls or a ceiling. I could sense the mounted wolf's head somewhere above us, its sunken yellow eyes watching me. *The Great Wolf can be merciless*, I heard Nafid saying.

"*Sab zarat!*"

My eyes jerked back to the old woman as she threw a

handful of what sounded like seed husks over the embers. The clinking shells snuffed out the orange light, but soon a deep blue glow replaced it, pulsing up through the smoke. It was accompanied by a strong animal smell.

The old woman grunted in apparent satisfaction and started into a repetitive chant. Each round came faster, all of them ending on a hard note, as though she were trying to create enough momentum to move something. Her dark lips worked and twisted until she looked certifiably insane. But before long something *did* begin to move: our space. I felt it turning slowly around.

She's opening a doorway, I thought, the idea coming unbidden.

I placed a hand against the ground to steady myself, my breaths picking up, my heart beating louder. Outside, the beasts behind the locked door began to bark, the savage sounds clambering over one another. The animal smell in the room grew stronger, more feral.

The woman ended the chant suddenly, and the movement stopped. The barking fell off into yelps and whimpers. My eyes shot around, senses on high alert. Something else was in the room.

The witch growled in a voice that no longer sounded human. When she lifted her face from the embers, large yellow eyes glared into mine. But they weren't her eyes, I realized. A giant shadow with a hunched back and peaked ears was taking form around her.

The Great Wolf, I thought.

He rose to all fours, eyes elevating high above Baba's head, and merged into the blackness. Baba remained sitting in her layers of robes, face fixed as though entranced. Buzurg stalked around the pit, his enormous form shifting in and out of the blue light, until I sensed him behind me. An aggressive heat radiated from him, more intense than anything I'd ever felt.

He sniffed my neck in great huffs. My animal heart thundered in my chest, and I felt an urge to fall onto my back, to submit, but I resisted. Submission to a threat had been trained out of me a long time ago.

Buzurg drew back, his growl rumbling through the room. The sound resolved into a deep voice in my head.

Why have you called me?

I cleared my mind of the strangeness of what was happening until I was completely focused. "I understand that you have chosen me to be the Blue Wolf, the Principal Protector," I said in tone both diplomatic and direct. "I'm honored, but I have other commitments. I'll help the Kabadi people, but not like this. I need to be returned to my human form."

You ask to abandon your duty?

Though menace coursed through his words, they struck a nerve. In my ten years in the service, I had never been accused of abandoning a duty. "This isn't something I agreed to," I said, anger climbing in my voice. "I have duties to my own people, to my family." I thought about Daniela and our future monsters, three or four of them. "With all due respect, the Kabadi people are neither."

You were born under the Wolf, he thundered, *or I could not have chosen you.*

Not knowing what he was talking about, I remained silent, letting my request stand.

Buzurg began to pace, his tread heavy and restless. I pictured great muscles bulking and shifting over his frame.

Without warning his teeth seized my neck and slammed me onto my back.

I struggled but couldn't get out from under his shadowy form. He shifted until his teeth were wrapping my throat. I tried to pry his jaws apart, but he didn't seem to be wholly material. I couldn't grasp anything. But that didn't seem to be a problem for Buzurg. One jerk of his head, and I would be throatless.

Look into my eye, he growled.

I stared up his muzzle to where his right eye gleamed like a star. And then it *was* a star, set against the black void around us. I felt disembodied as I watched the star separate into twelve smaller stars, each a different color. They took the shape of animals—the red star a bear, the green one a fish of some kind. But my gaze was drawn to the blue one, which was changing into a giant wolf. The animal stars spread and rotated into what looked like a large zodiac.

You were born under the Wolf, Buzurg repeated. *The Protector. You heed an urge to defend, negotiating when you can, killing when you must, exceeding at both. It is who you are. If you can look into the light of the Great Maker and refute this, then I will release you.*

Was he really giving me an out?

I opened my mouth to tell him those qualities were the result of my training, not being born under any star. But as I looked at the celestial animals, I couldn't form the words. The light of the blue wolf shone into me, and I was overcome by a sense of brotherhood—like with my own men, only more intense. In that moment, I couldn't deny its influence any more than I could abandon my team in battle. I felt my mouth close again.

Do you see? Buzurg said harshly. His teeth unclamped

my throat and he stood back, the stars disappearing from his eye. *I recognized your true nature. The transformation would have killed you otherwise. The pack is weak. It needs the leadership of the Blue Wolf.*

"What about you?" I asked. "Why can't you lead them?"

For the first time his eyes shifted from mine. *I've been relegated to the shadows. I have too little power here.*

Something in his tone told me not to pursue the question. "I can help in other ways," I insisted. "I can give the Kabadi weapons and ammunition, improve their fortifications. I can train them."

That will not be enough against the White Dragon.

I recalled my battle with the vile creature. "Who is he?"

He is an aberration. He is greed. He knows we are weakened and smells blood. You surprised him tonight, but he will return to test you. He is determined to end our line and claim the valley, even if it means tipping creation back into eternal night. You must not let him.

I didn't understand this talk of creation and eternal night, but I saw an opening. "And if I manage to keep the White Dragon at bay, the pack will be safe?"

They will be more secure, but they will not be safe until the next generation of warriors comes of age.

When he spoke of the warriors, a bolt of guilt shot through me. They were the blue-haired wolfmen the Kabadi had tried to hide in the infirmary when we arrived. But with Baine's command, that generation had been wiped out. The next generation was their children. A primal need to protect and lead them rose up inside me, but I forced it back down.

"I'll make you an offer," I said. "I'll hunt down and destroy the White Dragon. In exchange, you'll release me.

The pack will be safe. There will be no more need for the Blue Wolf."

The White Dragon is not easily hunted and even less easily destroyed, Buzurg said. *He is wily and powerful. More likely, he will destroy you, becoming more powerful still. Without their protector, the pack will be slaughtered.*

"I'm hunting him regardless," I said.

The Great Wolf growled at my insubordination, but he had already shown his hand. He needed me more than I needed him.

"If I'm going to be the pack's Blue Wolf, those are the terms."

After a long silence, Buzurg said, *Then you must strike while the White Dragon is still weak.*

I nodded, already thinking tactically. I would need as much firepower as I could gather. What about the handful of young men in the village who had helped repel the dragons?

No! Buzurg shouted, picking up the thought somehow. *Though the Wolf does not express himself in them, he is latent in their blood. They must remain alive to repopulate the pack. Their children may still become warriors or greater.* After a moment of brooding silence he said, *There are the beasts. If they accept your leadership, you can take them.*

"Beasts?" Did he mean the things behind the locked door?

But at that moment the old witch moaned, and the cube around her neck shifted. Buzurg swung his head toward her. *The da'vat is ending. I must return to the shadows.* He looked back at me with his large predatory eyes. *Be prudent in your hunt. If the White Dragon proves too great, fall back.*

You are all that stands between him and what remains of the pack. Between him and absolute darkness.

"Do we have an agreement?" I asked.

We do, Wolf, he said, and leapt across the pit of blue embers.

As he disappeared into the old woman, she picked up the rapid, lip-twisting chant as though she'd never stopped. I could feel the room rotating again, the doorway to what must have been the Great Wolf's realm closing. The woman wound down the chant, and the embers returned to orange. The darkness receded. I could see the room around us now, the mounted wolf's head a sagging parody of the powerful being I'd just spoken to.

Now I just had to pray that being would keep his word.

14

"How did it go, Sir?" Parker asked when I emerged from the shrine room.

"Interestingly," I said, accepting my camo pants that he held out. Stepping into them, I explained what happened in the *da'vat*. "He didn't change me back, obviously, but we came to an agreement."

"What agreement?" Nafid said.

"I destroy the White Dragon, and I don't have to play Blue Wolf anymore."

"White Dragon?" Parker frowned. "Do you mean that huge thing that was flying away when we arrived?"

"That's the one," I said, pulling my shirt on.

"Tell me everything that happened," Nafid said.

As I put my vest and pack back on, I gave a succinct report of the ceremony, from her great-grandmother's chanting to the Great Wolf returning to his realm. Nafid watched me intently as I spoke.

"Then there is much to do," she said when I finished. "But first you must eat and rest. Come."

Parker and I followed her from the building. Outside, night had paled into a misty pre-dawn, and the first ragged cries of roosters were rising in the village. The activity around the compound had thinned. Though wreckage remained everywhere, the dead were no longer lined up in the courtyard.

"Have the deceased already been buried?" Parker asked.

"We have a crypt underground," Nafid said, "where the dragons cannot steal them."

She led us across the courtyard into another building whose large front room was crowded with villagers sitting in concentric circles. Dusty, exhausted, and no doubt in shock, they ate in silence. Nafid spoke, and a group scooted over to make room for Parker and me.

No sooner had we sat on the dusty floor, the villagers began passing us cups of tea as well as clay pots of what looked like stew. The stew was, in fact, bread soaked in broth and topped with lentils, raisins, and succulent chunks of lamb. Ravenous, I scarfed mine down. The villagers seemed to appreciate this and several of them tried to pass me another pot. I showed my palms, but they insisted.

Nafid, who had taken a seat on my other side, said, "It is an honor for them to feed the Blue Wolf."

I didn't feel it was an honor I deserved, but for their sake I nodded and held up a finger to indicate I would have just one more. Though I paced myself this time, I could feel the watchful villagers ready to spring forward with another offer of food the instant I finished.

"I have some questions," I said, turning to Nafid.

"I expected you might."

"Where did the Great Wolf come from?"

She cast a glance at Parker as she sipped her tea.

"You can trust him," I said. "Nothing you tell us leaves Team 5. Isn't that right, Parker."

"Yes, sir," he replied.

"He came from the Great Maker," Nafid said. "You say you saw a light in his eye. That was the Great Maker, the light of Creation. The Great Maker then divided Herself into twelve Guardians, each one representing a quality, each given a place in this world to defend against the return of darkness. The Great Wolf is the third Guardian, protector of the valley."

"But the Great Wolf said he'd been relegated to the shadows," I pointed out.

"When humankind arrived, worship of the Great Wolf and the other Guardians followed. That worship bolstered the Guardians' power, but it also brought temptation. Several Guardians coupled with powerful priests and priestesses. The Great Wolf was one of them. He mated with a sorceress in this valley. As punishment, the Great Maker sent him and the others to a shadow realm, leaving their mortal descendents to carry on their role. It is how the world became so fragile."

"Interesting creation myth," Parker remarked.

I looked around the room to find the villagers watching us, several touching their wolf tooth pendants. Whether it was history or myth was irrelevant. "Spec Ops is about adapting to realities on the ground," I reminded my civil affairs officer in a lowered voice. "And right now those realities are whatever she can tell us about the elements in play." I turned back to Nafid. "Is that why there are men among the Kabadi with wolf attributes?"

"Yes," she said. "The attributes are passed from father to

son, though they are not always expressed. Some children show no wolf features, others show an even balance—those are the warriors—and in a small number of children they are fully expressed." I suspected in the last case she was referring to the "beasts" the Great Wolf had mentioned, the ones who had been clamoring behind the locked door. But before I could ask her about them, she went on. "In much the same way, the attributes of the sorceress are passed from mother to daughter."

"That explains the spell craft and light shows," I said.

"As well as why armies never successfully invaded the corridor," Parker put in. "If this is all true," he added quickly, though I could tell his brain was inching over to the new reality.

"So, your great-grandmother...?" I said to Nafid.

"She is the full expression of Nasreen, the sorceress who mated with the Great Wolf. According to our stories, there has never been another like my great-grandmother since Nasreen. She is the Great Wolf's link to our world."

"And that's how I was turned into the Blue Wolf," I concluded.

"Yes, the Blue Wolf is the manifestation of the Great Wolf's essential qualities."

"How old is your great-grandmother?" I asked.

"Baba is older than two hundred years."

When Parker made a skeptical face, I pointed to my own. He examined my hairy brow and long muzzle before waggling his head to concede that anything might be possible.

"She could live two hundred more," Nafid said.

"I have to ask," Parker said, leaning forward to see her better. "Where did you learn English? I mean, I would've thought with your isolation that would be difficult, but you're fully fluent."

"I learned from you," she said simply.

"Me?"

"Yes, from when you were translating earlier."

"Um ... even if something like that were possible, our exchange barely scratched the surface of the language."

"It didn't need to," Nafid said, gesturing into the air. "Once I learned where you were making the translations, I went there too. You have a well-organized system. Very easy to work from."

Parker sputtered. "Wh-what do you mean 'where you were making the translations'?" He tapped his temple hard enough to knock his glasses crooked. "It was all happening up here."

"Yes, and in the *Kollec*," she said. "That is where organized thoughts live. The *Kollec* is like a big building with many rooms, but you have to know which room you're looking for in order to enter."

Parker gave me an exasperated look before straightening his glasses and returning to his food. It was too much for him, which was just as well. We were starting to veer off topic.

"So how did the dragon shifters come into the picture?" I asked.

"In much the same way as our wolves. But in this case, the Great Dragon mated with a warlord of a region north of the Wari River."

"Wait a sec," I said. "The Great Dragon was one of the original Guardians?"

"Yes, she was the ninth Guardian, Opponent of the Great Wolf." Seeing my confused look, she said, "Creation requires opposing forces—positive and negative, you call them—otherwise, Creation collapses. When the Great Maker divided herself, she ensured each Guardian had an Opponent. For the Great Wolf that was the Great Dragon, champion of the high peaks."

I thought back to the lights I'd seen in the Great Wolf's eye. Though I'd been drawn to the blue light, I remembered seeing a white light across the zodiac in the shape of a winged creature.

"The first son of the Great Dragon and the warlord was Orzu, the White Dragon."

"The shifter who visited us last night? He'd have to be thousands of years old then. How is that possible?"

"Though a vestigial connection exists between our people and the Great Wolf, our men are not shifters. They remain as they are. Their power is never replenished. Over time they weaken and die. Not so for the descendents of the Great Dragon. When a dragon shifter returns to their human form, their dragon form merges into the Great Dragon. There it regenerates until the shifter calls on it again. Though a dragon shifter only comes along once every ten generations, they cannot die unless killed. For this reason, they have become very good at survival. Rarely have two dragon shifters been killed so close together as happened last night. Orzu was overconfident. He will not make that mistake again."

"The Great Wolf said something about him wanting this valley."

"By his dragon nature he is aggressive, while the human line from which he came makes him greedy. He prizes riches above all else. For centuries he has thrived in the opium trade, but his lands are nearly exhausted, while ours are the most fertile in the province. With them, he could triple his wealth."

"But why here?" I asked. "It seems like a shifter that powerful could go anywhere and take anything."

"Because his power is rooted to the place of his creation. The farther he strays, the weaker he becomes. He would be foolish to challenge anyone outside our province."

"And your wolf kind has kept him at bay all these centuries?" I asked.

"There have been nine great battles and countless skirmishes. Though the White Dragon has consumed many of our warriors, he is careful. He will only attack when he believes he has a decisive advantage. Even so, the Kabadi have always managed to repel him. But last night was different. He arrived knowing our warriors had been wiped out. Indeed, he was gloating over his prize as he toyed with us." Her green eyes fixed on mine. "But last night was the closest he came to being killed."

"Doesn't he risk destroying Creation, though?" I was beginning to understand something else that had seemed nonsensical when the Great Wolf told me. "Because with your line gone, there's no more opposition to the Great Dragon. Creation implodes, right? Darkness returns."

"The White Dragon does not believe the myths," she said.

"But then wouldn't the same be true if you destroyed the White Dragon?" Parker challenged. "Implosion and darkness and all of that?"

"He is just one dragon shifter, so no," Nafid replied. "There are many of his line, though not all of them became full shifters. As long as that line continues, so does the essence of the Great Dragon—which will continue to stand in necessary opposition to the Great Wolf."

"Couldn't another shifter just step into his place, then?" Parker asked. "Give you the same trouble?"

"Theoretically, yes. But the dragon shifters in existence are less powerful than the White Dragon and mostly solitary. The White Dragon contracts the greedier ones into his service. Otherwise, we would rarely see them. The natural opposition between the Great Wolf and Great Dragon keeps us apart."

"Mercenaries," I growled.

Nafid squinted slightly, as though referencing something. "Yes, that is the perfect word for them."

I sipped my tea and reviewed everything we'd just discussed. There hadn't been a lot of actionable information, but it was good background. I reached into my pocket and pulled out the laminated satellite map of the corridor. I spread it on the floor in front of Nafid. Some curious villagers craned their necks to see it as well.

"Here's your village and compound," I said, tapping the map. "The dragons came from up here."

"Yes," she said, pointing out the compound among the high peaks. "The White Dragon's fortress is here."

"Colonel Stanick mentioned that it was the resort of a wealthy poppy grower," I said to Parker. "He must have been referring to Orzu." I studied the image, trying to gauge the best route up the valleys and passes to reach the fortress while carrying heavy weaponry. Even in my animal form, I was looking at a half-day's journey. I then studied the fortress itself. The resolution didn't give me much except that it was smaller than the Kabadi's compound.

"Do you know anything about its defenses?" I asked Nafid.

"Scouts have gone up occasionally to gauge the threat. The walls are tall and strong. Human and kobold mercenaries patrol them while the White Dragon's nephew, Ozari, keeps vigil overhead."

"Sounds like a classic defensive setup," I said. "But what's a kobold?"

"They are like our warriors. Descendants of the White Dragon, they are born with human and dragon features, but they cannot shift from one to the other. A lone kobold is little threat, but they are strong in numbers."

"How many would we be talking about?" I asked.

"Fifty to one hundred kobold and human mercenaries."

Parker whistled. "And armed to the teeth, no doubt," he said.

I continued to study the fortress on the map. Something like that could be reduced to rubble with air support, but that wasn't an option. I took a mental inventory of my weapons and ammo. The .50 cal was heavy duty, but it wouldn't be enough against fifty to one hundred foot soldiers, plus at least two dragon shifters. With the Great Wolf denying me use of his men, I was either going to have to determine a way to sneak inside or find another backup force.

"The Great Wolf told me I could take the beasts," I said, "if they accepted me."

Nafid gave me a long look as she sipped her tea. "That would be unwise," she said when she lowered the cup.

"Why?"

"Though born to the Kabadi, the beasts have no humanity in them. They are full-blooded wolves, but they are not like the wolves in the wild. Ours are larger, stronger, and more bloodthirsty. They attack humans on sight, even Kabadi. We do not believe in killing our own, so we keep them in a secure hold. Shut away in the darkness, they have only become more fierce."

"Is there a safe way for me to assess them?" I asked.

"The only way to determine whether they will accept your leadership is to make the leader submit to you in front of the pack. That will require you to enter their hold."

"And if he doesn't submit?" Parker asked nervously.

"Then the beasts will attack en masse, and there are more than thirty of them."

I shook my head. Unwise? Even contemplating something like that felt stupid as shit. But some deep-down animal instinct was jumping at the prospect of challenging another leader for control of his pack. An intense heat broke out over my body. *Plus you need the backup*, a small but slightly more rational voice whispered.

"How soon can I go in?" I asked.

15

"It will be safer if they are fed first," Nafid said, switching her staff to her other hand.

It was midmorning of the next day, and she, Parker, and I were standing on the rooftop of the partially bombed building, looking down on a trap door reinforced with metal bands. Faint green currents ran along the bands, much like the ones I'd seen on the door inside the compound the day before. We had arrived by way of an outer staircase on the compound's backside—the same stairs Olaf would have used to tag the infirmary with his infrared strobe sticks.

Who is he in the Centurion scheme of things? I wondered, remembering his rapid healing from the night before.

But the anticipation of facing the pack leader surged inside me again, blowing apart thoughts of Olaf and Centurion, and flaring my nostrils. I could smell the beasts beneath our feet, could hear them leaping and snapping at one another.

"What do you suppose they eat?" Parker asked me.

I followed Nafid's gaze to an old man bringing up three sheep on tethers.

"Oh," Parker said as the old man dragged the bleating sheep over to us.

Nafid set a hand on the head of each animal in turn, which seemed to calm them. Nodding to the old man, she knelt beside the trap door and grasped the handle. Parker and I stepped back as the green energy dissipated.

She pulled the door open, and the old man brought the first sheep to the edge of the square opening. From the eruption of barking, a flash of blue muzzle and white canines appeared and seized the sheep by the throat. Cartilage crunched, and the sheep disappeared into the hold. It landed with a messy thud, its bleats immediately buried beneath a torrent of vicious growls and wet tearing. The man led the second sheep to the trap door with similar results.

When the third one was pulled in, I peered down to see a huddle of massive lupine bodies about fifteen feet below. The largest of them peered up at me, his graying muzzle plastered with blood and gristle. He bared his teeth before returning to his meal.

The Alpha, I thought.

Nafid closed the door. With a word and a tip of her staff, she restored the green energy. The door thumped and rattled several times before the wolves decided the feeding was done.

"Do you still wish to test your leadership with them?" she asked.

I understood now that she'd wanted the spectacle of the feeding to discourage me, but I nodded my head. "If they're as fierce as you say, I'm going to need them." And now that

I'd seen the Alpha, the animal part of me wasn't going to rest until I'd made him submit.

Beside me, Parker swallowed dryly.

"Very well," Nafid said. "I can lower you inside, but once I remove your protection you will be on your own."

"I'll cover you," Parker said, checking the chamber on his M4.

"You don't fire a shot unless I give the command," I warned him.

"Yes, sir."

"I will raise the door again," Nafid said. "When I do, step onto the opening."

I didn't know how that was going to happen without me falling, but I trusted her. I handed Parker my sidearm and shed my clothes. If I was going to dominate the beasts, it was going to be as the Blue Wolf.

When I finished, I nodded that I was ready. Nafid opened the door, but this time she spoke a sharp word. Green light from her staff spread over the opening in a web-like pattern similar to that which she'd used against the dragons, but more dense. The web gave a little when I stepped onto it, and immediately muzzles began slamming into its underside while snapping teeth labored to tear into it.

Parker watched me nervously behind his glasses.

I signaled for Nafid to send me down. Her lips moved as she lowered her staff. I began to descend, the web stretching up around me like taffy, wrapping me in a protective cocoon. When I cleared the frame of the opening, the beasts began attacking my protection from different sides, their pale eyes angry and bloodthirsty. Soon, the webbing settled onto the slippery floor where the three sheep had been ripped apart.

I eyed the beasts that circled me. Nafid was right. There was no humanity in them. They moved on all fours like wolves, but their bodies were more angular—and much larger. They growled and lunged at me in turn, green sparks flashing with each collision into the web.

"You all right?" Parker called down.

"Yeah," I answered. "When you're ready, Nafid, you can release me."

I hunkered and spread my arms. An instant later, the green net glimmered out, and foul, humid air rushed in, stifling my first breaths. The wolves crouched back on coiled muscles, mouths slavering. I was larger than each of them and probably carried a confusing scent: foreign, yet familiar.

A bug-eyed member of the pack growled from my right, then leapt forward. I swung my arm around and slammed the back of my fist into his muzzle. He yelped and flew from sight.

Two more wolves charged from the front. I drove a heel into one of their throats and brought a fist into the other's slatted ribs, incapacitating them both.

As my chest began to heave, I realized I was enjoying myself—until a sharp pain tore through the muscles where my neck and left shoulder met. A wolf had jumped onto my back and sunk his teeth in. Sensing weakness, another wolf sprang forward and latched onto my ankle. Then they all collapsed in at once, burying me beneath their weight and tearing teeth.

"Jason?" Parker called shakily.

From above, I must have looked like one of the sheep

being slaughtered. But inside the pile, I was still standing—and fighting. "I'm good!" I grunted as I crushed a wolf's nose with an elbow. I ripped open the side of another with my talons, drove a knee into a third wolf's gut, and then grabbed the scruff of the wolf biting my neck and slammed him down on the wolf still latched to my ankle. The injured wolves keened and limped behind the retreating pack.

I wheeled in a slow circle. Though blood dripped from my arms, legs, and gashed torso, I could feel the bite and claw wounds closing, the tissue stitching itself back together.

"Anyone else?" I asked in a gruff voice.

The pack shrank back farther, their growls milder, less certain. But one wolf had remained in the shadows during the melee, watching with luminous eyes, assessing my strengths and weaknesses. The pack parted as the giant gray-haired wolf stood and strode forward: the Alpha.

We circled one another in the gore-spattered arena. Usually steady in confrontations, my heart thundered in my chest. The captain in me needed to remain in control, but my wolf nature yearned to destroy.

The Alpha struck first, darting in to bite my left knee before ducking beneath the swipe of my claws. He feinted, making me swing again, then ripped at the tendons behind my other knee. Before the injuries could heal, the Alpha plowed his head into my stomach, the surprising impact too much for my crippled knees.

I'm thinking too hard, I realized as I fell. *Trying to push back against my animal instincts, to keep them from taking over, but that's only dulling my reaction time, slowing me down.*

I landed hard on my back, the Alpha on top of me, his bloody muzzle diving for my throat. I let go of my captain mind, my control. The frenzy that had been building inside me released. It poured from my lupine body in a snarling storm of thrashing, clawing, and biting, my animal intelligence knowing where and how to strike my opponent's vulnerabilities. I felt like a passenger in a car going three-hundred miles per hour, blood and hair flying past.

But when a hot copper taste flooded my mouth, I slammed on the brakes. I was on top of the gray wolf, teeth buried in his throat, ready to rip it out. A tongue lapped at my temple—the Alpha's.

He was submitting. I had won.

I relaxed my jaw, sparing the bloodied wolf, and helped him to his feet. He looked back at me, ears flattened, tail tucked, and shuffled into the mass of wolves, his pack now mine. I rose to my full height and looked over the assemblage of thirty-odd wolves. Some of them whimpered and pawed the ground, anxious to greet their new leader, but fear held them back.

"I need you," I said and immediately felt the message radiate through the collective consciousness of the pack. The wolves yipped and barked in affirmation. "*All* of you," I emphasized, meeting the nervous eyes of the former Alpha. "We have a mission against a dangerous enemy."

———

Two hours later, I paced the room Nafid had set up for me, a satellite phone pressed to my ear. Following my meeting with the wolves, I had cleaned up and then completed my planning and packing for our journey to the White Dragon's fortress. The wolves and I would be leaving in an hour.

The line clicked as it connected to a phone seven thousand miles away, in a world that couldn't have been more different.

"Hello?" Daniela said, her voice thick with sleep.

"Hey, honey."

There was a pause. "Jason?"

"Yeah, it's me. Sorry to be calling so late."

"No, no, it's fine, I'm glad you called." I could hear the sheets rustling and the headboard groan as she sat up. "Is everything all right? Your voice sounds completely different."

When I closed my eyes, I could picture her in the white boxers and tank top she slept in, the skin between her eyebrows folding into a small comma as she concentrated into the phone. She seemed so close. I tried not to think about how she'd react if I was standing in the room with her right now. "Probably the connection," I lied. "I'm calling from a sat phone."

"Can you video chat?"

"I'm actually not at the base. Which is partly why I'm calling."

"What happened?" she asked, her stern tone warning me not to sugarcoat anything.

"I'm all right. A last-minute assignment came up. I know I don't usually call in these situations, but it could back up my transfer date. I didn't want you to be kept on tenterhooks."

"I appreciate that," she said. "But something still sounds wrong. Your voice..."

"I might have come down with something," I said, looking over the thick hair and talons on my right hand.

"And you're taking care of it?"

"Absolutely."

I reflected on my impending battle with an ancient dragon shifter in exchange for returning to Jason Wolfe. It was so far outside the scope of my military experience that for the first time I felt uncertain before a mission. And that was the real reason I'd called.

I drew in a breath to tell Daniela I loved her, but my free ear suddenly cocked toward a sound: the *whump-whump-whump* of rotary blades.

Four helos. Still distant but heading our way. Parker had been handling communication, but he hadn't reported anyone coming. Was this Baine returning to claim more kills for Centurion?

"Hey, Dani? I'm sorry but I have to go. Daniela?"

Crap, I'd lost the connection again.

I tossed the phone onto my bedding, grabbed the cases with the .50 cal machine gun and ammo belts, and climbed the compound's tallest building. With one hand shielding the glare of the afternoon sun, I squinted toward the sound. After a moment I spotted them: Apaches armed with missiles. They were sweeping down the valley in attack formation, noses dipped.

I shouted for Parker as I opened the cases and began assembling the .50. I mounted it on the roof's broad retaining wall and loaded the belt of armor-piercing incendiary rounds. I then sighted the helos. I couldn't see the Centurion logo, but I wasn't taking any chances. At the first sign of hostility, I was going to light those fuckers up.

In my peripheral vision, I saw Parker burst into the courtyard below, squinting around in search of me. "Captain?" he shouted.

"Get up here!" I called. "We've got four Apaches incoming. I'm gonna need a feeder."

But instead of coming, Parker started waving his arms wildly. "Wait, wait! Those are our guys!"

I straightened from the gun and stared down at him.

"It's Team 5!" he said.

———

Parker jogged to keep pace with me as I stalked toward the gate in the compound wall. Beyond, I could hear the Apaches touching down in the pasture, the thumping of their blades winding down.

"I'm sorry, sir," Parker stammered, out of breath. "But Segundo made me promise to keep him updated. And when I told him about your mission, he said he was getting Team 5 into the fight."

"You defied an order."

"Yeah, but Segundo said—"

"I don't care what he said. I still outrank him."

Parker looked like he was about to add something then thought better of it. I growled and stormed ahead. I needed to be getting ready to head out, not dealing with a second-in-command who wouldn't take no for an answer.

I passed through the gate and swung toward the pasture to find Segundo and the team not only fully outfitted, but unloading more gear. I reached into a pocket and pulled on my balaclava to hide my monstrous face from the pilots. Spotting a stained scarf on the ground, I scooped it up and wrapped it around my neck. As I approached the team, I shrugged my arms at Segundo: *What are you doing?*

"Not my decision," he shouted.

"What in the hell are you talking about?"

He strode over to meet me. "I got a hold of Colonel

Stanick and gave him the song and dance about keeping the populace in our camp in the wake of the bombing. Stanick was furious at Centurion, and get this—he used a clause in their contract to have Baine arrested. That's right, the little shit's locked in a military cell. But Stanick didn't like the idea of you and Parker out here on your own, especially with enemy fighters in the region. He sent us back in with aid until we know the corridor is secure."

I narrowed my eyes at him. "And Parker's update about my mission didn't have anything to do with that?"

"Well ... it might have made me lobby harder than I would've otherwise," he confessed with a smirk. "By the way, it's good to see you too. I don't mean literally, of course. You look like a freaking nightmare."

I sighed as I accepted his clasp and let him pull me into a hug. "Look, I love you too, man," I said. "You know that. But we went over this already. This is my thing. I can't get the team involved."

"Hey, CENTCOM wants a secure corridor. That White Dragon you're going after? I didn't say a word to the higher ups, of course, but if he's threatening the people here, then he's a danger to the supply route."

"That's a bit of a stretch."

"Is it?" Segundo said. "Pete ever tell you the story about that thing attacking his buddy's Apache? These dragons don't discriminate, bro. They're a threat to the coalition's interests, which means they need to be eliminated. And that's what we do."

"You haven't seen them in action," I said. "Their scales are like iron plating. They can flatten buildings with a flick of their tails, freeze men solid with their breath. And we're going to be fighting them on their turf—a mountain fortress at over fourteen-thousand feet."

Segundo turned toward the team. "Yo, Dean!" he called to the senior weapons sergeant. "Can you bring that container over here?" As Dean lugged the big plastic container over, Segundo said, "Parker gave us the mission details, and we packed appropriately. Insulated suits in snow camouflage and…"

Dean arrived and pried off the container's lid. When I looked inside, I could only shake my head.

"Ta-da! Flamethrowers," Segundo announced, pulling out one of the sleek black weapons. "That's how you fight an ice blast, baby."

By now the rest of the team had gathered behind Segundo, all of them watching me, awaiting my decision. They had adapted to conditions, their fear from earlier sinking back beneath their determination to stand with their captain, to go to battle as a team. Nothing I said was going to dissuade them.

"All right," I said. As the team began to shout and pump their fists, I added, "But we're splitting. Half the team will come with me. The other half will stay and defend the compound." I turned to Segundo. "Pick the teams. I'll update the mission plan, then hold a briefing. This is going to be a nighttime raid, and we've got a long hike ahead of us. We need to leave within an hour."

"You got it, Captain Wolfe." Segundo paused mid salute and cocked his head. "Wolfe … Hey, that really suits you now."

16

The night wind whipped against my face as I pushed back the hood of my camo suit and peered over the snow-encrusted boulder. I didn't need night-vision goggles or binoculars to make out our target. The stone fortress was set in the crags against a mountain top, its defensive walls rising forty feet—almost as tall as the half-frozen waterfall above the fortress that crashed down the mountainside to eventually run through the fortress itself.

In the guard towers, I spotted mercenaries in winter gear manning heavy guns, while others patrolled the tops of the walls. Their numbers didn't appear especially robust. I raised a handheld radio to my mouth. "Wolf 2, Wolf 1. Quiet here," I said. "What about you?"

"*Same,*" Segundo answered. *"I don't think we were spotted coming up."*

Segundo had placed himself on my split team, putting Mick, our intelligence officer and third in command, in charge of the group that had stayed behind. In addition to me and Segundo were our two weapons sergeants, our senior engineer, and Hotwire, our senior commo sergeant.

"And no new chatter," added Hotwire, who was tapped into the enemy's radio frequency.

That didn't seem right, not for a creature as risk-averse as the White Dragon. Only a day earlier he had been injured and on the run.

I squinted up into the clouds that had blown in around midnight, the lowest layers brushing us with mist. Nafid had warned me a second time about the White Dragon's sadistic nephew, Ozari, the shifter who patrolled the skies, but I hadn't seen or heard him during our climb. We had taken the route the scouts had once used. It had kept us on the blind side of the mountain until about twelve-thousand feet, where we'd donned our snow camo suits and made our way over an icy pass, then up through a boulder field. The six of us were now concealed around the south side of the fortress where we'd be concentrating our attack.

"Wolf 1, Wolf 2. Still not seeing anything overhead," Segundo said. *"You?"*

"Nothing," I confirmed. "Move into position."

I looked back to make sure my senior engineer was coming, then grabbed the cases beside me and crept forward. I'd carried the bulk of our weaponry—almost five-hundred pounds worth—up the mountain with an ease that had both impressed and troubled me, distributing the loads before we'd split up.

After a couple hundred yards, I found a good spot and signaled my engineer over. While I set up the MK19 grenade launcher and M240 machine gun, he primed a set of explosive charges.

"Wolf 1 in position," I radioed.

A minute later Segundo and then Dean, the senior weapons sergeant, answered that they were in position as well.

"You have your assigned sectors. Start laying heat in thirty seconds."

"Good," Segundo said, "'cause it's colder than a witch's tit up here."

I stuffed in my ear plugs, gripped the handles of the MK19, and sighted in on the near tower. The mercenaries at the large machine gun lazed around, apparently clueless they were about to be lit up. According to Nafid, no one had ever attacked the White Dragon's domicile, including the wolves. Maybe that particular danger had diminished in the White Dragon's mind.

Not that I was complaining.

"Now," I said, thumbing the trigger. A stream of 40mm grenades thundered from the barrel and detonated around the tower's heavy machine gun. Mercenaries flew every which way, while their heavy gun canted to one side in a burst of smoke.

My teammates opened up on their targets with 203 launchers mounted to the undersides of their M4s, and the attack became a booming storm.

I switched my aim to the wall adjacent to the tower and sent more of the golf ball-sized grenades exploding over the heads of the scrambling mercenaries. Hot shrapnel ripped into them and dropped them from sight.

Air support would have been nice, but we had no planes, and the attack helos that had dropped Team 5 couldn't navigate in the powerful wind currents and vortices at this altitude. As I paused to check my weapon's feed, I made sure the enemy's heavy guns with an angle on us were now disabled.

They were. But the surviving mercenaries were organizing themselves along the wall, with more arriving. They popped up and down, automatic weapons flashing from their shoulders. Shots began pinging off the boulders around us.

"Keep a steady stream going off above them," I ordered.

"Eat death, lizard men!" Segundo shouted prior to a fresh hail of grenade fire.

I fired in bursts of four to six grenades, scattering more mercenaries, until my belt was spent. While the others continued firing grenades, I ducked behind cover, stripped off my camo suit, slung a flamethrower and the medium machine gun over my shoulder, and grabbed the duty my engineer had primed.

"Switch to small arms and pin them as best you can," I radioed. "I'm heading up."

"We've got you covered," Segundo said.

I eyed my target, a grate low in the wall through which the river from the waterfall exited. Nafid had told us about it—the one potential weakness in the fortification. I waited for my teammates to begin laying cover fire before setting out.

My legs propelled me nimbly through the boulder field as the intelligence in my animal muscles took over. The occasional bullet or two snapped past, but they were few and far between. My team was doing its job of keeping the enemy down.

Within a half minute, I was beside the frozen river. Beneath several inches of ice, water gushed through the grate. Unshouldering everything, I removed the shaped charges from their pack and began mashing them into where the poles of metal disappeared into the wall's thick stone. When they were all in place, I lined the detonation cord out along the wall. The firing from the mercenaries and my men chattered back and forth, but no rounds impacted around me.

I waited for the next sustained burst from above before squeezing the detonator. *Bang.* I returned and ripped the half-dislodged grate the rest of the way from the stone and ice, then slid into the opening on my back.

The tunnel proceeded for ten feet under the wall. At a far grate, I removed blocks of primed C-4 from the pack and pressed them against the ceiling at one foot intervals until I was back at the opening. I measured off the time fuse and stood. With thirty seconds to detonation, I gathered my weapons and hustled a couple hundred feet from the wall. Automatic fire continued to clamor from my teammates' positions as I took cover behind a boulder.

"Three ... two ... one," I whispered.

Red-hot flashes burst from the opening followed by a violent geyser of dust as the lower wall collapsed. With no support, the wall above followed, the vertical section dropping like a demolished building. A handful of mercenaries plummeted too, becoming buried in the cracked and pulverized stone.

Victorious whoops went up from the radio.

"I need you to soften up the inside," I said into my handheld.

A series of rapid *thump-thump-thumps* sounded as two of my men switched back to their launchers, lobbing grenades past the collapse and into what I'd identified from the satellite image as a courtyard. I picked up a few screams among the explosions—mercenaries who had arrived to defend the breach. The rest of my team continued to place automatic fire on the walls.

"Wind down the grenades, but keep up the suppressive fire," I ordered. "We're going in."

I stood and raised my fist. The giant wolves that had been crouching in wait burst from their hiding places in fits of barking and charged toward the collapse. The approaching pack—wolves that had journeyed up with us, wolves I now commanded—was awesome to watch. Within moments, the thirty-two of them, including the former Alpha, stormed past me. They clambered up the pile of smoking stones and into the fortress.

I arrived at the top of the collapse to find them already ripping into the surviving mercenaries. I experienced a burning urge to join my pack, to crash into the enemy and sink my teeth and talons into them. But with a trembling effort, I resisted.

Have to stay in control...

I brought the M240 to my shoulder—something I couldn't have managed for any length of time as Jason Wolfe—and used the high ground to mow down the mercenaries who were taking aim at the wolves. The armor-piercing rounds blew holes through their body armor and flung them back. Hot shell casings cascaded down my flexed thighs and clattered to the stones.

More mercenaries poured from a palatial-looking building that took up the far side of the compound, ending at the sheer stone of the mountainside. The fighters were mostly men with wild hair and sun-blackened faces, while the rest were reptilian with scaled snouts and slanted red eyes. Grotesque tails flicked at their backs. These were the kobolds Nafid had told me about.

Though the kobolds put up a more ferocious fight than the men, they were still no match for the wolves plowing into them. Black blood spouted from a pinned kobold's throat where one of my pack bit down and shook.

Once more I was tempted to join in, but Segundo and Dean hustled up beside me, M4s coughing rounds. The newly arriving mercenaries were so fixated on the rampaging wolves that by the time they noticed us, it was too late. Our firing tapered as the numbers of arriving mercenaries petered out. The wolves circled the corpse-littered courtyard, stopping occasionally to thrash the dying. Two wolves had fallen, I saw. Shot through the sides.

"No more movement on the walls," Hotwire radioed.

"We've cleared the courtyard, but there could be more inside." I said. "Still no sign of the dragons. Hold your positions in case we need to break contact and retreat. And keep one eye overhead."

"Yes, sir," Hotwire replied.

The machine gun still to my shoulder, I descended the collapse and entered the courtyard. Segundo and Dean followed, covering my sides and back. With no one left to maul, the wolves returned to us, their faces blood-drenched and excited. Segundo hadn't been thrilled about their coming, but now he patted one on the head and told it, "Good boy." The wolf bristled and snarled, but before it could snap, I caught its eye and shook my head.

"Good way to lose a hand," I told Segundo.

I checked the two fallen wolves, both dead, then signaled my teammates and the rest of the pack to follow me to the palace. We stacked beside the open door and listened. No sounds came from inside, not even breathing.

Segundo and Dean filed in behind me, and we covered each third of the room with our weapons.

My eyes absorbed everything at a glance: tall stone pillars, white marble tiles inset with diamonds, a pair of ornate stairways with banisters curving up to a second level, an arrangement of what looked like ice statues. Segundo, slower to process the visual info through his night-vision, gave a grunt of alarm, and a shot echoed from his M4. The head of the nearest statue exploded.

"Damn," he chuckled, realizing his mistake. "I thought those were people."

"They *are* people," I said, picking up the scent of blood and brain matter. I looked at the other statues: soldiers from various epochs frozen in ice, dozens of them. "Or were. Trophies of the White Dragon, I'm assuming."

"You think he's in here?" Segundo asked in a whisper.

I picked up a distinct reptilian smell when I sniffed the air. The kobolds' scent was similar, but this was warm and living. And where else would the White Dragon have fled to heal?

"We need to assume he is," I said. "And if he's still recovering, he'll probably be in his human form." I turned to the wolves who had stalked in behind us. "Search the palace," I said, the command propagating through our unique connection. "Kill any more mercenaries, but no women or children. Come get me if you find Orzu. I don't want you engaging him."

The wolves yipped in affirmation and took off, some sprinting up the stairs, others disappearing into rooms farther back in the palace. As they skittered off, a foul current of air streamed past me. I narrowed my gaze into a corridor that appeared to plunge into the mountainside itself.

I swapped the 240 for my flamethrower, signaled Segundo and Dean to do the same, and jerked my head for them to follow. I'd perceived correctly. The corridor ended at a high archway and became a cave.

"He's back here," I whispered in the growing stink. "And I was wrong—he's in his dragon form."

Segundo thumped his chest. "Let's Team 5 this mofo and get you home."

17

The cave tunnel opened into a series of caverns dominated by stalactites and stalagmites and shallow pools of ice. To our left and right were what must have been the mercenaries' barracks: deep spaces with fire pits, storage lockers, and tossed bedding.

"Place smells like shit," Segundo muttered.

Grunting in agreement, I filtered out those particular odors to focus on the dragon stench. We proceeded past the barracks. Several wolves joined us, which told me the palace was clear. I ordered them back to act as rear guards in case anyone or anything arrived from the outside.

After another hundred or so yards we stepped into an especially large cavern. I could hear the river running off to our left—but I was honing in on another sound. Beyond a pair of icy stalagmites stretching toward the high ceiling, the rumblings of deep breathing issued from a side cavern.

That was where the dragon stench was originating.

Giving hand signals, I took a position behind one of the pillar-like stalagmites beside the opening, while Segundo and Dean did the same behind the other. I motioned for them to stay put as I slipped around my pillar.

The cavern I peered into was high and deep. Cold wind gusted down through an opening far above, batting my hair. On the cavern's far side, I could make out what looked like a giant drift of snow and ice. But as my lupine eyes focused, I realized they were treasures: diamonds, ingots of platinum, and other precious metals. I was in some sort of vault.

The rumbling sounded again, this time interspersed by sleepy mutters. The treasure mound rattled and shifted. At the far end of the mound lay a dragon's head, the glittering scales blending in so well with the platinum and diamonds that I'd missed it at first glance. I examined the head for another moment then, making sure his eyes were closed, moved my gaze down the mound to the creature's tail. He was curled around the backside of the treasure heap.

"Is it the White Dragon?" Segundo asked when I returned to fill them in.

"Looks and smells like him," I whispered, taking off my pack. "And he's damn sure big enough. Might be our lucky day too. He's asleep. Got himself wrapped around the treasure like it's a body pillow."

"He didn't hear the explosions and all that shooting?" Dean asked.

"Either he's insulated from the sound back here, or he's a really deep sleeper." I opened the pack and removed a coiled steel hawser cable that I'd borrowed from one of the Apaches, each end featuring a reinforced loop. I threaded the cable through one of the loops to create a noose and held it up. "Just need to slip this around his neck and draw it tight."

"You've got cover," Segundo said, flipping on his flamethrower.

I took the lead as we all stole into the treasure room. I signaled for the men to hang back as we neared a mushroom-shaped stalagmite. It would make a good anchor. Wrapping the end of the cable around the stalagmite's stem, I forced the noose through the other reinforced loop and drew out the cable until it was taut. I then made my way toward the dragon's head, tugging on the cable to ensure it wouldn't slip from its mooring.

I was almost to the dragon when he shifted, creating a small avalanche down the near side of the treasure mound. His eyelids slid open, revealing the translucent plates that covered the black orbs of his eyes. Deep black pupils shifted and narrowed as though focusing in on me. I froze. I could feel Segundo and Dean tensing behind me, fingers on their triggers.

Long seconds passed before the dragon smacked his lips and exhaled in a weary mutter, his body settling back into place. I waited for his eyelid to close completely before resuming my approach.

Within moments I was beside his head, standing in the cold fog that issued from his nostrils. Extending a steady arm, I moved the noose around his snout, then canted the top of the noose back until it cleared the thick ridge of his brow. The dragon's deep breaths scraped in and out. The challenge would be working the noose beneath his throat, which was pressed flat to the stone floor. That was where I was counting on my animal strength and quickness.

Go time, I thought.

In a rapid sequence, I straddled the dragon's neck, jerked the noose to crank his head back, and then opened the noose out enough to work it under the soft flesh of his throat. The dragon reared to life, his giant wings thrashing and scattering treasure. I pulled the noose taut again, wedging the top part into a crevice between two spines on the back of his head.

"Gotcha, you son of a bitch," I said.

With me still aboard, the dragon climbed a good twenty feet before he ran out of cable. The throttling tension jerked him to the ground. I leapt off and rolled several feet to where I'd left my weapons. Snatching up the flamethrower, I flipped it on and felt it hum in my grip.

The dragon looked wildly around before trying to take off again. When he slammed to the ground a second time, a fragmented gulp issued from his throat. He was calling up a cold blast.

"His face!" I shouted, depressing the trigger and unleashing a gout of fire.

Segundo and Dean did the same. Steam plumed up and water rained around us as the dragon's ice blast became engulfed in a triple attack of pressurized napalm. With a strangled shriek, the dragon stumbled backwards. We cut our jets, but the napalm continued to burn over the blackened scales of his face, making him look even more demonic.

The dragon crouched low, talons warning us back. Then, using his tail as a booster, he thrust himself skyward. This time the anchoring stalagmite broke off at its stem and dangled from the hawser around the dragon's neck. He stroked toward the opening high overhead.

"He's getting away!" Segundo shouted, chasing him with a futile burst of napalm.

I swapped my flamethrower for the M240 and

unleashed a withering burst of gunfire. The fusillade tore through the creature's right wing, crippling him. The White Dragon shrieked as he began to lose altitude. I opened up on the left wing as he flapped and grasped at a wall for purchase.

The leather-like material of the wing was tough, but no match for the 240's armor-piercing ammo. A cluster of perforations appeared, and the dragon plummeted. Rocks spilled with him as he knocked into one wall and then another, talons clawing desperately.

He landed on the treasure mound with a splash of diamonds and rounded on us. "Fools!" he hissed in a sharp accent. "Do you know who I am?"

Flames ripped from Segundo's flamethrower, swallowing the dragon. "We could give two shits."

This time the dragon didn't bother with an ice blast. Bursting through the fire, he tail-lashed Segundo to the ground. Dean, who had been stepping forward with his own flamethrower attack, was met by the tail coming the other way. Dean flew through the air several feet before landing in a backward series of somersaults, his weapon clattering away.

As the dragon pounced to finish my men, I caught the dragging chunk of stalagmite he was tethered too and yanked. The force throttled the dragon and slammed him onto his back.

Before he could recover, I choked up on the cord. With a roar, I swung him into a wall. He landed amid a pile of rubble, legs pedaling as he tried to right himself. My chest and biceps swelled as I roared and swung him against another wall. The dragon gagged out a scream.

Spotting a pair of close-set stalagmites, I took off toward

them, dragging the dazed dragon behind me. The dragon's head and neck followed me through the narrow space, but not his enormous body—which was the whole idea. The dragon firmly wedged, I pulled with all my strength, the noose digging deeper and deeper into his leathery neck. His eyes widened above his pale, protruding tongue. His legs and wasted wings kicked futilely.

Segundo and Dean, who had both recovered, came around, flamethrowers aimed. But the creature would never spew another ice blast. His movements were already slowing, the spark of white fire fading from his eyes. After another minute, he stopped kicking altogether. The protective plates relaxed from his empty black orbs. I maintained the tension for another minute before easing back and uncoiling the cable from around my aching hand.

"Holy shit," Dean breathed. "We just fought a dragon. And won."

For the past twelve hours, I had been so absorbed in the mission that I had given little thought to what should or shouldn't exist in this world—only that the mission had to be accomplished. And that had meant killing a dragon. My relieved exhale became a chuckle, which turned into a hoarse laugh. My senior weapons sergeant gave me a perplexed look.

"Sorry, man," I said. "Just never thought I'd hear those words coming from a soldier who hadn't completely cracked. And here I am agreeing with you."

Dean broke into a smile. "And I never thought I'd be taking orders from a werewolf."

Segundo clapped my shoulder. "Speaking of which, should we go visit the witch? Get you looking halfway handsome again?"

Before I could answer, Hotwire's voice came through my handheld radio in a staticky burst. *"Just got an urgent message from Parker down in the valley,"* he said. *"They're under attack. Say again, they're under attack."*

"Who's attacking?" I demanded.

"The White Dragon."

"White Dragon?" Segundo repeated. "Then who the fuck is this guy?"

The three of us turned toward the stalagmites, where a young, naked man of Asian persuasion lay on his side. His neck was raw and scored where the noose had dug into his dragon form, but the blood bubbling from his cracked lips told me he was still alive. Barely.

"Must be the nephew," I said. Which meant that while we had been coming up, the White Dragon had been going down, dammit. And we were hours from being able to back them up. "Try to get them some air support," I radioed Hotwire. "Anyone you can find. We'll meet you and head down."

The wolf in me wanted to snap Ozari's neck. Instead, I stooped and slung his slender body over a shoulder.

"We might need him," I grunted.

18

Two hours later, I arrived in the valley and crossed the Wari river. Though I'd shed most of my gear to sprint ahead, I already knew I was too late. Hotwire had been sending me updates as he and the rest of the team made their slow way down. He hadn't been able to secure air support, but it wouldn't have made a difference. The White Dragon's attack had been as quick as it was violent. A mess of casualties lay in his wake—Parker among them.

As I raced toward the compound, I could see more buildings in ruins, several glittering with ice. I hustled up to the main gate, the breaths that heaved in and out of my chest clouding the chill air. Ozari, whom I'd stuffed into an insulated suit, slapped against my back, still out. I'd pushed myself to the limit, and for the first time as the Blue Wolf, I felt fatigued.

The inside of the compound was a chaos of downed buildings and villagers in rescue mode. It looked like a nightmarish replay of the night before, except the smells of blood and death were more potent. I spotted Mick, my intelligence sergeant, carrying an injured woman.

"Does anyone need to be dug out?" I shouted.

"No, sir! The buildings were evacuated before the dragon struck. Dead or alive, everyone's accounted for."

"Where's the rest of the team?"

"Mauli's doing trauma care and the others are manning the guns in case the dragon comes back."

"And Parker?"

He hesitated. "At the casualty point, sir. Follow me."

We wound past the destroyed buildings to a part of the compound that remained intact, emerging into a sheltered courtyard warmed by several fires. Among the victims knelt several women—the sorceresses—green lights swimming around them. I found Mauli setting up an IV drip for an unconscious man whose arms were bandaged. When my senior medic turned toward me, his eyes were dark and sunken into his face.

"Where is he?" I asked.

Mauli pointed past me. "I did everything I could, Captain. I'm sorry."

I turned toward the covered bodies and then drifted toward them like a sleepwalker. I was vaguely aware of Ozari sliding off my back and thudding to the ground as I knelt and pulled the blanket from the tallest one's face.

Parker's eyes squinted past me, brow furrowed, teeth bared in determination. It was as though he was stuck in time. If I couldn't have smelled the dead, thawing tissue, couldn't have heard the absolute silence in his vessels, I would have believed my civil affairs officer was still with us, still facing down the White Dragon.

But he was gone. And he'd done it for me.

As I looked at the first man I'd ever lost, I felt my mind wanting to go silent, like when Billy was having the blood drained from him sixteen years earlier. Instead, I placed my monstrous hand against Parker's chest.

"You're one of the best soldiers I've ever served with," I said, "and a damned good friend. I know you went down doing what you believed in. I know you went down fighting. I just wish I would've been there with you. As your captain, as someone you trusted, it was the least you deserved. I'll visit your mother when I get home. I'll make sure she knows how much we all loved and depended on you out here. Go in peace, brother."

I covered his face with the blanket, then stood and peered around, surveying the White Dragon's destruction. We'd had the same idea—to surprise the other. We'd failed in our respective missions but had imposed devastating costs. At the moment, his actions felt far more damning.

I caught sight of Nafid tending to someone. Though I couldn't see the person's face from my angle, I recognized her smell.

"What happened?" I asked.

"The White Dragon destroyed her shrine before I could get her out," Nafid said without turning. "Her magic spared her from death, but her legs were crushed."

I stood beside Nafid and looked down on her great-grandmother. In our prior encounters she had always adjusted her eyeless face to mine, but now, gashed and dusty, it was tipped back, as though she were taking in the stars. Her dark lips moved around a series of mumbles, while her bent fingers twitched over the wooden cube that dangled from her leather necklace.

My gaze moved down to her splinted legs. Nafid was

stroking the air above them with her staff, seeming to reinforce the waves of green light that rippled over them. "Will she be all right?" I asked.

"She is dangling between worlds. She may return to ours, or she may slip into the Beyond. Only the Great Maker knows."

"I'm sorry," I said.

"And I am sorry about your friend."

"The young warriors?" I asked quickly. "Are they...?"

"Yes, they are safe."

I studied the skies, but something told me the White Dragon would not be returning tonight. "Do you know where he went?"

"No, but *he* may."

I followed Nafid's narrowed gaze to where I'd dropped the White Dragon's nephew. He struggled onto his side and released a weak cough.

Ozari sputtered and shook as I dropped a bowl-full of cold water onto his face. We were inside a small room I'd unofficially requisitioned, a lantern glowing in one corner. The steel cables that secured Ozari to a wooden pallet dug into his wrists and ankles as he strained.

Refilling the bowl in a bucket, I dropped another dollop of the water onto his face. It landed with a slap. His eyelids moved for the first time, trying to blink back the water streaming from his black hair. Thanks to his dragon powers, he looked young, like a kid starting his freshman year of college. But according to Nafid, he was several centuries old.

I set the bowl down and stepped around to where he could see me. The black eyes that focused on me widened in surprise, then narrowed with hateful recognition. "Y-you are the invader!" he said in a thick accent. "You come to steal! Do you know who I am? Do you know who you steal from?"

"I don't want your damned treasure," I snarled. "I want to know where your uncle is. Orzu. The White Dragon."

"Guards!" Ozari screamed.

"You're not in your palace anymore, dipshit. And even if you were, your mercenaries are dead. How do you think I was able to turn you into a living wrecking ball and choke you out?"

Ozari's eyes relaxed suddenly and took on a strange glaze. For a second I thought I was losing him, but then I understood: he was peering into the plane Nafid had mentioned, checking on the status of his dragon form.

"Try it," I challenged. "That cord around your neck might be taut now, but if you shift, your neck is going to grow. I'll have no problem standing here and watching you strangle yourself to death."

The glaze left Ozari's eyes in a flash, and hate filled them once more.

"Where's your uncle?" I repeated.

"Go ask your momma."

I'd been insulted by an enemy before, but now my face burned beyond all proportion. "Oh, so that's how you want to play this," I growled, a sensation like hot pokers skewering my temples.

Before I could stop myself, I was leaping toward him, my right arm drawn back. I was going to split him open, spill his miserable guts all over the floor.

But a force arrested me. I looked down to find a glowing green web ensnaring me. I struggled from instinct, but my rage was already cooling, my reason taking hold once more. If I killed Ozari, I would lose anything he knew about his uncle's whereabouts.

"Allow me," Nafid said.

She walked up beside me, her robes blood streaked from helping her great-grandmother. After studying my face to ensure I was under control, she spoke a word, and the threads of light disappeared into the end of her staff.

"Go ahead," I breathed and stood back, massaging my temples.

I didn't like these episodes of control loss—and they were getting worse. I thought back to the White Dragon's words. Was the same spell that empowered my body starting to corrode my mind?

Ozari's eyes shot back and forth as Nafid knelt on the floor behind his head. "What is the witch doing?" he demanded.

Nafid pressed her hands to his temples and closed her eyes. He began to jerk, trying to shake her off him, but he went still suddenly as a wave of green light cascaded over him. His eyes stared at the ceiling, mouth open, as though he were beholding something heavenly.

"Orzu left him in charge tonight," Nafid said after a moment, her eyes still closed. "He began to patrol the skies, but the White Dragon's treasure called to him. A treasure he had long coveted. Before he knew what he was doing, he was wrapped around the wondrous weight of all that wealth. He fell into a drunken sleep. Your arrival awakened him. Your ... violent arrival." She winced and touched her throat as though she were the one being throttled. "And then he awoke here to coldness and wet. He was determined to say nothing about his uncle's whereabouts, yes, but his uncle had told him nothing. Only that he would be gone for several days and that he, Ozari, was in charge, that he was to defend the fortress."

Dammit, I thought, squeezing my fists. *Dead end.*

"But he'd never seen his uncle in such a state as when he returned last night," Nafid continued. Though it had seemed much longer ago, last night would have been after our encounter. "He was storming around the palace in his human form, half mad with rage. Ozari overheard him on the telephone at one point, telling someone he needed to meet with a buyer who would pay for his next opium yield in advance. He talked about funding an army to wipe out our valley and then hold it by force. He sounded determined."

"Couldn't he fund it with his treasure?" I asked.

"A white dragon can part with money, yes, but treasures are to be amassed. In the dragon's mind, they are measures of his worth. To lose even a small portion of one's hoard can cast a dragon into a deep depression or launch him into a vindictive rage. It is why the larger accumulations are so intoxicating."

Which explained why Ozari had been so out of it when we'd found him. "Is that where the White Dragon went?" I asked. "To find a buyer?"

Nafid nodded slowly. "His nephew did not hear this, but he made associations in his mind. I am trying to…" Her words trailed off as her brow creased in concentration. "Yes, his uncle has been courting a buyer in your United States, a man who pays top dollar for opium from this part of the world. But the buyer is paranoid and will only make deals in person. He lives in New York, a place you call Chinatown. His name is Wang Gang, though most call him 'Bashi.'"

I made mental notes of the information. The White Dragon must have swung through here en route to wherever he kept a plane, maybe to discourage an attack against his fortress while he was gone. I had undermined those plans, but the knowledge gave me no comfort. Not with Parker gone.

Nafid withdrew her hands from Ozari's head. "That is all I can see right now."

"That may be all I need to get started. And didn't you say the farther he strays from his place of creation, the weaker he'll become? Will he even be able to shift?"

As Nafid stood, green light lingered around Ozari's head, seeming to hold him in an entranced state. "It's unlikely," she replied, "but he'll have bodyguards."

Bodyguards or not, finishing him would require little more than a single high-caliber bullet to the head. Something I was equipped to do. The challenge, of course, would be getting to New York.

"I must return to Baba," Nafid said. "But she wanted me to give you this." From her gown, she produced the wooden cube I had seen around the old woman's neck and held it out by its leather strap.

I accepted it and turned the cube over in my hand. "What is it?"

"Many years before I was born, the White Dragon took Baba away. After three days, everyone thought her dead. But she staggered back to the village, her body battered and broken from torture, her eyes gone. It is said that to have seen Baba was to understand the White Dragon's evil.

When people asked how she escaped, she replied only that the cube had spared her."

I looked over the cube's strange inscriptions. An almond-like smell emanated from the dark wood.

"If there was magic in the cube once, I sense none now," Nafid said. "But a few minutes ago, in a moment of clarity, she insisted you take it. She said you would need the cube in your battle."

"Please thank her for me."

Nafid nodded as she walked past me, but then hesitated in the doorway.

"You should know something, Jason. As long as my great-grandmother lives, I can reach the Great Wolf through the portal she created—even if she cannot. I can perform the *da'vat* ceremony. I can see to it that the bargain is fulfilled. But should Baba perish, so too will the portal. Neither I nor any of my sisters will have a way to reach the Great Wolf. Meaning that even if you kill the White Dragon, you will remain the Blue Wolf."

19

"It can't be done, boss," Segundo said, shaking his head. "Not in the kind of timeframe you're talking."

It was four hours later, and my split team had returned from the mountains along with the wolves. I'd been on the radio for a chunk of that time, arranging for a Chinook to airlift Parker's body and deliver the village a large supply of food, medicine, building materials, and weaponry.

While that percolated through the channels, I had used Hotwire's computer to send a situation report, in which I described the attack as the work of the Mujahideen. I explained that Parker had become separated while pursuing the enemy into the mountains. We'd found him early this morning, frozen and succumbed to hypothermia. It was the first time I had ever lied in a report, but the truth would only get me pulled for a comprehensive medical eval.

And that was the biggest challenge right now: getting *anywhere* without the military seeing me.

"Easy there," I said to Segundo, irritation heating my

words. "This is a brainstorming session. I'm asking for ideas, not roadblocks. And right now, Mauli's idea has the best chance of getting me to New York."

According to Mauli, the military physicians in Waristan were so overburdened that they were signing off on medics' orders without reading them. Mauli's idea was to diagnose me with a malignant skin condition and then write an order that I be transferred to a VA hospital in New York that specialized in such conditions. He would get a physician at the main operating base to sign the stat order. Wrapped head to toe, I would be lifted out with Mauli escorting me.

"Look, I'm not trying to be a dick," Segundo said. "All I'm telling you is that even if you did get the order, you'd still be on the military's timetable. That's going to mean a ton of stops, a lot of waiting. You remember what happened when they sent Donnie out? It'll be a week by the time you set foot in New York."

I turned to Mauli for his opinion.

"I mean ... he *could* be right," my medic hedged.

"Great," I muttered.

"I'm telling you," Segundo added. "This isn't the military of ten years ago. It's stretched really damned thin, which helps with the order thing, but we're still talking fewer planes, fewer flights..."

"Unless you booked with Centurion," Hotwire cut in.

I narrowed my eyes at him. "Is that supposed to be funny? Centurion is the reason we're in this mess."

Hotwire showed his hands. "Hey, if time and discretion are the issues, then Centurion is an option. That's all I'm saying. They fly direct with mid-air refueling. You'd never have to disembark until you reached your destination. It will cost you a shitload, but it's the surest bet."

"How do you even know this?" I asked.

"I hack encrypted frequencies in my spare time. Just last month a soldier wanted out, some senator's kid. The military wouldn't release him, so his dad paid Centurion's transport division to include the kid on a cargo flight to his home state. I eavesdropped on the whole thing."

As Hotwire's commanding officer, I didn't want to hear about his illegal activities. But Segundo was right. This wasn't the military of ten years ago, or even five. Times had changed.

"Seems like a huge risk to their contract," I said.

Segundo blew a raspberry with his lips. "Centurion has taken over half the war. They could drop a bomb on the Presidential Palace on Monday, say 'oops' on Tuesday, and by Wednesday Centurion lobbyists and members of Congress would be laughing about it over cocktails. They do whatever the hell they want."

"They're not gonna help someone who cracked one of their rep's faces in half," I said.

Segundo shook his head. "Different departments, man. Transport probably doesn't even know, much less care, about what happened to Baine." He snorted. "Look who's throwing up roadblocks now."

"And hell, I can disguise your digital identity," Hotwire said.

"I think we should exhaust all options before even thinking about Centurion," I said thinly.

"Captain." Segundo leveled his dark Colombian eyes at me. "There *are* no other options."

I dragged a hand through the thick hair between my ears and paced the room. I pictured waves of armed kobold mercenaries storming the valley, a fleet of white dragons flying overhead. With or without the Blue Wolf, the Kabadi wouldn't stand a chance. All remnants of the Great Wolf would be wiped out, possibly casting the world into darkness. I needed to reach the White Dragon before he secured the money for his army. And, yeah, before the old woman passed on and I lost my future with Daniela. I stopped pacing and turned toward the team.

"How much are we talking?"

"It cost the senator fifty-five," Hotwire said.

"Thousand? Yeah, well, I don't have that kind of dough, so we can scratch that option."

"Do you have *five* thousand?" Segundo asked.

"I doubt they're going to let me pay on an installment plan."

"Yes or no."

"Yes, but—"

"Good," he said, then looked around. "Who else has five thousand? Savings, retirement, home equity?" He raised his own hand. When the rest of the team's hands went up, I saw what he was doing.

I shook my head. "I can't take your money."

"Don't worry, you'll never see our money," Segundo said with a smirk. "It's going straight to Centurion—as much as that fucking burns. Look, man, the White Dragon killed a brother. And he's damn sure not getting off on the technicality of the rest of us being cheapskates. We want as much skin in the game as you, and if we can't be there, it means contributing to the 'Grease the Dragon' fund. That's how Team 5 rolls." As whoops went up, he turned to Hotwire. "Call Centurion Transport and get Captain Wolfe on the next flight to New York."

"Hold it," I said, showing Hotwire a hand. I turned

toward Segundo. Suspicion prickled through me as I thought back to Team 5's return the day before. Something wasn't adding up. "Colonel Stanick didn't send Team 5 back to support me and Parker, did he?"

Segundo furrowed his brow. "What are you talking about?"

Though he looked convincing, I caught a souring of his scent. The rest of the room went quiet. Too quiet. When I looked around, a few of the team members averted their gazes.

I nodded knowingly. "He sent you to extract us."

"You really think we'd blow off an order from Colonel Stanick?" Segundo asked.

"The rest of the team, maybe not. You? Absolutely."

Segundo's jaw clenched as if he were about to launch into a defense of his innocence, but then he sighed and threw his hands up. "Stanick said the situation was too unstable. After consulting with CENTCOM, he decided to pull out and reassess. So yeah, he sent us to extract you."

I shook my head. "You should have told him I refused and then returned to base."

"We put it to a vote," Segundo said. "Help you fight the White Dragon or leave you here on your own. It was unanimous. And before you go beating yourself up, Parker was as vocal as any of us."

The rest of the team grunted in agreement, but I quieted them with a glare. "A vote?" I said. "We're not a high school debate team deciding what color tie to wear to the state meet. This is the military. We don't do votes. We follow a chain of command."

"Team comes first," Segundo said defiantly. "And I'd do it again."

"This is your future!" I roared. "Do you think you're going to get into OCS after this?"

"If we get you back, I could give a rat's ass," he said. "This is *your* future too. And I'm sorry, but when I introduce my kids to you some day, I don't want them screaming in fucking terror."

I frowned at Segundo's attempted humor and paced the front of the room again. I was angry because of what had happened to Parker. Angry at myself. I had put my team in an impossible position. Of course their first line of loyalty was going to be to me, a brother in trouble. That's the way Spec Ops units were designed to function. But this was bigger than me now. To be fair, it was also bigger than the U.S. military and the "Never-Ending War." The wolf in me knew this even if it made little rational sense.

My team was watching me, awaiting my next words. At last, I turned to Hotwire and nodded.

"Contact Centurion," I said.

I jolted upright, the strong smell of airplane fuel filling my nostrils, and realized the plane was no longer airborne. We were speeding down a runway. I checked my watch. Twelve hours since liftoff. That was about right.

Hotwire's intel had been good. Centurion Transport dealt in flights for the right price. He talked them down to an even fifty thousand, and with fifty percent up front—money he transferred electronically from our accounts—he secured a seat for me on a flight leaving in four hours. That done, I'd radioed Pete, asking for a second favor in almost as many days: getting me a lift to Centurion's airfield.

At the airfield, I was escorted by a member of the flight crew up to the bay door and into the cargo hold. To conceal myself, I wore a bulky flight suit, a scarf, and a mask that Mauli had made for me using bandages and medical tape so that I looked like a soldier recovering from a head wound. No one asked any questions, except if I needed to use the bathroom before takeoff.

As I settled in, I tried not to think about the fact I was leaving my team behind, minus Parker, or that they were jeopardizing their military careers to cover for me. Segundo would be sending periodic communications up the chain that insurgent attacks were frustrating my extraction. There was no telling how long that charade would hold, but my focus needed to be on my mission. Not on my teammates, not on Daniela, who had no idea where I was or what I was doing, and not on the fact I was going AWOL on a one-way flight to the States.

I would face the consequences when the White Dragon was dead. As my former captain used to say, in war it was often easier to ask for forgiveness than permission.

I spent part of the flight using my laptop and the plane's Wi-Fi to search for information on the man the White Dragon had gone to meet. Wang "Bashi" Gang headed New York's Chinatown mafia, an organization known as the White Hand. I found several stories dealing with Bashi's brutal rise to power, including accounts of him torturing and killing his own siblings in order to succeed his father, who had died a few years earlier. Bashi brought the same brutality into his reign as kingpin as he used to grow the White Hand's influence and territory. In addition to extortion, prostitution, and weapons dealing, the White Hand was involved in a major drug network that extended up and down the East Coast.

Hence the White Dragon's interest in Bashi as a buyer.

I couldn't find anything on where this Bashi was headquartered, though, which meant I was going to have to pick up the White Dragon's scent somewhere in Chinatown's fifty square blocks.

As the plane taxied to a stop, I unbuckled the harness that strapped me into my seat in the cargo hold and let out a monstrous yawn. I'd only managed a few hours sleep the last three days and was beginning to feel the strain.

Checking to make sure my sidearm was still in my hip pocket, I stood and zipped up my flight suit, adjusted my scarf and mask, slung my backpack over a shoulder, and lifted the case with my disassembled M4. Another advantage of flying with Centurion had been the issue of weapons. Being able to just carry them on and off made things a hell of a lot easier.

I shifted my weight as I watched the bay door. I'd never had a problem flying before, but in my wolf state the plane had started to feel like a coffin whose sides were closing in. The stuffy suit didn't help.

Within minutes, though, the bay door lowered, and a surprising flood of daylight burst into the hold, stinging my eyes. Ten thirty at night in Waristan meant two in the afternoon here.

A silhouette bisected the light. "Welcome to JFK International," a man said.

I grunted, raising a forearm to block the glare as I limped on stiff legs past the chained pallets of supplies. I expected to find the same crew member who had escorted me on board. Instead, out of the light emerged a short black man in a dark pinstripe suit. His lips grinned beneath a pencil-thin mustache that matched the color of his combed-back gray hair. When he reached the cargo hold, he extended a hand to shake.

"Burn wound," I said, retracting my gloved hand.

I didn't need anyone gripping my huge paw. Besides, the man was throwing off a sketchy vibe.

"Of course," the man said, sliding his hands into his pockets. He came to a stop in front of me at the top of the ramp, his grin reducing his eyes to slits. Something told me he knew I was lying. "I imagine you're in a hurry to get to where you're going, but I was hoping we could have a chat first."

"Like you said, I'm in a hurry."

"Sorry, I didn't introduce myself," he said quickly before I could step past him. "Reginald Purdy, head of Program Development at Centurion United." He started to extend his hand again but caught himself.

My gaze fell to the silver pin on his lapel with the Centurion insignia.

"Is there some sort of problem?" I asked, my gaze flicking past him. Four large Centurion soldiers stood at the bottom of the ramp, automatic weapons pointed downward. I edged over so the man was between me and them.

"Well, there's the matter of the remaining payment due on landing," he said. "Those were the terms, correct?"

I relaxed slightly. "Right. Let me contact my man and he'll make the transfer."

"Or perhaps we can waive the remaining payment in exchange for fifteen minutes of your time."

He was going to waive twenty-five thousand dollars for a fifteen-minute chat? Though I guessed to a hundred-billion-dollar company that would be like flipping me a nickel. "What do you want to talk about?"

"I'm here to make you an offer, Captain Wolfe."

I stiffened. There's no way this man should have known who I was. Hotwire had taken special care to cloak my identity. He'd sent the payment through encrypted channels that wouldn't expose me or my teammates. My nostrils opened out as the animal in me tried to draw a better bead on him, but all I could smell was his damn aftershave.

"What kind of an offer?"

"First, apologies are in order for the actions of our representative. Baine Maddox embedded himself in your team on his own initiative. Centurion never ordered him to do so. The bombing that followed..." Mr. Purdy, who possessed the mannerisms of an old-time lawyer, grimaced in a show of sorrow. "Horrible. As you may have heard, the military took Mr. Maddox into custody for his actions."

So much for Centurion's right hand not knowing what the left is doing, I thought, tensing anew. I glanced down the ramp to find the soldiers had shifted such that they had clean lines of sight on me.

"And Olaf?" I asked.

"He's being handled internally."

"I'll bet," I muttered.

"What you don't know," Mr. Purdy went on, "is that Baine lost his life two hours ago."

I squinted at him. "Baine's dead?"

"In the act of attacking a guard and trying to take his weapon, yes. By all accounts, Mr. Maddox was ambitious but also temperamental and reckless. And that's our failing. We're revising our hiring protocols as we speak."

"Good to know," I said thinly, wondering if Centurion

had had him killed to frustrate an investigation into his actions. But then another thought hit me.

Or to cover up the fact that Centurion had been contracted by Orzu to eliminate the Kabadi's warrior class.

I thought about Baine's push to bring Olaf along, about his insistence that the blue-haired men were enemy collaborators, about Olaf sneaking onto the roof to tag the building. It added up. Baine hadn't been looking for a commission from the U.S. military, which would have required a review to determine whether the targets were high value enough.

He and Centurion had been in the pay of the White Dragon.

"But that's all preamble," Mr. Purdy continued. "I felt we needed to clear the air on the matter of Mr. Maddox before proceeding. Dispel the cloud of mistrust. So let me cut to the chase." He removed a folded handkerchief from the front pocket of his jacket and touched it to each corner of his mouth. "After the bombing, we kept a surveillance drone in the area to assess the damage. With our exceptional video capacity, we can monitor details as small as six inches from an altitude of 20,000 feet. Do you know what that means?"

The thick hair over my skin bristled hotly. When I only glared at him, he continued.

"It means we saw everything, Captain Wolfe. I know what you look like beneath your disguise. I know about your transfiguration. I know about your newfound abilities."

My breaths cycled harshly. "Is this some sort of extortion job?" I growled.

Though I towered over the diminutive man and

possessed claws that could separate his head from his body, his eyes twinkled amicably. "Oh, far from it," he said. "We'd like to offer you a position with Centurion."

"Because of this?" I gestured to myself. "Sorry, but I don't plan on staying this way beyond the weekend."

"I confess to not knowing why you came to New York. We had eyes on you, not ears." His grin returned. "Yes, even the mighty Centurion has its limits. But a little deduction told me it had to do with finding a cure, which you're now confirming. That's where Centurion can help you."

"How?" I challenged.

"Not all of the work of Centurion's bioengineering division is made public, but they've had some astonishing breakthroughs in the past few years. Tissue regeneration, for example?" When he cocked an eyebrow, I understood he was referring to Olaf, Baine's sidekick whose arm had practically grown back overnight. My eyes must have betrayed the connection because he nodded. "And cases like his are just the tip of the iceberg. Give the bio division a year, and I'm confident they can restore you to your former self."

"I don't have a year," I said. "And anyway—"

"You're going to take care of it this weekend," he finished for me. "What I'm offering, then, is a contingency plan. If for some reason this weekend doesn't pan out as planned, you have a second chance through Centurion."

I thought about what Nafid had told me about the portal to the Great Wolf depending on her critically-wounded great-grandmother remaining alive. Even if I succeeded in killing the White Dragon, I could remain stuck as the Blue Wolf.

"In exchange for what?" I asked.

"A year of your service."

"And what would that entail?"

"Heading a division of special operatives," he said.

"No matter what I've become, I'll never be a *mercenary*." My lips wrinkled around the word. "Thanks, but no thanks."

"What if I told you that you wouldn't be fighting people, but monsters?" he called as I stepped past him. "Like the ones who killed your childhood friend."

I stopped.

"What was his name?" Mr. Purdy asked, as though to himself. "Billy Young?"

"How in the hell do you know about Billy?"

"Before making offers of employment, we do extensive background checks. The police report with your testimony remains on file at the Jefferson County Sheriff's Department. Make no mistake, Captain Wolfe, those boys who thrust a knife into Billy's neck and took their turns sucking him dry were not human. They were a breed of vampire. Those are the kinds of creatures your division would be pursuing. Creatures who hurt people like Billy."

For a moment I was back on the river bank, watching Billy's dimming eyes beside the blood-slurping leader, the one with the scruffy blond beard and dirty John Deere hat. The local paper had called them Satanists.

But a breed of vampire?

"I've thrown a lot at you, so here," Mr. Purdy said, holding out a business card with his name and number in small print against the Centurion logo. "For right now all I ask is that you hold onto this. Regardless of how things turn out, give me a call. We'll talk some more. And as a gesture of good will, today's flight is on us. The money you paid up front will be refunded."

I nodded for no other reason than that my men would no longer be on the hook.

"Can we offer you a ride somewhere?" he asked.

"I'll catch a cab."

"Very well. At the bottom of the ramp, take a left. There will be one waiting for you at the end of the big warehouse, beyond the security gate. My men will let you out. And, Captain Wolfe..."

I turned.

"I do hope we hear from you."

20

I asked the cabbie to wait while I drew money from an ATM then ducked into a used clothing store. I picked out a large trench coat and floppy hat and then had the cabbie drive me through Chinatown, street by street.

Coming from Waristan, where most of my assignments had been in rural or mountainous areas, the crush of buildings and traffic was overpowering. I had been to New York City only once before, and briefly, while attending a training at Fort Bell on Long Island. I vaguely remembered the smell of traffic, but now my nostrils flared at the multiple layers of exhaust streaming through my cracked window. And that was to say nothing of the other scents: fish, incense, hot grease, stagnant water, garbage, and people.

Lots of people.

Picking out the White Dragon's scent was going to be more challenging than I'd thought. For right now, though, I just wanted to get the lay of the neighborhood. General recon.

"Pull over here," I said after about thirty minutes.

The cabbie laid on his horn and swerved his cab past a line of street vendors to the front of the store I'd indicated: Mr. Han's Apothecary.

I paid the cabbie and stepped out. Thick currents of pedestrians streamed around me as I adjusted my coat and hat, the second meant to cast shade over my bandage mask. But everyone seemed to have places to go and things to do. No one gawked at the strange seven-foot-tall figure.

I strode toward the apothecary, rereading the handwritten sign I'd spotted in the window: "Room for rent."

A sharp *tring* sounded as I ducked beneath a string of paper lanterns and into the pungent-smelling shop. The inside was a crammed arrangement of shelves holding dried herbs, powders, and an assortment of oddities that made no sense to me. I edged my way around a fish tank filled with live scorpions and found myself in front of a small Chinese man perched behind a register.

"How can help you?" he asked. "Have good, good sale on raven beak."

"Yeah, no thanks," I said. "I'm actually here about the room for rent. Still got it?"

When he glanced at my rifle case, I was sure the transaction was a bust. But he surprised me by saying, "Yes. Upstairs room with bathroom and Wi-Fi. Good view back alley. One t'ousand a month."

"How about for the week?"

"No rent for week. Only month." When he saw me hesitate, he added, "Come with free energy juice." He ducked beneath his counter and reemerged with a large mason jar. When he opened the lid, a greenish liquid inside hissed and released a fermented gas. The smell almost knocked me over. "Made with tiger testicle. How you say, fill you with piss and vinegar."

"I'll pass on the energy juice, but I'll take the room."

"Good. I show you now." He shouted something into a curtained back room and then led me out of his shop. After locking the door behind him, he walked to an adjacent door and unlocked it.

The room was at the top of a narrow flight of steps. It was simple, and the bed had been built for someone half my height, but it was in my target area and discreet. Anyway, I didn't plan on spending much time in the room. I paid him the thousand, and he handed me the keys and a slip of paper with the Wi-Fi code.

"Energy juice be ready for you after unpack and chill out," he said, forgetting that I had declined it.

When he left, I set my pack and rifle case on the bed and walked over to the window. I gazed over the steam-shrouded rooftops of adjacent buildings, then down at an alley with a narrow creek of swill running down its middle. A group of children were kicking a ball around at the far end.

I had no intel sources here, just a spec ops background and my enhanced senses. Assuming Orzu had flown here immediately after the attack, he'd have an eight hour head start on me. With the advantage of mid-air refueling, I'd probably trimmed that lead by a couple of hours, but I was still behind.

With the memory of the flight came Mr. Purdy's offer to join Centurion in exchange for a cure. I quickly shoved the thought back down. I needed to focus. And anyway, it wasn't going to come to that.

I unpacked the laptop, set it on a small desk in the

corner, and removed my bandage mask. As the screen powered on, I felt an urge to check on my team, but Hotwire had warned that any communication I sent or accessed would be stamped and likely flagged by the military's system. Even with the laptop's login and GPS disabled, the chain of servers would tell them I was no longer in Waristan.

Maybe it was just as well—again, for purposes of focus.

I logged onto the Wi-Fi and pulled up a map of Chinatown. I'd already formed a good internal map of the neighborhood's layout during the cab ride, noting street names as well as the smells associated with them. The second had happened automatically, another feature of my new abilities.

Now I planned my route on the screen, eating a couple of MREs as I did so. I would start on the neighborhood's perimeter and spiral my way inward. The redundancy would give me second and third chances to pick up the White Dragon's scent, versus starting at one end of Chinatown and working my way toward the other.

"Time to get moving," I said, closing the laptop.

I polished off a third MRE and drank a half gallon of water straight from the bathroom's tap. I then stepped into a pair of camo pants and strapped a ballistic vest over my shirt. I covered everything with the huge trench coat. If I stood in a hunch, the coat's skirt covered my feet. A good thing because the bandages were starting to go ragged, revealing sections of blue hair and black claws.

In front of the mirror I hesitated before putting on my bandage mask and scarf. The hairy face peering back at me was impossible, with its peaked ears, yellow eyes, and lethal muzzle, but there it was, and it belonged to me.

For now.

I dropped my sidearm into a pocket, distributed grenades and magazines into the others, and then hefted the gun case. I was almost through the doorway when the satellite phone I'd left in my pack began to ring. I hesitated. *Could be Team 5*, I thought. *And they'd only be calling if there was trouble.*

I returned into the room and dug out the phone. "Hello?"

"Is this Jason?"

I swallowed dryly, heart slugging in my ears. "Daniela? How did you get this number?"

"You called me a couple of days ago, remember?"

"Right, yeah." I didn't think satellite calls showed up on caller ID, but apparently they did. It was good to hear her voice, so good, but I could feel the second hand ticking away. "What's going on, baby? Is everything okay?" Her tone had sounded strained.

"That's what I'm hoping you can tell me. Where are you?"

"Still on that assignment I told you about. In fact, I'm sort of in the middle of it."

"No you're not."

Her words landed like a slap across my face. "Say again?"

"You're not on an assignment, Jason. I just got off the phone with your colonel. He says you've gone AWOL. He wanted to know if I'd heard from you. Now will you tell me what's really going on?"

Colonel Stanick had found out about my absence? How? And what did that mean for Team 5? The light through the window seemed to go gray, and the room wavered. I sat down hard on the bed, nearly breaking the frame.

"Jason?"

"Yeah, I'm still here. I need you to listen to me, Daniela. First off, I'm fine. There's just something I need to do. Something important. When I finish, I'll report back to duty and be home shortly. You don't need to worry."

"But you were on the verge of being transferred. I ... I don't understand."

"I know you don't." Hell, *I* barely understood. "But I'm asking you to trust me on this."

"I *want* to trust you, Jason, but this doesn't sound like you. Not your voice, not the things you're saying, not the things you're doing. There are military police watching the house."

"Military police?" But that was standard procedure. They were there to apprehend me should I turn up.

"I have this feeling in the pit of my stomach that something's happened to you, something awful, and you're not telling anyone. If you need help, baby, you need to tell someone. You need to tell *me*."

I closed my eyes.

"But you won't," she said flatly when I didn't answer. "Can you at least tell me where you are?"

"I'm in the States."

"The States! Where?"

I didn't want to lie to her, but I wasn't going to put her in a position where she would have to lie for me.

"I can't say right now."

"Don't do this to me, Jason. Don't shut me out."

Daniela didn't deserve this. Not after two years of solid commitment. But even as I thought this, the muscles over my body cramped and tensed. I could feel my heart rate picking up. The animal in me was getting agitated, restless for the hunt. "If I told you, it wouldn't make sense right now," I said. "I'll explain everything when I get home, baby. I promise."

"That's my fear. That you're not coming home."

Without warning, a blood-red fury jagged through my head. "I'm just asking you to fucking trust me!" I roared.

A stunned silence fell over the line. I panted into the receiver, dizzy, wondering what in the hell had just happened. I had never yelled or swore at Daniela before. But she was standing between me and the hunt, and in that red bolt of rage, I'd had an image, a horrifying image, of slashing her aside with a clawed hand.

It's the wolf. I'm losing control of him.

As though coming to the same conclusion, Daniela said, "You're not Jason," and hung up.

As I lowered the phone from my ear, I considered calling her back, but not like this. Not with my heart pounding a mile a minute, my mouth bone dry, and a high ringing in my ears. I couldn't trust what I would say. I might lose it even worse. I needed to find and kill the White Dragon before whatever I had become consumed me. Then I would explain everything to her. I tossed the phone aside, took my gear in one arm, and left the unit.

Slamming the door behind me, I bounded down the steps to begin the hunt.

21

Though I maintained enough presence of mind to follow my pre-planned route through Chinatown, I couldn't prevent my wolf nature from compelling me to move at a rapid trot.

I dodged around traffic and hordes of pedestrians, colorful storefronts passing in a blur. I only plowed into one person, a wasted man mumbling about soft pretzels. I caught him, set him on his feet, and was gone before he knew what hit him. Before long, the bandages unraveled from my feet. Even so, no one gave me a second glance—maybe a case of New Yorkers having seen it all.

The only ones that seemed to know what I truly was were the dogs that cowered on leashes and the cats that hissed and bristled at me from alleyways. But that was all peripheral—as well as everything that had happened in the last three days. All of my neurons were on peak alert for a single reptilian scent. It was just after six o'clock when I found it.

I stiffened to a stop at an intersection on the western

side of Chinatown and raised my muzzle. Testing the air in each direction, I pivoted toward the south. There. The scent was leading down Mulberry Street. I chased the scent through the din of odors, past several intersections, the signal growing stronger.

When I was almost on top of it, I forced myself to slow to a walk. I was in a quieter part of the neighborhood now. A park lined with ginkgo trees appeared to my right where old men played board games on picnic tables and women practiced Tai Chi in the grass. Something told me a seven-foot man with wolf feet might attract more attention here.

I hunkered down as I continued to stalk the scent—a scent I could almost see. Like tendrils of smoke, the White Dragon's trail drew me toward an unassuming cluster of tenement apartments opposite the park before slipping beneath a large roll-down steel door.

The White Dragon is inside that building.

My heart slammed in my chest, the wolf begging me to sprint across the street and burst through the door.

No, I thought, digging my talons into my palms. *We may only get one shot at this. Need to recon the building, identify entrances and exits, see what kind of security is set up.*

If Orzu was inside, he was likely meeting with Bashi. That there was no one pulling security outside didn't mean anything. During my research I'd read that Bashi was so paranoid he never slept in the same place two nights in a row. In which case he probably wouldn't want a bevy of armed guards announcing his whereabouts. They could be monitoring the entrance in plainclothes or concealed behind the building's dark windows.

I continued past the roll-down door and circled the block. On the south side, beside a dumpling shop, a brown metal gate separated the sidewalk from a back alley that ran behind the tenements and street-level businesses. I completed my circuit, finding no other access points to the building.

Back at the roll-down door, I caught my captain's mind going to explosives and split teams, but it was just me now. I could climb an adjacent building, create a sniper's nest, and wait for the White Dragon to emerge, but where would that be? Front entrance or back alley? It was a coin flip, and if I chose wrong, I could lose my shot.

That left either attempting to sneak inside or forcing my way in and trying to reach my target as quickly as possible. I didn't like either option, frankly.

"Yo, big man!" someone called.

I peeked over a shoulder to find a group of Asian teens in white suits and slicked-back hair walking toward me. I recognized them from one of the articles I'd found online. They were enforcers for the White Hand, the ones who made sure the residents and businesses in Chinatown paid their protection taxes to Bashi. They were also in charge of general security in the neighborhood. Black pistol grips protruded from their waist bands.

As I lowered my head, the enforcer in the lead sped his pace. "Hey, I'm talking to you!"

I talked my wolf down. Wasting them would only draw unwanted attention—especially here. Pretending not to have heard him, I made sure my feet were hidden and started in the other direction. Another group of enforcers rounded the corner ahead of me and spread across the sidewalk.

"Shit," I muttered.

"What's your hurry?" the lead one asked as the two

groups merged into a circle around me. Though they all looked similar enough to pass for cousins, he stood out for being taller and possessing one of those things a person couldn't fake—the deadened eyes of a killer.

I felt the wolf in me interpreting his stare as a challenge. Against every instinct, I lowered my gaze and slouched further down. "Just walking," I said.

"This is a residential area. You've got no business here."

"Guess I got lost. I'll head back up this way." I was trying to sound as docile as I could, which was hard when adrenaline was dumping into my system and every word emerged a deep growl. I went to edge past the leader, but his hand clamped down on my gun case.

"What's in here?" he demanded.

My breaths panted in and out. "I said I was leaving."

"What's in the case?" he repeated, drawing his pistol and pressing it under the brim of my hat. The barrel mashed against my right temple. "You make me ask a third time, and I'm popping you in the fucking head."

It only took me a heartbeat to gauge my immediate surroundings. Eight other enforcers, most of them now congregated opposite their leader. The weapons they drew were a variety of pistols, all chambered in the 9mm to .40 caliber range. The leader was holding a Beretta 92 against my head.

Which meant I would have all the shots I needed.

In the instant it took for the leader's eyelids to slide down into one of his slow blinks, I seized his gun hand, shoved his finger from the trigger guard with my own, and jerked him in front of me. When his lids popped back up, his weapon was aimed at his fellow enforcers, and he was covering me like a flak jacket. Not comprehending what had just happened, the enforcers hesitated.

I didn't.

The shots banged out in a chain as I pivoted the leader's arm around, rapid-flexing my trigger finger. The enforcers dropped in a circle, red blooms spreading across their chests. In two seconds and a cloud of smoke it was over. Only the final enforcer had time to get off a shot before I struck him twice. I felt his bullet slam into his leader's spine and stop.

I released my protection and watched him collapse to the casing-strewn sidewalk. Ironically, his once-deadened eyes now showed desperate glimmers as he struggled to hold in the life that was leaking from him.

"Never grab another man's gun," I said, holding up my case.

I emptied the Beretta's final shots into him, then tossed the spent weapon onto his stomach. The wolf in me swelled at having answered his challenge with lethality. But I'd also caused a god-awful commotion, which the ringing in my ears was just one testament to. In the park, the Tai Chi session had broken apart in chaos while game pieces clattered from picnic tables, the old men fleeing as fast as their aging limbs could carry them.

Only one option now, I thought, turning to the roll-down door.

I opened the gun case and hastily assembled the M4. I slammed in a mag, chambered the first round, and slung the canvas strap across my body. Jamming the claws of my left hand into the edge of the steel door, I grunted and peeled it to one side. Shots from inside spanked what remained of the door and sparked from the metal frame.

Need to approach this like any operation, I thought. *Can't use my quick healing as an excuse to get careless.*

I angled my M4 around the door and fired off a suppressive burst. A glimpse inside showed me a room that had been converted into a garage. Three gleaming cars were parked in a line. The gunfire had come from a short set of steps beyond. Automatic weapons. Nine millimeter from the sound of it. Two shooters—for now. I had to assume more were coming.

I fired another burst, then entered low, using the luxury cars as cover. Answering fire cracked and caromed overhead.

Still high from dominating the enforcers, the wolf in me wanted to rush the men. But I could tell they weren't practiced. Instead of coordinating their bursts, they were firing simultaneously—and wasting a lot of ammo. I waited until I heard the click of an empty chamber, then popped my head up and down. The other shooter reacted predictably, emptying his own mag. Too easy. I leapt onto the car and in two quick bursts from my M4 dropped them both.

Shouts sounded from a large room beyond the flight of steps, and a door of thick security bars began to descend. Still on top of the car, I bounded forward, the impacts of my giant feet crushing rooftops and hoods. The door was halfway down by the time I cleared the steps.

I slid into the doorway on my knees, my left hand catching the descending door and bracing against its hydraulic power as though I were attempting a one-armed military press. I released a tight arc of fire, cutting down the four men running toward me across the two-story room. Stray bullets cracked into a giant LCD-screen television and a wall of high-end stereo equipment.

Two more armed men had hung back. Their next bursts were wild, the recoil jerking their barrels around. Even so, two bullets hit me before I could release the door and move behind a pillar on the room's near end. One bullet slammed into my chest plate, the other buried itself in my thigh. I grunted in pain as the security door ground to a broken slant behind me.

I switched out for a fresh mag and slapped the bolt release while the men kept spraying my end of the room. I waited for a lull in the shooting before peeking out. The men had taken positions behind two other pillars across the room. Firing off a burst with one hand, I dug a grenade out of my coat pocket with the other. I flicked off the safety clip, withdrew the pin, and lobbed the grenade across the room. I fired another burst, then ducked behind my pillar. The men shouted an instant before the grenade detonated in a rattling explosion, sending razor-sharp shrapnel flying everywhere.

When I emerged, the men were down—one dead, the other well on his way. The explosion had also dropped one side of the wall-mounted LCD television, shattering the screen. I checked back the way I'd come, making sure my six was clear, before sprinting past the spill of brass casings and up a flight of steps.

I couldn't help but appreciate Bashi's ingenuity: converting what looked from the outside like a modest tenement building into one grand apartment. The question was how much security personnel he kept around him. I'd already dropped eight of them. And Nafid had mentioned the White Dragon would have bodyguards.

The pain in my thigh dulled as I bounded up the stairs. I could feel the tissue healing from the bottom, forcing out the bullet. The flattened round dropped down my pant leg and clattered off behind me.

I soon arrived at a corridor that gave onto several rooms. The White Dragon's scent was drifting from straight ahead—an open room at the end of the hallway, where I could make out a large table. From the looks and smells of it, I had interrupted a dinner meeting in progress.

I dug for another grenade, cooked it for one second, and hurled it the length of the corridor. It bounced off the table and rolled out of sight, exploding a second later. I wasted no time, making quick checks of what turned out to be bedrooms and offices as I moved down the hallway.

When I reached the dining room, I peered through the smoke into each firing sector. The lavish room, which featured a gold-accented table and chairs as well as a huge chandelier, was empty except for the large koi fish in a pond that ran around the room's perimeter. At the shrapnel-splintered table, I noted the scattered place settings. There had been three principals at the meeting: Bashi, Orzu, and someone else—a clean surface scent with a musky undertone.

But where in the hell had they gone?

The only other opening was over a small bridge that led to the swinging doors of a kitchen area. I could hear someone cowering inside, no doubt the staff. I had no fight with them. Anyway, the White Dragon's scent didn't lead there. It was trailing to the right—where there was nothing but solid wall.

I dropped my gaze to the koi pond. A sheet of glass that would have been hard to detect with human vision lay flat over the water. A hidden bridge.

Which means, I thought, my gaze roaming the paneled wall, *there's also a hidden door.*

I stepped onto the glass and pushed against the wall, looking for a seam, a switch—something. Though it had only been a minute or so since I'd ripped open the garage door, it was still a minute. And that time gap was swelling. I could feel the White Dragon slipping away.

Stepping back, I raised a heel and drove it against the wall. My foot disappeared through the wood with a crunch. I tossed another grenade through the hole and took cover. The detonation shook the room.

I returned and kicked out the hole until it was large enough for me to peer through. I was looking at a landing at the top of a spiral staircase. About two floors below, I could hear a revving engine and a second later the scream of rubber over concrete.

Damn, they're taking off.

I broke through the hole and sped down the stairs, landing in a small garage in the rear of the building. A black SUV that had just backed into an alleyway was lunging into drive, tires laying down rubber again.

Bursting into the littered alley, I opened up with my M4. A cloud of white particles exploded off the vehicle's back window, but the glass was made of a polycarbonate that the rounds could smash but not penetrate. I dropped the muzzle. Rounds flashed off the car's plated body before nailing the rear right tire. Shredded rubber blew from the tire in chunks, but I was thwarted again—this time by a polymer donut that maintained the wheel's form.

I crouched as rounds cracked against a nearby cornice. Automatic gunfire from behind. I wheeled to find a pair of kobolds shooting from the cover of a leaking Dumpster, red eyes narrowed above their flashing barrels.

I released a burst to force them down, then dropped to all fours to chase the escaping SUV. The M4 slipped off me in the process, but I couldn't go back for it.

My hands and feet pounded through foul puddles as I sped past stacked crates and lines of trash bins. Up ahead, the gate I'd seen during my recon was sliding open—but slowly, allowing me to close the distance. The driver cut back and forth, trying to keep me from coming up beside them. I faked left and then sprinted right until I was even with the rear wheel I'd shot up.

When the SUV veered toward me, I planted my outside foot and met the body with a lowered shoulder. The SUV fishtailed away, bouncing off a mini Dumpster in a burst of sparks, then slammed against the backside of a building on the alley's other side. The approaching gate was fully open now, but the SUV was approaching the narrow space at a bad angle. The vehicle's brake lights flared as the driver tried to adjust in time. He couldn't.

The angry keening of metal on metal sounded as the SUV ground halfway through the opening—and got wedged. Distressed shouts, one of them a man's shrieking voice, sounded from inside the vehicle. The rear tires screamed, but the result was only a cloud of smoke. From the smell of burning rubber, a thread of the White Dragon's scent leaked out.

I pulled my pistol from my pocket and seized the rear door handle. Something nailed me in the left hip. A shout tore from my throat and my hand dropped from the door. I fell, writhing, onto my back. It was like someone had bored into my hip with a half-inch drill bit and then filled the hole with acid.

From up the alleyway came the sound of footsteps. I flipped over to find the kobolds running toward me, tails slapping the pavement, weapons still firing.

One of them had hit me, but with what?

Rounds flashed from the asphalt. The pain spreading, I breathed between my teeth and raised my pistol. Two cracks. The kobolds' heads snapped back and their reptilian bodies dropped to the pavement. I craned my neck toward the SUV. In its struggles, it had shimmied enough to begin scraping the rest of the way through the opening.

Can't let him get away.

I struggled to stand, but my wounded hip dropped me. Using my hands, I hobbled toward the vehicle. With a final keening, the SUV lurched out onto the street. It turned sharply left and began to accelerate away. I emerged behind it and rose onto one leg.

The block was empty—everyone no doubt scared off by the shooting. I jammed a hand into my coat pocket and seized a grenade. My one chance was to heave it ahead of the vehicle and hope a blast into the undercarriage would cripple it. I armed the grenade and drew it back, but as my arm came forward, a voice bellowed from the other end of the block.

"Vigore!"

A force plowed into my back like a defensive end hitting a quarterback's blindside. I was driven to the asphalt, the grenade tumbling from my grip and falling well behind the fleeing SUV. I squinted from the grenade, but the detonation was muted and no shrapnel flew past.

The SUV squealed into a sharp right turn and disappeared.

Heart slamming, mind warping with pain, I sprang onto my hands and feet to face my attacker. From the end of the block, a man armed with a glowing sword and what looked like a short staff approached. A long coat flapped around his calves with each stride. I didn't know who this son of a bitch was, but he'd just denied me a chance to destroy the White Dragon. As far as the Blue Wolf was concerned, that marked him as an enemy.

With a growl I tore off my scarf and mask and sprang toward him.

22

I bounded my four-hundred pounds toward him, blood-red rage compensating for my disabled hip. From the man's vantage, I must have looked like a nightmare: ears pinned, eyes blazing, lethal teeth bared. But instead of fleeing, the man planted his feet in a wide stance and shouted, *"Protezione!"*

White light flashed from the end of his staff. Only yards from him, I rammed head first into a solid wall.

I staggered back, his image blurring briefly, before I shook it off and lunged again. My pain and fury were driving me now. But the wall of light between us wouldn't budge.

"I'm assuming that pile of bodies out front is your work?" he said.

I circled, clawing and ramming the wall, but it encompassed him completely. From a dim place I remembered the threads of light Nafid could create from her own staff. Was this man some sort of sorcerer?

"Not that I have any love for Bashi's enforcers," he went

on, pivoting to keep me in front of him. "But still ... a demon's a demon."

Demon? I tried to say, but all that emerged was a savage bark.

"Respingere!" he cried. The light encasing him exploded outward, blinding me and knocking me ass over end. I rolled for several yards, pain detonating through my lower left quarter each time my hip slammed into asphalt.

Why wasn't I healing?

By the time I righted myself, he was above me, thrusting his sword down. The flashing blade clanged off the ballistic plate over my chest. He had been going for my heart. I roared and lashed a clawed hand at his face. My nails raked his light shield, spilling sparks. He staggered back.

Sensing weakness, I hobbled to my feet. His eyes fell to my wounded hip. Blood had plastered my coat to my side, and I could feel it spilling down my leg.

"Ouch," he remarked, then shouted another one of his Italian-sounding words.

The same force that had plowed into my back now rammed my left hip. The pain felt like a grenade going off. Roaring, I collapsed to my knees.

I didn't know who this sorcerer was, but he was determined to end me. Panting, reeling with pain, I crouched back to spring before remembering my pistol. I grabbed it from my coat pocket, took aim at his head, and fired until the slide locked open. Every shot sparked harmlessly from his shield.

"Vigore!" he called.

A fresh force lifted me and slammed me onto my back. I struggled to sit up, but I couldn't move, could barely breathe. Light danced around my head—*his* light, I realized. When I tried to bring my hands to my head, I found it encased in a dome.

Struggling, I pressed myself to my hands and right knee and began crawling toward him. My lungs seared with each breath while a pounding pressure built behind my eyes until I thought they would explode. Beyond the dome, his image flashed and wavered. My heart missed a beat, then caught up in a panicked gallop. He was suffocating me.

I stretched an arm toward the sorcerer, then dropped into blackness.

———

I peered down the church aisle, past the crowded pews, my pulse quickening in anticipation.

Segundo, my best man, stood beside me, arms bulging beneath the sleeves of a black tuxedo jacket that I suspected he'd ordered small on purpose. Beside him stood Parker, then the other members of Team 5, all of them smiling. And I was smiling too, grateful they could all be here with me today.

"Enjoy the moment," Segundo whispered. "But then you've gotta get back to the fight."

I was going to ask what he meant when the organ started and Daniela appeared at the end of the aisle. Her white dress gleamed as her father walked her through the shafts of sunlight pouring through the chapel windows. She was perfect, everything I could have wanted in a partner. I had never felt happier.

And then her father was walking her up the steps to the altar, kissing her cheek, clasping my hand in both of his, and retiring to the pews with the rest of our family and friends. I turned to face my bride, taking her hands in mine. I smiled into her strong, trusting eyes. But as the pastor began the ceremony, her brow crushed down and her gaze turned hard.

"Don't do this to me, Jason," she said.

I peeked around. "Do what?"

"Don't shut me out."

My heart staggered. There was something familiar about her words—some truth in them, even—but I couldn't understand why she would be saying these things now, at our wedding. The pastor continued the ceremony, speaking calmly, smiling beatifically, as though we weren't having what sounded like the start of an argument two feet in front of him.

"Whatever this is," I whispered, "can we discuss it after we're married?"

The chapel dimmed, casting Daniela's face in shadows. "Something's happened to you—something awful—and you're not telling me."

Before I could answer, the chapel's rooftop disappeared in a roar of tearing wood and smashing glass. I looked up, expecting to see a tornado-black sky. Instead, I beheld an enormous white dragon, its malevolent face leering down at me. Daniela screamed, but not because of the dragon.

When I looked down, my hands were covered in blue hair, and my black nails were punching through her skin. Blood soaked into the sleeves of her white gown as she struggled to pull away.

Staring at my face in horror, she screamed again.

Dreaming, I realized, my heart pounding sickly in my chest. *I'm dreaming.*

Fragments of who I was, the creature I had become, coalesced in my waking mind. Sensations returned to my body. I was in a fetal position on my right side, but not on a rough asphalt street. The ground beneath me was smooth, warm. Pleasant waves rippled through me, making it hard to open my eyes. The once-explosive pain in my left hip barely throbbed now.

"Are you going to kill him or what?" came a tired woman's voice.

"*Banish* him," a man's voice corrected her. "And that's proving easier said than done," he muttered above the rapid flipping of pages, as though he were searching for something in a book.

"Ugh," the woman said. "It's making me ill just looking at him."

"Then don't look at him," the man shot back. "No one's forcing you."

"It's not like there's anything else to do in this infernal dungeon," she muttered.

"Dungeon? Really? I don't know too many dungeons that serve braised pork chops with raspberry sauce to their inmates. Especially when said inmates are feline."

"I'm only feline because *you* made me that way."

"Yeah, that's called mercy. Would you rather I'd decapitated you?"

The woman muttered a few curses before returning to her original point. "I'd rather you decapitated *him*. He is without a doubt the ugliest thing I have ever seen. And that's coming from a succubus who's spent time in Hell."

My lashes became unstuck, and I willed my eyelids open.

The face of a fat orange cat with green eyes stared back at me. "Lovely," she said. "The mutt's awake."

A cat commenting on my appearance, strange as that was, was the least of my concerns right now. Where in the hell was I?

I pushed myself up until I was sitting and peered blearily around. A large wall of books rose to my left. To my right, a table cluttered with nonsensical odds and ends ran alongside a railing. When I peered down, I saw I was still in my trench coat and camo pants, sitting on a large, glowing symbol that had been painted onto the concrete floor. A few feet away, the cat's bored face warped slightly. I reached a hand toward her but was blocked by an invisible field.

The cat cleared her throat. "Everson, darling?"

"Huh?" the man answered from behind me.

"I said he's awake."

I turned to find the sorcerer I'd battled in Chinatown standing with an open book at his chest. He looked to be thirty-something with mussed, dark hair and an intelligent face. He'd shed his coat from earlier, revealing a wrinkled white shirt rolled past his elbows and a thick blue tie that hung loosely from his collar. He stopped reading and blinked down at me from above a pair of reading glasses.

Everson. Where had I heard that name before?

And then it clicked with what Mauli had told me.

"You're that wizard who works for the mayor," I said.

He removed his glasses and gave me a quizzical look before setting them and the book down on the desk behind him. "Guilty, though past tense," he said. "The working for the mayor part, anyway."

When he turned back to face me, he was holding a cane. The bold smells of wood and metal told me it was the same staff he'd used against me earlier, and that the blade was hidden inside. But he didn't wield either as a weapon now. And with my wolf back under control, I wanted to keep it that way.

"I'm Jason Wolfe," I said carefully. "A captain in the U.S. military."

Everson's head tilted back as I rose to my full height. I staggered once, but caught myself against the hardened air. Like so much in the last few days, I didn't understand the field containing me. It appeared to align with the edge of the circle, rising around me in a solid column. I pressed both arms against the field until my giant muscles trembled, but it wouldn't yield. I was trapped. The thought sped my breathing, but I willed it back under control.

If I lost my cool, the cat would get her wish. This guy was powerful.

"Everson Croft," he said in introduction, then added in a mutter, "though everyone seems determined to call me 'Prof Croft.' I guess it rhymes nicely." He nodded past me. "The forty pounds of attitude over there is Tabitha."

The large cat slitted her eyes at him.

"I think there's been a mistake," I said. "When we were fighting back there, I heard you say something about me being a demon?"

"Well, that's what my alarm indicated," Croft replied, peering over at a hologram beside his desk. The pale glowing image represented Chinatown, but when the wizard waved his hand through it, the image zoomed out to show the entire city. "You didn't respond to the usual banishment spells, though. And despite appearances, you're not a lycanthrope exactly—even though the damage the silver inflicted on your hip suggested otherwise."

I massaged the spot where the round had entered. It was healed now ... but silver?

"I thought the silver's charge might be interfering with my magic so I removed the bullet," he said. "Didn't make any difference, though."

"Why are you telling him all of this?" Tabitha asked with a sigh. "Just finish him."

"Because I think better out loud," Croft replied testily. He began pacing his end of what looked like a loft-level space. Beyond the railing, I could see a large living room with a flagstone fireplace below. The field was blunting my sense of smell, but these two appeared to be the only ones in the apartment. Fortunately, Croft's bent brow suggested I was a problem he was determined to solve rather than *finish*, as his cat had put it. At least for now.

Regardless, I had to get the hell out of here, had to pick up the White Dragon's scent again.

"Look, I don't know much about magic," I said, "but the reason you might be having trouble figuring me out is because I was cursed. In Waristan. An old woman carved this into my cheek, and I took on the abilities of an entity called the Blue Wolf. I'd tell you the whole story if there was time, but there isn't. I'm in pursuit of a being called the White Dragon. He was meeting with Bashi in Chinatown tonight, trying to close a huge opium deal. The consequences of that deal could be catastrophic if I don't stop him."

Plus, I'll be stuck like this, I thought, the nightmare about Daniela coming back to me.

"How fanciful," Tabitha scoffed.

"I'm not lying," I growled, rounding on her.

Safely beyond the field she met my bared canines with a smirk. "Touchy, touchy."

I pressed a fist to the glass and closed my eyes. So much at stake, and I was letting a talking cat get under my skin.

"He might actually be telling the truth," Croft said.

I turned to find him halfway up a rolling ladder, his fingers running along a row of bindings on an upper-level bookshelf until he found the volume he was looking for and carried it down. The pages flew past his face as he flipped through them.

"Waristan, you said?"

"Yeah. The Wari Corridor in Wakhjir Province."

"Aha!" He stopped at a page and pushed his reading glasses back on. "The Wakhi people."

I nodded fervently. "That's right."

I watched Croft's hazel eyes pulse back and forth as they moved down the page, his lips frowning. "What you're saying is consistent with the creation myth of that region. The Great Maker split into Twelve Guardians, each designated to defend a different aspect of the 'World,' as they called it. Of course to them, the World was their corner of present-day Central Asia. But still, those beliefs appear to have held enough power to manifest the twelve Guardians into a planar existence. At some point, the Guardians' qualities comingled with the physiology of those who worshipped them, producing hybrids and shifters. Fascinating..."

With that word—"fascinating"—I realized how much this Prof Croft reminded me of Parker. The memory of my friend's frozen body reinforced my need to get out of here, to find and kill the White Dragon.

"Which brings us to your case." Croft leaned toward me, his gaze moving between the open book and the scar on my right cheek. "Yeah, that's the mark of the Great Wolf all right. And that also explains why the alarm went off. The ward picked up the presence of a strong extra-planar energy—which ninety-nine out of a hundred times is going to be a demon. But it would have taken someone super powerful to marry the qualities of the Great Wolf to you."

"A two-hundred-year-old sorceress, according to the great-granddaughter."

"That would do it."

"And here's the thing," I said urgently. "If I don't stop the White Dragon, he'll wipe the remnants of the Great Wolf from existence, creating some sort of imbalance—one that could undo creation."

"In that particular plane, maybe," Croft said. "Again, we're talking about a very provincial belief system. I doubt it would have repercussions beyond that part of Central Asia, or even beyond the plane in question. Once created, these entities—the Guardians in this case—will do anything to preserve themselves. And that has apparently meant conscripting you into their war."

"Regardless," I interrupted, "you know I'm not a werewolf or a demon. I'm a danger to no one besides the White Dragon—a mass murderer—and anyone who protects him." I'd managed to control my wolf nature thus far, but now my words emerged in menacing growls. "You're holding a U.S. soldier in wartime, something the military frowns on. You need to release me."

"I've put in a call to my Order," Croft said, "a wise and powerful group of magic-users. I'm just waiting to hear back."

"I don't give a damn about your *Order*." I could feel my eyes blazing as my breaths hissed through my bared teeth. Every minute I stayed here was another minute the White Dragon had to finalize the opium sale and purchase his army. Regardless of the implications to creation, the entire valley, including my men, were in peril. "Release me. *Now.*"

Croft cocked an eyebrow. "Even if the Order can dispel the curse?"

23

"Dispel the curse?" I echoed.

"You know, make it go away," Croft said.

My clawed hand fell from the field. "The Order can do that?"

"Magic bound the qualities of the Great Wolf to you, which means magic can also unbind it. It would have to be powerful, though." The rims of Croft's irises seemed to glow as he looked me over. "You see, the binding force is like thousands of threads stitching you to the entity in question."

I nodded, remembering the threads of light the Kabadi sorceresses could manifest.

"But the threads are stubborn, not to mention regenerative," he said. "When I still thought I was dealing with demonic possession, I could only break through a few at a time, and when I did, more sprouted in their place while the rest bound you more tightly. I didn't want to push it."

I considered what the wizard was saying. If this Order of his could dispel the curse, then I would be restored to my old self. I wouldn't have to worry about the old woman's health anymore, or whether I could control my wolf nature. No more violent rampages. I would be Jason Wolfe again, not a bloodthirsty animal. But would I be able to defeat the White Dragon as a human?

"How long are we talking for the Order to get back to you?" I asked.

"There's honestly no telling."

"Then, no, I can't wait. I have people depending on me."

"Well ... we still have to wait for the Order. You're probably everything you say you are"—Tabitha, who I thought had fallen asleep, made a scoffing sound—"but you're also walking around with an extra-planar entity. One that seems to have anger-management issues."

"When he's *attacked*," I said through gritted teeth. "Can you at least let me out of this thing while we wait?"

Croft showed his hands. "With all due respect, I don't think that's a good idea."

"Why not?" I growled.

"You couldn't see yourself a couple of hours ago, but I could. Believe me, it wasn't pretty."

"So you're, what? Quarantining me?"

"Listen, it's for your safety as much as mine. If that silver bullet hadn't been in your hip, I'm not sure I could have gotten you here. I might have had to, you know..." He drew his cane across his neck.

"The *bullet* was what was making me crazy," I said, remembering the mind-warping pain I'd been in. "I'm under control now." But even as I said that, my nostrils flared. My breathing was speeding up again, dammit. My heart pounded like a jackhammer. I couldn't stay in here, couldn't...

I pursed my lips to slow my breaths. I had to keep the wolf down. Had to keep him from coming out.

"What's he doing?" Tabitha asked Croft. "Lamaze?"

I ignored her and focused, but it was like trying to dam a raging river. I began hitting the field with the sides of my fist. Moderately at first—to give my body something to do, I told myself. But before long, the blows were landing like sledgehammers, making the entire office shudder. Books rattled on shelves and slid from the table. A clay pestle broke against the floor.

"Good God." Tabitha said as she stood and backed away.

But no one was more horrified than me.

My jaws began snapping at the field, trying to find something I could latch onto and tear open. My claws followed suit, slashing the energetic barrier in a wilder and wilder frenzy. Beastly barks and snarls exploded from my muzzle, along with copious amounts of slobber. An image of tearing the wizard and his cat to shreds gashed through my mind. I tried to banish the thought, but instead I began throwing myself against the field, determined to get to them.

Croft had seized something from a storage container under the table—a glass tube of liquid. He threw it at my feet. As the glass shattered, he bellowed, *"Inspirare!"*

As though a vacuum had been turned on, the pink vapor rising from the smashed tube was suddenly sucked inside the field, filling my space with the cloying smell of flowers. I jammed my claws against the bottom of the field, searching for the opening, but I couldn't find one. I resumed my attack on the field, but the vapor was filling my head, fogging my thoughts.

"If you can hear me, Jason, that's a sleeping potion," Croft said. "Probably not strong enough to knock you out, but it should act as a depressant, calm you down. Just let it work on you."

My blows weakened as I sagged to my haunches. Before long, my claws were merely grazing the field in lazy strokes. I watched it all through drooping lids as if from a foggy distance.

"In any case, I hope you see my point now," Croft said.

I nodded in drunken concession. If there hadn't been a barrier between us, I would have tried to kill him. And if I couldn't control myself, how in the hell was I going to hunt down the White Dragon in a city of several million?

As Croft studied me, he managed to look both thoughtful and sympathetic. God, he really was like a white version of Parker. I drew my lethal hands from the field and examined them a moment before clasping them in my lap.

This was bad. This was *really* bad.

The brassy ring of a telephone sounded from downstairs. Croft excused himself and climbed down a ladder. Tabitha remained behind, arranging her bulk on the table again. She licked a paw and combed it over an ear.

"Everson means well, but he has a habit of bringing home lost causes. *I* was once a femme fatale, a real man killer. In the very literal sense. A soldier like you would have been meat in my hands. Now look at me, bathing in my own saliva." She made a face but resumed grooming herself. "Best case, you'll end up a poor prisoner like me."

I could hear Croft's voice downstairs, but with the distortions caused by the field, I couldn't make out what he was saying.

He returned upstairs several minutes later. "That was the Order."

I staggered to my feet. "And?"

"And," he said, walking over to the metal table, "they advised me to give you a concoction with wolfsbane. Supposed to dampen the mood swings. Then I can let you out."

I nodded in relief. "Make it fast, please."

He pulled some items from beneath the table, including a portable range and cast-iron pot, and set them on the tabletop. As the pink vapor dissipated from my confinement, I wiped my muzzle with my coat sleeve and tried to shake the fog from my head. On the other side of Croft's body, liquid gurgled into the pot. He threw, pinched, and tipped in other ingredients and began stirring with a wooden spoon while chanting a series of foreign-sounding words.

A couple of minutes later, steam began rising past his body. He stopped chanting and snapped off the range. When he turned toward me, he was holding the small pot with an oven mitt.

"How are you going to get it in here?" I asked.

"It's a one-way barrier," he explained. "Just drink half."

He extended his arm, careful, I noticed, to keep his mittened hand away from the field. Sure enough, the pot passed right through. I took the pot in my hands and held it to my muzzle.

"Smells terrible," I said.

Croft gave an apologetic shrug. I looked at him another moment. Maybe it was his similarity to Parker, but I decided I could trust him. Not like I had much choice. I tilted the pot back and drank down half of the hot, sludgy mixture. It tasted like clay. But as the concoction settled in my stomach, I felt the animal part of my mind unclenching. Croft could apparently see something happening because he nodded.

"It's working." He stepped back and whispered, *"Disfare."*

The field dispersed with a sudden outrush of air that fluttered the pages of the open books lying around and made my ears pop. Tabitha watched warily as I stepped from the circle.

"In most cases that's good for about forty-eight hours," Croft said, taking the pot back and funneling the rest of the brown concoction into a plastic water bottle.

"That should be all the time I need. I made a deal with the Great Wolf. Destroy the White Dragon and I go back to the way I was."

"Good, because that was something else I discussed with the Order. The only one who can restore you is the sorceress who originally bound you—in accord with the entity to whom you're bound, of course. The senior magic-users of my Order *could* restore you, but it would have to be an incremental process so as not to harm your psyche. We'd be talking ten years."

Great, another fallback plan, I thought morbidly.

I checked my coat and pants pockets but they had all been emptied.

"Oh, here," Croft said, lifting a large paper bag from beside his desk and handing it to me. Inside was my pistol as well as magazines for it and my M4, which I'd lost back at Bashi's. "I took this off you too." He reached into a tan corduroy jacket slung over his chair, produced my wallet, and held it out to me.

"You lifted my wallet?" I said half jokingly as I took it from him.

"I found your military ID inside, which made me realize you'd been possessed or transfigured rather than popped into existence wholesale. That's why I brought you back here."

"Where is here, anyway?" I asked, sticking the wallet, weaponry, and other items into my pockets. He had even bagged my scarf and bandage mask.

Croft turned toward his hologram. "We're in the West Village. In fact, in this building right here." He pointed to a block, and the hologram zoomed in on an apartment building that looked like a four-tiered wedding cake. "Top floor." He waved his hand through the image, and it zoomed out again, but with the apartment building now glowing purple. If I hadn't been so pressed for time, I would have studied the 3D representation more closely. The detail was amazing.

"And Chinatown's here?" I asked.

"That's right. You planning on going back to Bashi's?"

"You talk like you know him."

"I, ah, met him once," he said, massaging his right pinky finger. "That was enough."

"Well, I need to pick up a weapon I ditched there. Then I'm going to look around, see if anyone knows where they went. If I can get into the White Dragon's general proximity, I can pick up his scent again." I didn't want to think about how long those odds were. Instead, I pulled the wooden cube from the bag and held it up by its leather thong. "Any idea what this is?"

Croft took it and turned it over in his fingers, examining the inscriptions. "These are symbols of protection," he said at last, "but I'm not feeling any magic in them. Where did you get it?"

"From the same sorceress who turned me into this."

"Interesting relationship you two have," he said, handing the cube back.

"You're telling me," I muttered as I pocketed it.

"Take this too." Croft tossed me the plastic water bottle with the wolfsbane concoction. I caught the bottle and slipped it into a pocket inside my coat. "In case the last dose starts to wear off."

"Thanks for your help."

"Oh, I'm coming too," he said, slipping into his corduroy jacket.

I stopped at the top of the ladder and turned. "Why?"

"I was really hoping you'd say, 'The more the merrier.' But since you ask, the Order wants me to keep tabs on you while they look into the consequences of the Great Wolf's line being wiped out."

"But why keep tabs on me?"

"The wolfsbane is only a temporary fix."

"I thought you said it was good for forty-eight hours."

When Croft dragged a hand through his hair, I narrowed my eyes at him in suspicion. "Under the best-case scenario, yes," he said with a sigh. "But we may not be looking at best case right now."

"The hell is that supposed to mean?"

"These episodes of control loss ... They're getting worse, aren't they?"

"Yeah," I admitted. "They have been."

"Look, bonding spells are really hard to pull off—even for a practiced magic-user. I'm probably a good fifty, sixty years from even attempting something like that. I mean, you're marrying what is essentially the power of a divine entity to a person. That requires tremendous constitution on the part of the person but also tremendous precision on the part of the practitioner. It's like trying to balance a refrigerator on a single nail hammered into the floor."

"Are you saying the sorceress screwed up?"

I thought of Nafid's great-grandmother scuffing blindly around her cluttered shrine, worshipping a rotting wolf's head. Maybe the White Dragon had been right about her.

"I'm saying that if she was off by even this much"—Croft held his first finger and thumb a few millimeters apart—"then the fridge slips a little, a little more, until finally..." He clapped his hands together.

"The wolf nature overtakes me," I said coldly.

"Without a human constitution to mediate the powerful impulses, you'll descend into savagery. Which is why I need to stay with you."

"To chaperone me, in other words."

"Pretty much. But I'll just be observing."

"Yeah, I've heard that before," I muttered, thinking about the mess Baine had caused.

"Unless I see innocents endangered," he amended. "Otherwise, you're free to pursue your objective, I won't stop you. Of course, I can't help you either. That's coming from the Order."

"Fair enough. How long are we talking until I can't control this anymore?"

"The wolfsbane should slow the process, but judging by the episode a little bit ago? Not long."

"We're wasting time then." I put on my mask and scarf. "Let's go."

24

"Next block, next block!" Croft shouted at the cabbie from the backseat.

The driver, who barely understood English, smiled, bobbled his head, and continued edging past the police barricade as he turned onto the stretch of Mulberry Street that ran between the park and the front of Bashi's converted tenement building. Ahead, police cruisers were clustered in the road, red and blue lights flashing. On the sidewalk beyond, investigators moved among the covered victims: the gangbangers I'd gunned down.

"Great," Croft said, sliding down in his seat. "He's going to drive us right past the crime scene."

I lifted my mask above my muzzle. "Stop!"

I hadn't spoken to the driver to that point, and my monstrous voice startled him. He braked hard, his eyes moon white in the rearview mirror.

"Now turn around," I said, showing him with a black talon.

The cabbie nodded rapidly and performed a jagged

three-point turn. He took off back the way we'd come. Back outside the barricade, I guided him to the street that ran along the south side of the block.

There wasn't a police presence in the rear, but that didn't mean they weren't inside. The victims were all piled in front of the ripped-away steel door after all. It wouldn't have taken much detective work to find the bullet casings in the garage and more dead bodies beyond. The kitchen staff I'd been counting on for info was probably being questioned.

Croft was apparently thinking the same. "Sure you want to do this?"

"I want to at least see if my M4 is still there."

"If you're worried about being ID'd from your weapon, I have a friend on the force I could talk to..."

"Thought you weren't supposed to help me."

"Well, I wouldn't so much be helping as tip-toeing around some complications."

"I'm actually more concerned about a lack of firepower. Right here," I told the driver. He pulled over sharply, anxious now to be rid of us. The last thing we needed, though, was to get stranded in Chinatown with the NYPD nosing around and the White Hand on high alert.

"Maybe you should stay in the cab so he doesn't drive off," I said.

"I'll have him idle around that corner," Croft said, reaching over and plucking a hair from my ear.

"The hell was that for?"

"To keep tabs on you."

I glared at him, then grumbled and got out. As the cab droned away, I approached the damaged gate and peered into the alley. I could see the blood that had poured from my hip as well as the kobolds' blood farther down, but their bodies were gone. Someone had removed them.

I raised my nose and sniffed. I wasn't sure if it was the concoction I'd drunk or some lingering effect of the silver, but my senses didn't seem as sharp now. Even so, I caught wafts of human scent.

Edging through the gate, I hurried up the alleyway, careful to stay in the shadows, alert to every sound. When I arrived at the place where I'd lost my M4, I swore. Not there. Someone—or more likely a team—had picked up the bullet casings too. I wondered now if the idea was to limit the police activity to the dead White Hand enforcers out front. Cleaning up the evidence would keep the police out of Bashi's place until he could work his paid contacts in the department to wipe his name from the investigation.

I eyed the garage door I'd emerged from earlier that evening. Closed now.

Someone's probably inside who can tell me where Bashi took the White Dragon.

"Yeah," I muttered, "someone armed with silver bullets."

The Blue Wolf had a weakness, and there it was—silver. That it had come from a kobold's gun suggested the White Dragon had been expecting me. Had Centurion tipped him off?

I could be walking into a trap. But if I left now, I'd have nothing.

I pressed an ear to the garage door. Hearing no one inside, I dug my claws underneath the door and lifted with my legs. The metal bent and folded. When there was enough space, I sniffed to ensure the garage was clear, then drew my pistol and ducked inside. A black Hummer sat in the space abandoned by the SUV, its engine still warm.

Someone *was* here.

Leading with my pistol, I wound my way up the spiral staircase. At the wall I'd kicked through, I stopped and peered into the dining room. The table had been cleared, and I could hear water running in the kitchen. I stepped through the wall and pressed my back beside the doorway leading onto the corridor I had come down earlier. A quick look showed that it was empty.

I darted past the corridor and stopped to listen outside the swinging doors to the kitchen. The water shut off suddenly. The clinking of dishware followed. Sounded as if the kitchen staff was back to work.

I parted one of the swinging doors slightly. A woman with black hair and a formal white shirt stood to my ten o'clock, most of her back to me. She was loading dishware and pots from a deep sink into a dishwasher. Alone.

I eased through the door, hunkered behind a large prep island, and came up quietly behind her. In a single motion, I pinned her arms to her sides and cupped her mouth with my other hand, muffling her startled scream.

"I'm not going to hurt you," I said.

She writhed and kicked my shins.

I gave her a firm shake and clamped her harder. I hated doing this, but there was no other way. "Listen," I growled. "I need to know where Bashi went. Tell me, and you'll live. I've already killed twenty people tonight. I'll have no problem adding you to the tally."

The last part was a lie, but I'd sold it. Eyes wide, the woman nodded and murmured beneath my hand.

"In a whisper, understood? Anything you tell me is

going to be in a whisper."

I waited for the woman to nod again before relaxing my hand from her mouth. "I don't know," she gasped. "I swear."

"Where *might* he have gone?"

She shook her head. "I don't know."

"How long have you been working for Bashi?"

"T-two years."

"Doing what?"

"Working in kitchen. Cooking, cleaning."

"Okay. So you work at this address. Where else?"

I didn't know how many properties Bashi operated out of, but if she even worked at one other one, that would be a start.

"Just here," she whispered.

I shook her again. *"Where else?"*

"Just here, just here. I swear."

She was too scared not to be telling the truth. And it made sense. If Bashi was as paranoid as he sounded, he would keep his support staff compartmentalized. Damn. I'd hoped to avoid any more armed men tonight, especially since silver had entered the equation, but I wasn't going to have a choice.

I cocked my head toward a doorway opposite the swinging doors. "What's back there?"

"Walk-in pantry and freezer."

I patted her down, relieving her of a smartphone in her back pocket. "I want you to go into the pantry, close the door, and remain there for twenty minutes. Do you understand?"

She nodded quickly and was turning to go when a bullet splintered one of the swinging doors and cracked past my head. I shoved the woman down behind the prep island and hunkered beside her with my pistol. More shots cracked past us. My nose picked up the bite of silver.

"Stay down," I told the woman.

I fired around the island, then peered out. The space between the batting doors showed the dining room filling with armed men. I looked down at the cowering woman. Had she been placed in here as bait? My gaze cut to her phone on the counter. Damn, it was on—and probably connected to wherever the men had been lying in wait, listening to our exchange.

But that didn't matter. What mattered was that I was trapped. And even if I had it in me to use the woman as a human shield, I could tell by the intensity of gunfire that she was expendable. Whoever, or whatever, was shooting at us wouldn't hesitate to take her out if it meant getting me in the bargain.

During a lull, I popped up and fired twice, dropping one of the shooters.

As I came back down, a grenade clattered along the tile floor, coming to a rest off to our right. I shoved the woman around the island and crouched over her. Shrapnel tore across my low back and exposed shoulder as the explosion shook the kitchen and blew a wave of dust around us.

In the ringing aftermath, I grabbed the woman's arm and pointed to the back door. "Is there an exit back there?" I shouted.

She blinked at the dust caking her lashes and shook her head.

"Okay, crawl into the freezer, but leave the door open a crack!"

The metal hull would protect her from the projectiles, but little good that would do if she suffocated inside. She coughed and crawled over the blood-spattered tiles as the shooting resumed.

Shards of metal dropped from my healing wounds. No silver in the shrapnel, anyway. But it was still in the bullets winging past. If even one of them nailed me, I'd be in the hurt locker big time.

To my left stood a huge stainless steel fridge. Keeping the island between me and the doorway, I crawled over to it, seized its sides, and ripped it from the wall. The condenser tubing in back crashed as I heaved the fridge around and shoved it in front of the swinging doors—one of them barely hanging on now.

The large refrigerator covered the opening save for a one-foot-high gap on top. Rounds thudded into the stainless steel, but the fridge was built like a tank. Nothing was getting through.

I turned and made for the back door. If there wasn't a rear exit, I would have to improvise. Beyond the door, a short corridor ended at a wall with a fuse box. To my left, cold air fogged from the freezer's cracked-open door.

I was contemplating the fuse box when I heard a familiar clatter behind me. And then another, and another. My assailants were shot-putting grenades over the top of the fridge, loading the kitchen. The woman started when I swung the freezer door opened and joined her inside.

"Plug your ears!" I said, closing the door again.

She got her fingers into her ears just as the grenades began to detonate. Concussions rocked our bunker. The explosions went on for several seconds, shrapnel tearing through the kitchen's back door.

When the detonations stopped, I signaled for the woman to stay put as I opened the door wider to listen. I didn't know if any of my assailants had military training, or if they were just hired guns, but after an assault like that, the room would typically be breached. Sure enough, I could hear the refrigerator scraping over the tile floor, making room for the men to file through. Another man would be acting as a spotter through the top of the gap.

"Behind the island," I heard someone mouth. "Blood trail."

As footsteps entered the kitchen, I opened the fuse box and hit the main switch. The lights went out. From the kitchen, whispers sounded, and the footsteps became retreating shuffles.

Only one of the men put two and two together, but by the time he opened fire into the back corridor, I was on the island, my talons ripping through his neck. I landed on one of the retreating men's backs, my four-hundred pounds smashing him head-first into the tiles. A third man swung his rifle toward the sound. I seized the barrel, wrenched the gun from his grip, and drove the stock end into his gut. He wheezed and went down hard.

Righting his weapon, I aimed past the fridge into the dining room, cutting down two men scrambling for cover. The rear one glanced back, his final image a blue-haired creature illuminated by gunfire. The wolf in me relished that. A third man escaped down the corridor toward the front of the building.

I took off after him. Needing info, I couldn't let him get away.

Halfway down the corridor he heard me and spun to shoot. But I was already on top of him. I smashed the weapon from his hands, then seized his wrists and drove him to the floor. My right knee mashed into his gut. Unable to breathe, he thrashed his head back and forth. Though he was dressed in street clothes, his rifle and body armor were military grade, and his blond hair had been brush cut.

"Who do you work for?" I growled. "Centurion?"

If they'd been in the pay of the White Dragon once, then it stood to reason they were under contract again—this time to eliminate me. But then why wouldn't they have done so on the plane? Was their game to keep me from Orzu long enough to flip me to their side. I eased off the man's gut to allow him to answer.

"Fuck Centurion," he grunted.

"Where did Bashi take Orzu?"

"I don't know what the hell you're talking about."

I flashed a black talon in front of his face. "Would losing an eye spark your memory?"

But before the man could answer, footsteps echoed from downstairs in a room-clearing sequence. Two sets began climbing the stairs, flashlight beams lancing ahead of them.

"No one move," a woman's voice hollered. "NYPD!"

Crap. I didn't need to tangle with the police. I flipped the man over and dug out the wallet in his back pocket. "Hey!" he cried.

I punched him in the back of the head hard enough to silence him for a while, then bounded back toward the dining room. There, I grabbed one of the downed men's rifles—an M4—and hit the opening in the wall just as the corridor began to glow with the beams of the arriving officers.

I took the spiral staircase three and four steps at a time until I was back in the garage. Ducking under the door I had bent up earlier, I was met by the sounds of tires smashing through puddles. Red and blue lights flashed down the alleyway.

"Up here!" someone called.

I craned my neck to see Prof Croft standing on the rooftop of the adjoining building. I slung the rifle across my back and, grabbing window ledges, propelled myself up the five stories until I was over the ledge. I landed beside the wizard, whose staff was crackling with energy.

"Police heard the gunfire and explosions," he said, taking off across the rooftop. "Whole block's going to be sealed off any second."

Sure enough, all around, police sirens were wailing.

"Thought you had a friend in the department," I said.

"I do, but ... well, I sort of have a thing for her. And this could look bad."

I rolled my eyes. "Where's our ride?"

"Three blocks east."

At the end of the block, we stopped and peered down. Cruisers were staked out at the intersections. I eyed the building across the street from us. It was about the same height as the one we were standing on.

"I can use a force invocation to get us across," Croft said, "but its imprecise, and the landing could be a little rough."

"Stay there." I backed up and then sprinted toward the ledge.

"Oh, c'mon," Croft said, holding his arms out. "You're not planning on—ungh!"

I seized him around the waist as I leapt. We arced over the street and thudded onto the next block of rooftops with room to spare. I ran several feet to exhaust our momentum before setting Croft back down.

"A little warning would've been nice," he said, straightening his coat.

"Wasn't time."

I took the lead, charging around rooftop gardens and clothes lines. Croft followed. The end of the block was clear. Declining my invitation to climb onto my back, Croft stepped off the ledge to drop the five stories. A few feet before impact, he shouted a word. A force blew from the end of his cane, softening his landing. I came down on hands and feet beside him, and we ran the next block to where the yellow cab was parked.

"Thanks, Kumar," Croft said as we piled into the back seat.

The Bangladeshi driver was too busy cranking the ignition key and swearing at the dead car to respond.

"Oh." Croft uttered another one of his words, and the engine roared to life. "Only way I could get him to stay put until we got back," he whispered to me. "Where are we going anyway?"

I pulled the wallet I'd confiscated from the shooter and opened it with a rip of Velcro. I turned it so the ID behind the plastic sleeve was right-side up and stared at it for several seconds.

"Shit," I muttered.

"What's up?" Croft asked.

"Those guys were U.S. military."

"The shooters?"

I nodded, my thoughts going a mile a second. The driver watched me in the rearview mirror, awaiting what he no doubt hoped would be the final drop-off location.

"My apartment," I said to him at last. "I'll tell you how to get there."

I needed the sat phone.

25

"So what's the plan?" Croft asked as our cab weaved through Chinatown.

In my peripheral vision, I could see the wizard watching me as I stared down at the wallet. I had no leads on the White Dragon, but I was looking at the ID of a man who had just tried to kill me—which could prove a lead in itself. If U.S. military personnel were involved, I needed to determine to what extent. That meant finding out whether this guy, John Paul, was still active duty and in what capacity. The next step would be hacking into whatever he was using for communication. If he was involved in keeping Orzu safe, he might drop his whereabouts.

I'd put Hotwire on it, one of the most capable commo sergeants in the military—and a soldier who, I'd recently learned, wasn't afraid to bend the rules.

"I need to make some calls," I replied to Croft. "It's right up there," I told the cabbie.

As we pulled in front of the apothecary shop, Croft said, "I know this place—Mr. Han carries some of the best dried arachnid in the five boroughs. Great for stealth potions. You're staying here?"

"Next door, actually." I fished the keys from my coat pocket. "I'm not sure how long I'll be. You're welcome to come up."

I still wasn't keen on being chaperoned, but Croft was staying out of my way as promised, and had even helped me out at Bashi's. Plus, there was his similarity to my former civil affairs officer. As with Parker, I felt strangely responsible for him—powerful wizard or not.

"Thanks, but I'm going to duck into Mr. Han's for a few items," he said.

I checked my watch then peered out at the dark shop window. "Is he even open?"

"He keeps odd hours. Plus I'm sort of a preferred client."

I grunted and opened the car door. The cabbie appealed to us with forlorn eyes and broken English that he be allowed to go home, but I noticed that the cabs had become scarcer after dark, and I needed transport. I made eye contact with Croft as he got out of the cab's other side. Catching the message, he spoke another of his words and the engine died.

"Wait here," I told Kumar, who was already swearing and banging the steering wheel. "We'll be back in a bit."

On the sidewalk, Croft grabbed my arm. "Hey, how are you feeling?"

I paused. In the heat of battle, there hadn't been time for a self-check, but I hadn't lost my cool once. "In control," I replied. "That wolfsbane drink you gave me is working."

"Good," he said, even as concern lines deepened around his dark gaze. He was thinking about the deteriorating bonding spell. Though he hadn't said it, I knew that if I descended into full savagery he was under orders to kill me. "Just don't forget you have another dose if you need it."

I nodded, patting the breast of my coat where the liquid sloshed in its bottle.

As Croft tapped on the shop door with his cane, I unlocked the door beside it and made my way up the narrow stairwell. I would call Hotwire on the sat phone and give him the info on this John Paul. He could take it from there. I would also get an update on Team 5, learn whether they were still in the valley or back at base after Stanick had discovered I'd left.

I swore at myself for putting my team in that position and even more so for alienating Daniela. I remembered the emptiness in her voice before she'd hung up. With the wizard's concoction, I felt I could talk to her now. I would call her after speaking to Hotwire, I decided.

But as I inserted the key into the lock, my nostrils flared. Someone had been in here recently. Someone familiar, though I couldn't place the scent. My ears angled toward the click of a floorboard on the other side of the door.

The person was still inside the apartment.

I shoved the door open as I dropped to the floor, the M4 I'd ripped off the soldier in firing position. The intruder stood across the room, his tall figure outlined by the window that overlooked the alley. His back had been to the door, but now he turned toward me. Beneath his iron gray hair, the stern lines of his face waxed into view.

My finger froze over the trigger. "Colonel Stanick?"

"On your feet, Captain," he said sharply. He was dressed in full uniform. "And lower your weapon, for God's sake."

My gaze dropped to his hands. He was unarmed. I removed the strap from around my body as I rose and set the weapon on the bed. At this close range he couldn't do anything without me reaching him first.

Colonel Stanick's rigid gaze moved from my monstrous feet to my hands and then up to my face. The bandage mask and scarf were back in place, but he studied the contours of my jaw and brow with a tight expression that was hard to read. At last his eyes came to a rest on my fiery yellow irises.

"How did you find me?" I asked.

"We used Daniela's call to triangulate your position. She didn't know."

He didn't need to add that last part. Daniela would never have knowingly set me up, no matter how hurt or confused she'd been. But I was thinking more about the timeline. From when I had talked to Daniela until now had been about six hours. I relaxed slightly. That would have been more than enough time for Stanick to have been flown from D.C. to New York.

"Now do you want to tell me what the hell is going on?" he asked, snapping on the desk lamp. Dark yellow light flooded half the room.

"First, who told you about this?" I gestured to myself.

"Why do you think someone told me?"

"Because you wouldn't have recognized me otherwise. My body's different. My voice is different." Also, Colonel Stanick hadn't reacted in surprise, which was still setting off alarm bells in my head. Especially after finding a military ID on the gunman back at Bashi's.

"Parker contacted me."

"Parker?"

"Two days ago, before he died in action." He held up a stiff hand. "Don't be upset, Jason. He was concerned about you, as we all are. He told me what happened, about you contracting this ... condition. I sent the team back in to evac you, but you wouldn't go with them. Parker told me you were under the impression you had to destroy some sort of dragon. Is that true?"

"Where are they now? Team 5?"

"I asked you a question, Captain," Stanick snapped. "Is that true?"

He continued to stand ruler-straight on the far side of the bed. As I met my commander's gaze, I felt my shoulders straightening and my feet coming together. I wanted to tell him the truth—he still had that effect on me. But there was no way in hell he was going to accept my version: sorceresses and curses and a war between ancient Guardians.

I cleared my throat. "I honestly couldn't tell you, sir. Whatever happened to me seems to have affected my mind. My thoughts are in constant chaos. I've been seeing things that aren't there. The men were just following my orders."

Stanick watched me for several moments, his mouth a taut line, before nodding. "Was that what brought you to New York? This same delusion about needing to kill a dragon?"

"I ... yeah, I think so."

"I want you to listen to me, Jason," he said, coming around the bed. "I believe you when you say your team was just following orders. They're committed to you. But they also aided and abetted your desertion. They're presently in detainment awaiting general court-martial."

Blood rushed to my face. "You can't do that, sir."

"You know me, Jason. I give you room to freelance out in the field, but I expect you to obey the chain of command. Desertion is a grave violation of the UCMJ." I started to protest, but he held up his hand again. "In this case, though, there were extenuating circumstances. You've clearly contracted a serious illness. Why else would you be chasing dragons? We need a physician to evaluate you. That will support what you're saying and explain why you coerced your team into aiding you. They'll be exonerated, and you'll receive treatment. I'll see to both. And no matter how long that treatment takes, your position at the training battalion will be awaiting you."

"Evaluate me where?" I asked.

"Fort Bell. On Long Island Sound."

"Fort Bell? I thought it was decommissioned."

"Only partially."

Though the lines in his face remained stern, Stanick's eyes softened with concern. He'd always treated me like a son. But going with him would mean turning myself in to the military. That would spare my teammates and reassure Daniela that I was safe and receiving care—ineffective as that care would be. But it would also give the White Dragon carte blanche to wipe out the Kabadi. And then what? A descent into world darkness, as the Kabadi believed? Or only the end of some minor line of Guardians, as Croft seemed to think. Either way, I'd be breaking a promise I had made to Nafid and the Great Wolf.

"It's the only way, Jason," he pressed.

As I considered my options, I felt my pulse racing, my body heating up. *Not now, dammit.* I stooped forward and massaged my temples with the thumb and middle finger of my right hand.

"What's wrong?" Stanick asked.

Grunting, I paced in a circle. My chest heaved with coarse breaths. My senses were returning to a razor-sharp keenness, crowding out my rational mind. The wolfsbane potion was wearing off. *This soon?* I thought worriedly. Shoving back against my wolf instincts, I pulled the water bottle from my coat pocket, unscrewed the lid with trembling hands and chugged down the muddy concoction. Almost immediately my heart rate steadied. I tossed the bottle away and, hands propped against my thighs, took several calming breaths.

"You all right, Jason?" Stanick stepped closer.

I shot an arm out, seized the front of his shirt, and slammed him against the wall beside the bed. The lines of his face spiraled toward his gasping mouth as his hands grasped my wrist.

"You almost had me," I snarled.

"Wh-what are you talking about?"

"It was a good story—no one would have been able to question him—but Parker didn't tell you shit."

"Put me ... down!" he grunted.

"Everything you learned about me came from Orzu, the White Dragon. He must have forgotten to tell you about my sense of smell."

When I'd first entered Bashi's dining room earlier that evening, I had picked up three scents: Bashi's, the White Dragon's, and one that had been unfamiliar—clean, but with an undercurrent of musky sweat. With my senses dulled, I hadn't made the connection to the scent filling my room. But the sudden return of my wolf nature had established it. The two scents were one and the same.

"Put me down," he repeated. "That's an order!"

I jacked him higher, until his head was touching the ceiling. "So now that we know who you're working for, let's go back to the beginning. CENTCOM didn't order Team 5 to the Wari Corridor, did they? You did. And you embedded Baine from Centurion, instructed him to order an airstrike. You knew how outraged I'd be. You knew I'd demand punishment. So you used your position to have Baine incarcerated. All part of 'the plan,' you probably assured him. Until you had him killed to cover up your involvement."

"This is the ... delusion talking," he managed, his face reddening.

"Then why don't you tell me why you were having dinner tonight with Bashi and Orzu?" He struggled instead of answering. "I think I've got that part figured out too. I noticed you got yourself a seat on the poppy-eradication task force last year. Imagine you learned a lot: the big growers, the major opium networks. You eventually set your sights on Orzu—a grower in a remote province no one cared about. In exchange for a percentage, you would help him expand his holdings while putting the more visible growers out of business. Less competition would mean more money. A bigger slice of the pie for you."

"How dare you—"

I shook him silent and continued. "Orzu explained his interest in the Kabadi's valley. Probably asked you to clean them out. But an airstrike on that many civilians would demand an investigation, right? That's when you decided to send the Centurion patsy in with Team 5. Make it look like he was after a commission, then shut him up. Unopposed, Orzu could then take care of the valley. Neither of you knew *this* would happen, though."

I pulled my scarf and mask away and watched Colonel Stanick's eyes go stricken with horror.

"That's right. I was cursed. I then helped thwart the White Dragon's attack that night. Still, you didn't want your fingerprints on that valley, so you arranged to meet Orzu here. The plan was to secure Bashi as a major buyer, fund the White Dragon's army, and claim the valley whether I was down there or not. Only I was here. And I got to your meeting a lot faster than you thought I could."

The men I had confronted at Bashi's just now had probably been a military security detail for Colonel Stanick. They wouldn't have been given info outside those parameters, meaning John Paul was going to be a dead end. Fortunately, I had a new source of info.

"The only question," I said, giving my commander another shake, "is where the White Dragon is now."

Stanick had stopped trying to talk. Instead, he was struggling to pull something from the right pocket of his pants. I readied my talons, but when his hand emerged, he was holding a folded-up piece of paper. He shook it out and held it toward my face. I felt my grip on him falter. It was the image of Daniela I had printed off and packed.

"Is that supposed to be a threat?" I growled.

"It's an appeal to reason," he grunted. "Set me down so we can talk."

I snarled at him, then opened my hand suddenly. He landed beside the bed, knocking over the end table and lamp on the way down. I watched him pull himself to his feet, swipe a hand through his hair, and then straighten and re-tuck his shirt with sharp, indignant gestures. The photo of Daniela had fallen beside him. I picked it up and tucked it into a pocket.

"Consider what this will do to her," he said.

"What the hell's that supposed to mean?"

"We're a country at war, Jason. Young men and women are sacrificing their lives every day. How do you think the country is going to look at a soldier who deserted his team and then murdered fellow soldiers back home? How do you think they're going to look at his fiancée?"

"I didn't murder anyone," I said between my teeth.

"I've got four dead soldiers a few blocks away that say otherwise."

"So you're admitting to everything I've said just now."

"I'll play no part in your sickness," he replied. "But delusional or not, your actions will have consequences—for Team 5 as well as that lovely young lady. The penalties for aiding a deserter are stiff, especially when fratricide follows. And that shadow *will* follow Daniela."

Stanick might have turned out to be a conniving son of a bitch, but he was right. Best case, I would be ending the military careers of ten good men and condemning them to prison sentences, further dimming their prospects.

I could hear Segundo saying "We're still behind you, bro. Do what you've gotta do." But could I, knowing the cost? And Daniela. Even someone with her strength had a breaking point—and believing that her fiancée had gone on a murderous rampage might be it. That was to say nothing of the stigma she'd bear. I imagined the saintly light she carried being snuffed out and never coming back.

"I don't know that our treatment will help you," Stanick continued. "But *you* can help those you care most for." He smiled tightly. "That's what the Jason Wolfe I know would do."

"Treatment," I snorted. "Do you mean lethal injection?"

"Like I said, your radical change in behavior would be explained medically. And no one would ever have to know about the murders." He paced past me and stopped at the door. "Look, Jason. We lose soldiers to illness every year.

Yours would just be another tragic case, and I mean that in the sincerest sense of the word. You are, and will remain, the best captain I've ever worked with. No one regrets what happened more than I do."

"I bet," I snarled.

"And you're right to worry about her," he said, his gaze dropping to the pocket where I'd slid Daniela's photo. "I imagine an emotional blow like that could drive a woman to suicide."

I thought back to what Daniela had said about military police watching her house. My lips wrinkled from my teeth. "You lay one finger on her and—

Stanick turned his head toward the window. The glass shattered, and fire exploded through my right shoulder. I collapsed against the wall, vision blurring, lungs gasping for air. He'd had a sniper set up on an adjacent rooftop, one who had just nailed me with a silver round.

"Consider that a warning," Stanick said, opening the door. "Do anything but report to Fort Bell, and the next one will be a head shot. Your friends and fiancée will then be beyond your help." As blood poured between my fingers clamping the wound, he checked his watch. "You have two hours."

"Too chicken shit to take me with you?" I challenged.

Colonel Stanick's thin lips pinched together. "Though you gain nothing by killing me, I'd rather not take the chance. You're out of options, Jason. The imaginary dragon you're after has flown, and there's no way you're beating him back to Waristan. Fort Bell by midnight."

The door closed firmly behind him.

26

By the time Croft tapped on my door, I had picked myself up off the floor, leaned the mattress over the window to block the sniper's view, and stuffed everything I thought I would need into my backpack.

"Come in," I grunted.

"Hey, I just got off the phone with—" Everson stopped in the doorway and stared from the bloody mattress against the window, to the blood trails that went back and forth over the carpet, and at last to my blood-soaked shoulder. "What in the hell happened?" he stammered, rushing up to where I was kneeling.

Without awaiting an explanation, he dropped the neatly-folded paper bag he was carrying, and tented his fingers over the wound. He spoke a resonant word. The bullet wiggled in the ragged hole, sending sharp spikes of pain through the tissue, before ripping free. The relief was almost immediate—as was the healing. Croft examined the flattened bullet in his palm before tossing it into the trash and cleaning his hands with a kerchief.

"Who shot you?" he asked.

I shook my head and tapped an ear to say someone could be listening. Croft nodded and then drove his staff against the floor. With a shouted *"Disfare!"* an orb of white light flashed from his cane, flattening my hair and burning a bright afterimage into my irises. To my left, the lamp's bulb exploded, while across the room something crackled. By the time I blinked my sight clear, smoke was drifting from my laptop and the sat phone on the desk.

"Heh, sorry about that," Croft said. "But it should be safe to talk now."

"I had a visitor," I said thinly, then proceeded to describe the encounter.

Croft listened, a fist propping his chin, brow furrowed. By the time I'd finished, he had stepped to one side of the window, out of the firing lane, but his expression hadn't changed.

"The dragon has flown," he repeated to himself before seeming to return to the room. "If true, that could be really bad. I just got off the phone with one of the higher ups from my Order. Turns out that what you were told about the end of the Wolf clan affecting creation has some merit."

"In what way?"

"Well, under normal circumstances the effect would have been very local, as I'd suggested. Limited to the plane the Guardians inhabit. But there was a huge disruption through a multitude of planes recently. Chaos itself tried to burrow its way into our world, and—"

I circled a hand for him to get to the point.

"Well, without going into too much detail, there are still a lot of tears in and around our world. Members of my Order are repairing them as we speak, but we're still exposed to planes we wouldn't otherwise be exposed to. The Guardians' realm is positioned such that should their particular system of polarity collapse, it would have a seismic effect on our world. Massive floods, earthquakes, rivers of molten lava. We're talking End Times-type stuff."

"So the White Dragon has to be stopped," I said numbly, thinking about Daniela and Team 5. "No matter what."

"Yes, which also means I'm no longer on the sidelines," Croft said.

"Is there someone from your Order in that area who could head him off?"

"Unfortunately, our most powerful are pretty far flung at the moment—some in other dimensions—trying to stitch the fabric back together. It's a coordinated effort. Super delicate. Diverting their power elsewhere could have the same effect as the collapse of the Guardians' realm. Or worse. The magic-user I'm in contact with is working to pinpoint the White Dragon's location."

"Is that something you can attempt?"

"Not without some material off him. Something cellular would be the most potent—hair, blood, a scale—but anything that his essence might have rubbed off on could also work."

I thought for a moment before shaking my head. I didn't have anything like that. My one encounter with him had been almost three days ago, and I hadn't taken anything during the raid on his fortress. "But if Stanick is telling the truth, I guess we already know where he is," I said darkly. "Or at least where he's headed."

Meaning I was staring at mission failure.

"Why didn't Stanick have you killed tonight?" Croft asked.

The question was so pointed that I turned to face him. The light from his staff cast long shadows down his face and gleamed from his intelligent eyes. In the aftermath of my encounter with Stanick, and with silver poisoning my system, I had been thinking only of how to spare Daniela and Team 5. But that was a good question.

Why *hadn't* Stanick killed me tonight?

I thought back to our mission the week before. My orders had been to kill General Zarbat and capture Elam, the Mujahideen leader with whom he was colluding. That was usually the way our missions went. Shoot to kill unless the enemy possessed something useful. But what did I have that was useful to Stanick?

"I think the answer goes back to the Kabadi belief system," Croft said. "The blood and vital organs of those descended from a Guardian are potent—especially to someone from the line of an *opponent* Guardian. The fresher the blood and organs, the more potent the effect."

"Nafid mentioned the long line of warriors the White Dragon had consumed in battle. She also explained that the Kabadi buried their dead in a deep crypt to prevent dragon shifters from stealing them, presumably for the White Dragon."

"Which was probably how he grew so powerful," Croft said. "Now imagine how much *more* powerful he'd become if he could consume the one who embodied the qualities of the Great Wolf."

"The Blue Wolf," I said in understanding. Which may have explained why the White Dragon kidnapped and tortured Nafid's great-grandmother all those years ago.

He'd wanted her to bring the Great Wolf into the world. She refused and escaped. "So you think the White Dragon is still in the city?"

"If there's one thing a dragon values over wealth, it's power. The thought of being able to consume you, to increase his power two or threefold, would pound like an incessant drum in his head. The urge would be overwhelming. Knowing you're here—and vulnerable? Yeah, he hasn't gone anywhere."

I nodded, remembering the way the White Dragon had stared down at me in the village when he realized what I was. The hunger and fascination that had filled his moonlit eyes.

"I surprised him at Bashi's tonight," I said, integrating Croft's information with the sequence of events. "After his escape, he and Stanick had time to plan. Stanick knows my commitment to Daniela and my team, so he uses it to force my surrender. Not to euthanize me, but to incapacitate me and turn me over to Orzu. Back in Waristan, Orzu consumes me as the White Dragon and finishes off the rest of the Kabadi at his leisure. He would no longer even need an army."

"I think you're on point with all of that," Croft said. "Where did Stanick tell you to turn yourself in again?"

"Fort Bell," I said. "Stanick said it had been partially decommissioned, but I'm pretty sure it's out of service." Which made sense. Stanick wanted to keep his fingerprint as small as possible. He had already taken a risk by getting his security detail involved. Of course there was enough strange shit in New York that they probably weren't asking too many questions.

"Is Fort Bell a big place?" Croft asked.

"Huge," I answered. "It's also secure. A good place to keep Orzu safe."

"We can go back to my place to see if my hologram is picking anything up over there. Might be able to hone in on an exact location."

As I pulled on my trench coat, I was already doing the initial mission planning in my mind. We would have a little over an hour to set something up. "I'm going to need to know every magical feat you can pull," I said. "Especially those that involve accessing a military base."

"I can run through them on the way."

"You can begin by getting us out of here unseen."

An impish grin spread over Croft's face as he lifted the paper bag he'd dropped and gave it a little shake. "Good thing I just went shopping." He peered into the bag, looking like a kid about to show off his Halloween haul. "Oh, Mr. Han wanted me to give you this."

He pulled out a plastic bottle, a swampy green liquid fizzing inside, and handed it to me. Recognizing it as the "energy juice" that came with the rent, I started to pitch it into the trash can before Croft stopped me.

"Wait, wait, Mr. Han's a master at that particular brew. Potent stuff. It taste's nastier than stale piss, but it will restore your strength like that." He snapped his fingers. "I'd hold onto it."

I grunted and slipped it into my trench coat.

"First up," Croft said, digging back into the bag, "a projection spell."

The spell involved me standing in a circle of copper filings while Croft chanted and strange currents moved throughout the room. He finished with a shouted word, and I found myself staring at an exact likeness of myself. I snarled on reflex, but my likeness showed no reaction to my presence. Instead, he began walking aimlessly around the room.

"He's not material, just a temporary reflection of you," Croft explained. I passed a taloned hand through him as he walked past us. "The projection will hold up for about thirty minutes, which will convince anyone watching that you're still in here. As for us..."

He signaled me to stand beside him and raised his cane in front of him. *"Oscurare,"* he uttered. The stone in the staff went dark, but it didn't stop there. The stone drew in the ambient light around Croft until he was hard to see, even with my wolf vision. I noticed the same darkness concealing me as well.

"Works on infrared and night vision too," Croft said.

He opened the door behind him and signaled for me to go first. I passed through the doorway, my pack and M4 slung over the same shoulder. He followed. Aiming his cane back through the cracked-open door, he spoke another word. Inside, I heard the mattress flop to the floor.

"The illusion is complete," he whispered, closing the door.

We descended the steps quietly and slipped out the front door. I kept waiting for the suppressed cough of a sniper's shot, but the darkness concealed us like a glove. We made it to the taxi and climbed into the backseat. Croft restored the engine and instructed Kumar to drive us back to his apartment. The cabbie, who appeared resigned to his fate, drove in silence.

I peered around to make sure we weren't being followed, then nodded at Croft.

"Right, the magical things I can do..." the wizard said, and began going down the list.

We pulled in front of his apartment twenty minutes later and hurried up the three flights to his unit. As Croft triple-bolted the door behind us, Tabitha yawned and shifted her giant bulk on a divan.

"Still knocking around with the wolfman, I see," she muttered.

I ignored the remark and turned to Croft. I hadn't been able to stop thinking about Stanick's threat against Daniela, and now I knew what I had to do. The decision made, the final piece of the mission plan clicked home.

"While you check the hologram, I need to make a call," I said. "Then I'll lay out the plan. If the White Dragon is where we think he is, I know how this is going to go."

27

My body jostled heavily in the backseat as the cab slowed, then came to a stop. A powerful light glared against my closed eyelids—the spotlight at the gate. I listened as the driver side window powered down.

"Oh, yes, hello?" came the cabbie's distressed voice.

"Who are you?" a soldier's voice barked. "This is a restricted area."

"Oh my God. It horrible."

"What's horrible?" the soldier demanded.

"This man ask me drive him here, then he, I don't know, he stop talking, stop breathing, I think."

A scuff of soles, and another light glared over my closed eyes.

"I need you to step out of the vehicle with your ID."

"Yes, yes," the cabbie said quickly.

The door opened and the cabbie stumbled out. Following the soldier's inspection of his ID, I heard the telltale signs of a pat down.

"Sit right there, and don't move," the soldier said.

"Yes, I sit."

I heard the breathing of two soldiers, one on each side of the vehicle. I had to imagine their faces and pointed weapons—probably M4s or SCARS. I could smell the chambered rounds of silver.

While one of the soldiers covered me, the other opened the trunk, rifled through it, and slammed it closed. Footsteps rounded the cab, then stopped as the soldier knelt to inspect the underside of the vehicle. The hood went up next before dropping again with a bang that shook the cab.

Now the backseat door opened. A glare hit my face, then fell away. I could almost feel the subtle heat of the flashlight playing around my feet, shining into my open coat, and then lingering on my bloody shoulder before returning to my head. A hand unwound my scarf, removed my hat, then seized the top of the bandage mask and pulled it away. Following a muttered curse of revulsion, the soldier shone his flashlight over my slack-jawed face, searching for the least flicker of life.

At last a dry swallow sounded. The soldier came nearer, and two fingers dug through the hair on the side of my throat in search of my pulse. A sour fear radiated from the pores of his hand. After several seconds, the soldier withdrew quickly and slammed the door.

"Your man just arrived in a taxi," he radioed, "but he's cold and got no pulse."

"What do you mean 'no pulse'?" Colonel Stanick's militant voice answered.

"He's slumped out in the back of the taxi, blood all over his coat, and he's not breathing or beating. He's DOA, sir."

Stanick swore. "How long has he been like that?"

The soldier posed the question to the cabbie.

"I not know ... ten minute?" the cabbie answered.

"The driver says ten minutes," the soldier reported.

I picked up bits of broken dialogue from Stanick's end before he said, "Bring him in here right away."

"What about the cab driver, sir?"

I felt my ears try to cock toward the radio, but under Croft's cataleptic spell, I couldn't move. How easy or difficult our mission would become hinged on Stanick's response.

"Just hold him there until we're done."

Something inside me unclenched. Right answer.

"Yes, sir." The soldier then addressed his partner. "I'll take him through if you want to babysit Apu over there." I heard a clunk of metal and pictured the security gate sliding open.

"You a hundred percent sure he's a stiff?"

"Look at him. He's not breathing. He's got no pulse."

"Yeah, but a bullet through the head would remove all doubt."

"Hey, hey!" the cabbie called. "I drive twenty mile. Who going to pay me?"

"Sit your ass back down!" the soldier who'd proposed shooting me shouted.

"He's all yours," his partner snorted. The cab rocked as he landed in the driver seat and slammed the door behind him. The cab started forward, gaining speed down the main drive of the decommissioned base.

That's right, I thought. *Deliver me straight to the White Dragon.*

After a couple of turns, the cab stopped. The back doors opened, and I picked up five new smells.

"Stanick wants him inside right away," one of the new soldiers said.

Hands grabbed me roughly by the arms and coat and hauled me out onto asphalt. I landed hard on my back, arms flopping out to the sides. After removing my coat, and patting down my pants for anything bulky, the soldiers took a moment to arrange themselves before one lifted me under the shoulders and two more grabbed a leg each. I heard the soldier who had driven me running ahead of us, opening doors. The two remaining soldiers covered me with weapons that bore the now-unmistakable scent of silver.

"Ugly sonofabitch," one of the soldiers carrying me grunted.

"Stanick said he's some sort of mercenary who needed to be eliminated."

"Put down is more like it," a third soldier said. "Though looks like someone beat him to it."

We took a right, and the acoustics changed; the men's breaths and footfalls suddenly echoed from distant walls. Wooden boards creaked underfoot. We were in the gymnasium. I remembered running suicides in here as part of my training stint.

"Set him right there," Stanick said.

I was dropped onto a large cot, where I lay stiffly, rigor mortis beginning to set in.

"Back to your posts," he ordered the men.

Amid a chorus of *yes sirs* their footsteps retreated. The men's scents swirled behind them and diminished. Now only four remained: two men up in the stands, whose weapons marked them as snipers, Colonel Stanick, and the strong, reptilian scent of Orzu, the White Dragon.

Human footsteps approached at a rapid clip, and the White Dragon's scent grew stronger. "Idiot!" he cried. "Why did you shoot him? You told me the threats would bring him here."

"Yes, but Jason can be very prudent. I felt I needed to drive the point home." For the first time, Stanick sounded unsure of himself. "And didn't you tell me the silver would only be lethal if it struck a vital organ?"

"Or leeched into his bloodstream," Orzu shot back.

"Well, he's here now," Stanick said. "I've delivered him."

"Yes, *dead*. Meaning I derive almost nothing."

"Dead or alive, I've fulfilled the original agreement. The valley is yours now."

"I don't care about the valley right now!" Orzu erupted. "Oh, don't worry, you'll get your precious payment. I am a person of my word. But I won't forget this slight, white man."

"I-I'm sorry," Stanick said.

"Leave me. And take your men. I may still be able to siphon off the pittance that's left," he grumbled. It was the voice of a man who had just seen the value of his stock portfolio triple and then flatline in the same day.

But as Stanick and the snipers paced off and the doors closed behind them, I was hit by the first stab of doubt. Though Orzu was near enough for me to reach up and snap his neck, I remained paralyzed, the ache of rigor mortis from the cataleptic spell spreading through me still. And that was the problem—everything had progressed too quickly. Orzu intended to consume me here.

I was entirely dependent on Croft now.

"Stupid idiot," Orzu muttered, still thinking of Stanick.

I could hear him fussing with something beside me before I picked up the unmistakable sound of a blade sliding from a leather sheath. From a numb distance, I felt the cold metal pressing into my neck. He would drink my blood first, then extract my organs.

A pair of gunshots echoed from the corridors outside the gym, and the blade paused.

The gymnasium doors banged open. *"Vivere!"* a voice gasped.

Life returned to my body in a burst of heat, and my eyelids popped open.

I had imagined the human version of the White Dragon to be lithe and powerful, much like his reptilian counterpart. But the man holding a dagger to my neck was short and round with thinning gray hair combed into a ponytail. He wore a black suit, the jacket embroidered with dragon patterns, his shirt collar open to a hairless chest and a white gold chain. As I drew an arm back, I had the feeling our final confrontation was going to be short and sweet.

Orzu's jowly face had slackened at the intrusion, but when his pale eyes fell to mine, his jowls clenched with fresh determination. Before he could drive the dagger home, I brought my arm forward. The punch collapsed his paunch and drove him from midcourt to one of the three-point lines.

Orzu landed hard on his back, the dagger clattering away from his outflung arm.

With a groan, I heaved my still-heavy legs over the side of the cot, pausing as the gymnasium swooped and spun.

"Here!"

I turned to find the cab driver running toward me, now wearing the uniform of the soldier who had stayed to watch him. But Kumar's face and form were melding back into Prof Croft's as the transmogrification spell left the wizard's system. He tossed me the bottle of Mr. Han's energy juice.

"It'll act as a catalyst," he said.

"The soldiers?" I asked as I caught the bottle and unscrewed the cap.

"All detained in a holding circle. I didn't bump into Stanick, though."

I chugged down the sour, burning concoction, then tossed the bottle away. "Find him. We can't let him leave the base."

Everson nodded and spun back toward the doors, an energy shield taking shape around him. I stood and stalked toward Orzu. Mr. Han's juice had already cleared my head, and now it was working on my limbs, injecting fresh fuel into the reviving muscles.

Orzu rose onto the seat of his pants and blinked several times. When his eyes steadied, he began kicking himself backwards, the heels of his shiny black shoes scuffing the court.

"H-hold on, Texan," he stammered.

I stooped for the ornate dagger, picked it up, and flipped it in my hand. I would have preferred a clean pistol shot, but this was the next best thing. I didn't want to soil my muzzle or talons.

"We can talk."

I narrowed my yellow eyes at the man who had murdered Parker. "There's nothing to talk about," I growled.

Orzu rolled onto his hands and feet and tried to scramble away. I stepped on his right ankle, bones crunching as I placed my full weight on him. The fat man howled in pain. Without comment or ceremony, I eyed the spot on his back where his heart would be and brought the knife down.

The tip punched through the fabric of his jacket, then smashed into something solid. The blade snapped at the hilt and clanged away.

He wearing some kind of body armor?

Digging my talons into the center of his back, I tore his jacket and shirt away. Not body armor. Orzu's skin had solidified into a mosaic of white scales that were growing and spreading. The son of a bitch was shifting. But how? We were thousands of miles from his place of origin.

I lost my footing as his body bulged and lengthened. And now wings were erupting from his back along with a spiny crest that thickened into dense plates along his spine. As the wings spread and batted to life, I leapt forward and seized the still-shifting dragon around his throat with both arms.

There was no way in hell I was letting him get away.

The White Dragon chuckled. "Surprised?"

The muscles in my arms trembled as I squeezed harder. I noticed his throat scales were no longer leathery, but hard, as though his growing neck now featured additional armor. With a thrust of his wings the White Dragon lifted off, tail lashing through his falling clothes.

Don't know how I mistook his nephew for him, I thought as I clung to his neck. *So much larger, more powerful.*

"Yes, I kept a special dragon form in reserve. In the event of emergencies."

The White Dragon circled the court once, then shot toward a large semi-circular window at one end of the gym. With an explosion of glass we were through and climbing over the decommissioned base. I grunted as my back healed from several deep cuts, and redoubled my grip.

"But honestly, there is no one more surprised than me," he said. "Here I thought your colonel had blundered the whole affair. But look at you, as full of vim and verve as a young dog."

If I can't get to his neck, going to have to try his eyes.

But when I dug my talons into the edge of protective plating over his right eye, he twisted, nearly pitching me off. Swearing, I wrapped his neck and held on as the wind blasted against me. Alone in the air, he would have the advantage. I would be vulnerable to his ice attack on the ground.

But what in the hell could I do to him up here? I spat out another curse.

The White Dragon laughed. "Is that distress I hear? There are no helicopters to help you this time. No missiles. You brought a friend, I see, but my new form is impervious to magic—a special gift from the Guardian herself. One time use, but I plan to make the most of it. And after tonight, I will be equal in power to the Great Dragon. A god on earth. It's a pity the crazy old woman involved you in this, but she has given *me* exactly what I want."

He climbed as he spoke, the air growing colder and colder as the base dwindled into the lights dotting Long Island. Before long, I was gasping for oxygen.

But the White Dragon began to slow. With a final flap, he tucked his tail and thrust his head down, and I found myself squinting past his ear to the black expanse of Long Island Sound.

"It's just a matter of getting you off my back and into my mouth."

He pinned his wings to his sides, and we dove like a plummeting mortar toward the water.

28

Long Island Sound spiraled closer and closer until we were slamming into it. The impact shot through me like a monster dose of Novocain, and everything went numb.

I recovered to the sensation of frigid, foaming water ramming up my nostrils and down my throat and the awareness that I was no longer holding the White Dragon. I flailed and kicked, until I saw the moon's pale glimmer through the boiling water and used it as my guide. But the force with which we'd hit was still driving me down, and I could feel the White Dragon somewhere beneath me, his mass and velocity creating a powerful suction.

I bared my teeth and drove my arms against the drag and pull, kicking with everything I had. The suction effect was abating, but that only meant the White Dragon was slowing, about to come back up. I pictured him climbing toward my flailing legs, his jaws open...

My head broke the surface with a ragged gasp, and I hacked and squinted through the salt water streaming from my hair. I spotted Fort Bell along the shoreline, but we had landed a good quarter mile from it. Still coughing, I put my swimming training to use and surged toward it. I needed to get to land before the dragon spotted me.

At that thought, the water around me began to bubble. I stroked harder, but when I peered into the black depths, I could see the moonlight flickering over a growing luminescent form.

Not gonna make it, I thought, even as I tried to speed up. *Gonna have to fight him in the water.*

"Wolfe!"

My ears cocked toward the distant voice—Croft's.

"The raft!" he shouted.

When I slowed to try to see what he was talking about, something thumped me in the side of the head. I turned to find a ten-by-ten-foot platform of weathered boards over a thick slab of barnacle-encrusted Styrofoam. Croft had evidently unmoored the raft and sent it out to me.

I wasted no time hauling myself aboard. "I'm on!" I called back.

Like a hundred horsepower motor had been strapped to the rear of the raft, it tipped back and took off toward shore. In our wake, the water continued to bubble and froth—and then the White Dragon burst up like a geyser.

He climbed thirty feet above the surface, water raining from his giant wings. His neck telescoped as he peered around, white fire burning in the depths of his eyes. When he spotted me, pleasure drove his mouth into a sharper grin.

I glanced toward the approaching shore. *C'mon, Croft.*

With powerful wing thrusts, the White Dragon lowered his head and sped toward me. A series of grunts boomed from his chest, and in the next moment a frosty blast plumed from his mouth. I could hear the swells of water behind me crackling into ice. I edged toward the front of the raft as the frigid attack billowed nearer. I could see Croft on the other side of the base's security fence, at the edge of a mock town used for urban-warfare training.

The cover of buildings would be good—if I could get there.

As the plume drew nearer, my wet fur stiffened into a crunching cast and my teeth chattered violently. The raft was gaining speed, though, its flat bow breaking through the skein of ice spreading over the water.

A hundred yards from shore, the White Dragon's head appeared through the dissipating frost and lunged, ears pinned, bone-white teeth gleaming. I reared back an arm, planning to land a hammer blow to his snout, but something seized me around the waist. With a sharp yank, I was shooting through the air.

The White Dragon's head descended, and the raft I'd been standing on burst into splintered planks and chunks of Styrofoam. Docks passed beneath me, then land, and soon I was over the perimeter fence and descending into a jumble of concrete and plaster buildings. The force that had propelled me now set me gently beside a police station in the mock town.

"Over here," Croft whispered.

I turned to find him in an alleyway beside the police station, light fading from the etched symbols in his sword. I hurried over to join him.

"Did you find Stanick?" I panted, cold water pooling around my feet.

Croft shook his head. "I gave up the search when I

heard the commotion back in the gym." I swore inwardly, but it was out of my hands. "I thought you said Orzu couldn't assume his dragon form."

"That was the intel I received," I said. "Apparently his Guardian keeps a form in reserve for special occasions, one that can travel. It features extra armor and is resistant to magic."

While Croft frowned in thought, I listened for the dragon.

"With the amount of energy a form like that would take to sustain," the wizard said at last, "especially over distance, I'm guessing it has a short shelf life. It might just be a matter of waiting him out."

"Doubt he's going to lay down till that happens."

"That's actually a good thing."

"How is that a good thing?" I growled.

"The more energy he expends, the faster the process."

I nodded in understanding. That *was* a good thing. "So it's a matter of staying one step ahead of him," I said, "making him wear himself out."

"And though he may be impervious to spells, he'll still be susceptible to invocations."

"Not that I know the difference, but I hope you're right 'cause he's coming."

I'd been listening to him flap above the water, circling in search of me, but he must have picked up my scent, because now he was driving in full bore. I would have given anything to test his armor with a sustained assault from a Ma Deuce. But save for the rifles belonging to Stanick's security detail, the base was weaponless. And the rifles wouldn't get it done.

"It's me he's after, so I'll play the mouse," I said quickly.

"I just need you to throw interference—as much as you safely can—but try to stay out of his sight. His ice breath is lethal."

"Roger that," Croft said, drawing the shadows of the building around him.

The gusts of the approaching dragon grew in intensity, making the flag in front of the police station rustle and snap. Nafid's great-grandmother had foreseen this moment somehow.

I reached into a pocket in my camo pants and pulled out the small wooden cube on its leather strap. She had given me the cube for a reason. I looked at the inscriptions in the wooden faces, half expecting to find them glowing with power like the symbols in Croft's sword had been a moment before, but the deep scratchings appeared as inert as ever.

I tied the ends of the thong around my neck anyway and stepped out into the street.

The White Dragon was coming in low, the weight of his tail knocking through a section of concrete-block wall that surrounded the mock town. When he spotted me, his grin steepened again, but there was a hardness there now.

"You are a *stubborn* one, Texan."

"I could say the same about you."

I waited until he was a half block from me before darting past a café and down a side street. The White Dragon slipped behind me like an eel. As I bounded down the street, I could hear his body cleaving between the old cars parked along the sides of the street, flinging their smashed and shattering bodies into the sides of buildings.

"Death or madness, Texan," the dragon called. "Not much of a choice, really."

At the end of the block I took a hard left, then another. Though it had been several years since my training here, the layout of the mock town remained etched in my mind. There were a few dead ends to avoid, but otherwise the streets were mine for running the dragon ragged.

It already seemed to be working. Tiring of the chase, the White Dragon climbed back above the town. Hearing the telltale grunts of an impending ice attack, I bounded toward the blue-domed mosque in the town square. I cleared the steps and broke through the front door. Chased by a blast of frost that spread into an icy veneer over the arabesque tiles of the entranceway, I slid for several feet before reaching unfrozen floor again, the pads of my soles burning with cold.

I was barely staying ahead of him, but I remembered what Croft said: every attack cost the dragon energy.

For the first time, he screeched in frustration, the sound like spikes in my ears. Plaster began raining down in chunks. When I peered up, I could see talons punching through the roof. The dome tore away with a violent roar and crashed into the square outside. My brief glimpse of the night sky was occluded by a pair of wings, followed by another storm of deadly frost.

The edge of the blast caught my right leg as I burst out the back door. The pain was immediate, biting deep into my marrow. I staggered out onto a back street. From the top of the mosque the White Dragon raised his head, eyes glinting as he recognized my weakness.

I bounded hard, the lame leg healing but not quickly enough. Each time I planted the foot, it felt like broken glass was being ground into the muscles. Behind me, the White Dragon began to grunt. I took a hard right, but he was above the buildings again. I searched both sides of the street for a door. Nothing. I must have looked like a mouse in a maze to the White Dragon as his grunting grew. He wouldn't miss this time.

"*Fuoco!*" Croft shouted.

A jet of fire seared through the night. I looked over my shoulder in time to see it explode around the White Dragon. He reared in surprise, coughing out his gathering ice blast in a cloud of wet vapor.

I made the next street, where there were plenty of doors to duck inside. But I slowed, my gaze backtracking along the trail of smoke until it reached Croft. He'd come out into the open to invoke the fire that had spared me, and though he was retreating into the shadows again, the White Dragon had spotted him. With a pair of sharp wing strokes, the dragon changed course.

"Meddler!" he screamed.

I turned and raced toward them. "Hey!" I shouted. "It's me you want!"

But the White Dragon's hatchet face was aimed at Croft. His throat convulsed with a fresh series of grunts. Croft barely had time to shout in alarm before the white plume swallowed him. My heart thundered in my chest.

When the frost cleared, Croft was a hoary statue, one foot pinned to the street in a running stance, the other poised toward the next step he'd never take. An image of Parker as I'd last seen him flashed through my mind.

"So much for your *assistance*," the White Dragon hissed, turning toward me.

But I had leapt and seized the end of his tail. With a roar, I swung him through the market stalls and into a two-story municipal building. The building crumbled on impact, concrete bricks crashing over him. I bounded toward him. My horror at Croft's fate was burning through what remained of the wolfsbane potion, leaving only blind animal rage.

Before the dragon could lift his head, I was on top of him, hands snapping the long, slender bones of his wings, foam-lathered fangs tearing into the leathery fabric. The dragon thrashed and kicked, screeches of pain renting the air. When his throat began to convulse around fresh grunts, I seized his mouth in a wrestler's hold and began punching him in the side of the head. If I couldn't exhaust his dragon form, I would beat all hell out of it.

And damned if it's not working, I thought from a distance.

The white flames in the orbs of his eyes were thinning, fading.

A shot cracked. My ribs blew open on the right side, and I toppled backwards into a pile of broken bricks. Panting, I craned my neck to see Stanick approaching from the far side of the square, smoke drifting from the barrel of an M16.

I tried to push myself up but collapsed again. When I looked down, I could see my liver glistening through my wounded torso. He'd hit me with a hollow-point round laced with silver.

"He's down," Stanick called. "Take him!"

The White Dragon rose, shaking the brickwork from his body. He flexed and extended his wings several times, the broken bones snapping back together, the torn leather fusing into faint scars. The white fire climbed back into his eyes as he peered down from his lengthening neck.

"Well done, white man," he said to Stanick without moving his gaze from me. "I recant what I said about you earlier. Consider us back in business." A slippery tongue emerged to lick the dragon's salivating lips.

I tried to back away, but his front leg came down, pinning my torn torso. I grunted in pain.

"I'm truly sorry, Texan. Fate cast you and your friends on the wrong side of the war. *You*, most of all. Under different circumstances, I might have considered you for a security position."

In a dim tribute to my childhood friend, I threw my head forward and spit in his face. The White Dragon began to grin, but as my head dropped back to the bricks, the cube over my chest shifted, drawing his gaze toward it. His grin faltered, and the flames in his eyes wavered.

Fear?

He recognized the cube, the object Baba said had spared her. But if he was resistant to magic, why should he fear it? As the almond odor emanating from the wood reached my nostrils, the answer hit me.

It wasn't what the cube could do—it was what the cube contained. And though I'd never smelled the exact scent before, I'd heard about it during lectures on chemical warfare agents.

I brought both hands to the cube and tugged and twisted.

The White Dragon thrust his mouth down in an attempt to stop me, but not before the cube's bottom released and I was holding the end of a short spine infused with concentrated cyanide—the poison I had been smelling.

His teeth crunched around my wrist. With a grunt, I rotated the hand and thrust the spine into his pale tongue.

The White Dragon stiffened, eyes wide. In the next

moment he was shrinking back to his flabby human form. Hissing through pain, I seized him and spun on one knee so he was covering my body.

Stanick, who had been poised to shoot again, raised his head slightly.

"He's paralyzed, not dead," I growled. "But if you want to finish the job, go ahead."

"Aren't you forgetting something?" Stanick called.

"What's that?"

"Your girlfriend? Your teammates?" He pulled out a cell phone and held it up. "I give the word, and one's dead and the rest are ruined. Is that what you want?"

The pain goring my side was making me see spots, but as a distant sound entered my hearing, I managed to grunt out a laugh. "The problem with you, Stanick, is you always sucked at reading people. Your assessments were all over the map. I was just too professional to say anything."

"I'm serious, Jason."

"Oh, you were right about my loyalty to Daniela and my teammates," I continued, the thumping sound continuing to swell in my hearing. "I'd do anything to protect them. Die for them, even."

"Release him, Jason, and the deal still stands."

"You didn't count on me taking a hard right, though. You figured that for Captain Jason Wolfe, committed U.S. soldier, there were avenues I wouldn't consider, moral boundaries I wouldn't cross."

Stanick could hear the arriving choppers now too. He craned his neck around before returning his apprehensive gaze to me.

"What did you do?" he demanded.

"I called in the mercenaries."

The four black choppers swooped down, flooding the intersection where he stood with spotlights. "Colonel Stanick," a voice echoed from the loudspeaker. "This is Centurion United's Enforcement Division. You're under arrest for the killing of Centurion associate Baine Maddox, pursuant to Article Four, Section Eight-Two of the Public-Private Cooperative Defense Agreement. Lay down your weapon." Gunmen leaned from the bay doors with rifles. "I repeat, lay down your weapon, or you will be shot."

Stanick stared around at the hovering choppers, his gray hair whipping in the rotor wash. He made a decision then. Setting his mouth in a determined line, he dropped his rifle and ran. For someone who had always appeared dignified, his limbs kicked from his body in an ungainly dance. He made it all of ten feet before a wall of light flashed in front of him.

Stanick struck it face first and collapsed onto his back, out cold.

"What did I miss?" Croft asked, rounding a corner, his staff dimming.

Relief poured through me. I started to move toward him before realizing I was still holding the paralyzed body of the White Dragon. I lowered my grizzled muzzle to his ear.

"The thing about Texans," I whispered, "is that we like to settle up the old-fashioned way."

I snapped his neck and slung his corpse aside.

29

As two of the helos set down in the square, Prof Croft hustled over to meet me.

"How did you survive the ice blast?" I called, the words thick in my mouth. My right elbow was pinned to my side, trying to hold in the shredded tissue, but blood was soaking into my camo pants in a torrent.

"Why don't we worry about you right now, tough guy," Croft said, arriving in front of me. "Let's take a look." He helped me lift up my arm, then drew his breath in sharply. "All right, this is going to sting a little."

I stared above his head to where men in black uniforms were emptying from the helos and aiming their rifles at Stanick, who was still down. Croft uttered a word as he passed a hand over the wound. The silver-infused bullet fragments tore free, but there was already so much pain, I hardly felt it. He then seemed to speak to his staff until the embedded stone pulsed with white light. The light wrapped my wound like gauze, sedating the pain. When I looked down, the ribs were reconstructing themselves, tissue growing back in healthy layers.

"I invoked a shield," Croft said, straightening.

"Huh?" I blinked, groggy from the healing magic.

"That's how I survived the ice blast. An instant before it hit me, I invoked a shield. But with the temperature differential, the shield shrunk over my body like cellophane. It was enough to insulate me, but it took a while to form the word to disperse it." He moved his jaw around, as though still trying to loosen it up.

"I'll take your word for it," I said, clapping his shoulder. "Just glad you're still with us, buddy."

Croft looked from Orzu's body to where the Centurion agents were dragging Colonel Stanick toward one of the choppers. "So I guess this is mission accomplished then, huh?"

I stared at Croft for a moment. Parker had said something almost identical not too long ago.

Before I could answer, one of the Centurion agents came trotting over. He was middle aged with a serious face and white hair at his temples. He studied my wolfish face for a moment before thrusting a hand forward to shake mine. "Captain Wolfe? I'm Agent Dunn, the one in charge of this operation."

I thought back to the moment in Croft's apartment when I had stood by the phone, turning Reginald Purdy's business card over in my hand. A core part of me had rebelled at calling in the mercenaries, but if I wanted to protect Daniela and take down Stanick, Centurion was my best option. When Purdy answered, I detailed Stanick's crimes against Centurion. Purdy assured me that Centurion's forensic technicians would get on it that night. If there had been communications between Stanick and Baine, Centurion would uncover them—and move to apprehend Stanick immediately. I gave them the location of Fort Bell, where Stanick would be.

I also explained how he was using Daniela as leverage. Purdy promised to deploy security agents from Houston to Beaumont. Even had Stanick carried out the threat to make his call, the agents would have nailed his goons before they moved against Daniela. That was my other reason for aligning myself with Centurion—they offered a global reach.

"Thanks for coming," I said to the agent.

"You were right," he said. "Colonel Stanick and Baine communicated through an encrypted network. Stanick promised him a hundred grand for the air strike, then had him arrested and executed. The techs found additional links to drug lords, but that's all being passed on to your military high command."

"Ouch," Croft said. "Sounds like someone's going to be spending his retirement in maximum security."

I nodded as I watched the men load Stanick on to the chopper.

"I understand we're flying you back to Waristan," the agent said to me. "The plane leaves at 0300. We have a helo heading past JFK. We can give you a lift."

"I appreciate that," I said, "but we have a cab to return."

When the agent's brow furrowed in question, Croft added, "We sort of borrowed one from a friend to get here."

Yeah, I thought, *as well as some of his hair to make your potion.*

After casting the cataleptic spell on me, Croft had completed his transmogrification. He'd become Kumar long enough to fool the perimeter guards and for us to gain access to the base. And now Colonel Stanick was in custody and the White Dragon was dead. To that extent, it *was* mission accomplished.

"Well," the agent said uncertainly, "I guess I'll let you two get going, then."

We arrived back at Croft's apartment to find Kumar snoring on the couch and Tabitha flattening her ears in irritation.

"I'll have you know," she said, "I came *this* close to eating his soul."

We awakened Kumar, paid him generously, dropped his keys into his hand, and bid him farewell. As Croft ushered the confused driver out, something told me he was going to take the next couple of days off.

I looked over my blood-matted body. "Mind if I grab a shower?"

"I thought you'd never ask," Tabitha muttered, wrinkling her nose.

"Go for it," Croft said. "Spare towels are in the closet beside the sink."

As I stooped beneath the steaming jet of water, a soup of blood, dirt, and suds swirling around my wolfish feet, I rolled the wooden cube between my fingers. I felt a strange but powerful bond with Nafid's great-grandmother now. She had foreseen my confrontation with the White Dragon and helped me.

I had no way of contacting Nafid—I had taken her satellite phone—so I didn't know the old woman's condition. But something told me she would hold on long enough for me to return, for the *da'vat* ceremony to restore me. Following that, I would spend as long as needed in Waristan to meet with military officers regarding Stanick's activities and to ensure my men were exonerated.

And then I would return home to Daniela.

When I emerged from the shower, my mouth watered at the smell of steak and onions sizzling on the range. Croft was just hanging up the telephone. "Notice anything different about yourself?" he asked.

"Besides feeling like I just lost ten pounds worth of filth?"

His mouth leaned into a smile. "No, your wolf nature. You're controlling it."

Now that he mentioned it... I turned inward. The snarling, bristling presence was still there, but distant, no longer threatening to overwhelm me as it had been for the last several days.

"That was the Order," he said. "With the death of the White Dragon, balance was restored to the twelve Guardians. Orzu's power was warping the polarity between the Great Wolf and Great Dragon. *That* was the reason for your deteriorating control, not the quality of the binding spell."

"So I'm out of danger of succumbing?"

"The Order said intense stress could still lead to episodes of control loss. But as far as a permanent slide...?" He shook his head. "Apparently your particular makeup was a good fit for the Blue Wolf."

I remembered the Great Wolf's insistence that I had been born under his star.

"Look, I know you've got a lot going on," Croft said, walking into the kitchen, "but I'm going to put this out there anyway. What we did tonight is what I do for a living. Protecting our world from interplanar beings, especially the nasty ones. Because of the rips in our world, my Order is outmanned right now. Outwomanned too, but you get the point." The pan sizzled loudly as he flipped the steaks and stirred the onions. "I'm under orders to assemble a team, and I could really use someone with your knowledge and skills."

He was peering at me through the smoke above the range, one eyebrow cocked expectantly. We *had* made a good team tonight. And though a little on the disorganized side, Croft was someone I could definitely see working with again.

"I appreciate the offer," I said. "I really do. But my priorities right now are to my fiancée and team."

Croft nodded in understanding. "I had to ask. I'll give you my number before you go. If the Order can help you in any way, let us know." He snapped off the flames. "In the meantime, let's chow."

I broke into a toothy grin that made Tabitha flinch.

"Hell, yeah."

30

Shaggy sheep scattered in all directions as the Black Hawk descended and set down in the green pasture. It was early, the sun just peering over the mountains along the Wari Corridor to the east. Peach-colored light spread over the orchards destroyed by the dragon's frost. The dead trees had since been removed and replaced with saplings. The same light highlighted the top of a complex of wooden scaffolding that rose around the compound's destroyed buildings.

I allowed a tired smile. The Kabadi would endure.

Several child shepherds watched as I disembarked and strode through the grass toward the compound. Their hair was blue. I waved to them, the next generation of warriors, defenders of the valley.

Ahead, a familiar figure emerged from the compound gate and descended the path toward me. Her headdress and tailored robe were dark, signifying mourning. It wasn't until we arrived in front of one another and I saw the sadness in her green eyes that I knew for sure.

"She passed away," I said.

Nafid nodded. "Early this morning. I'm sorry."

"No, I'm sorry," I said, hugging her gently. I half expected her to resist the gesture, but she gripped my low back and pressed her head against my stomach. For the next minute her body shuddered quietly. She took a moment to wipe her eyes dry before standing back.

"He's gone, isn't he?"

I nodded. "Orzu the White Dragon is no more."

"I felt it. I believe his nephew did too. Ozari killed himself trying to shift."

"And the man who ordered the bombing is being punished."

Nafid lowered her eyes. "Then you have done all you said you would ... and yet, there is no way to hold the *da'vat*, no way for the Great Wolf to restore you. You will remain the Blue Wolf."

I thought about my last mission in Waristan, training and then executing Zarbat, assigning his number two to leadership. My job had been to shift the men like pawns, all in the service of a more powerful agent. And now I had become one of those pawns, a soldier conscripted into a cosmic struggle between the Great Wolf and Great Dragon. I'd never known what to make of karma, but something told me it was staring me in the face.

"I understand," I said. I had braced myself for the possibility.

"Late last night, in her final moment of clarity, Baba announced that the Blue Wolf would protect all. I'm not sure what she meant, but you have a home here if you like. You would be revered."

I looked over the village and lush fields, where the child

shepherds continued to watch me, then around at the steep, thrusting peaks. The place resonated deeply with my wolf nature. For him, this *was* home. But when my eyes returned to Nafid's, she could see that Jason Wolfe would not be staying.

"What will you do?" she asked.

To keep my wolf nature from the military, I had authorized Centurion to act as my legal representation, defending my desertion as a patriotic act to bring Colonel Stanick to justice. They were also going to ensure my men were cleared. Given Centurion's clout, they would have little problem accomplishing either.

But there remained the question of Daniela.

I couldn't return to her like this, a blue-haired creature with two-inch canines. It wasn't that I thought she would reject me—Daniela was too good for that. But if there stood even the slightest chance I might lose control, that the wolf might harm her, then no, I couldn't.

That left two options: Centurion United or Prof Croft and the Order.

Centurion had promised me a year to a cure, but it would mean contracting as a mercenary. A weekend marriage of convenience was one thing—and their legal representation had been offered pro bono—but this would fundamentally change the soldier I thought I was. As for Croft, I could easily see working with him, a wizard fighting the good fight for all the right reasons. But he had put the time to a cure closer to ten years.

I blew out my breath as I met Nafid's soft gaze.

"I guess I have a decision to make."

31

One week later

My heart beat like a bass drum as I stood in a dapple of late afternoon sunlight and knocked on a red door. Inside the house a pair of Weimaraners burst into barking. Their race to the front door was followed by a set of footsteps and calls for them to quiet down.

The lock on the door handle released, followed by the sound of the bolt sliding back. I swallowed and moved the flowers to my other hand. The door opened. She was stooped over, grasping one dog by the collar while moving her yoga pants-clad hips to keep the other one from thrusting past her.

"Daniela," I said.

She raised her face, lips already turned up as though to make a wry comment about her hyperactive dogs, and froze. Loose bangs from her tied-back hair fell across her staring eyes.

I couldn't help but laugh. "Don't I get a hug?"

In the next moment, she slammed the door behind her and threw herself around me. Ankles clasped against my low back, she began kissing me all over my clean-shaven face. I closed my eyes and held her, inhaling the complex odors of her hair and body. At last her lips pressed against mine, something I had been waiting a long time for.

"You big jerk," she said when we separated, giving my chest a thump. "Why didn't you tell me you were home?"

I'd called her from Waristan to tell her everything was all right, that she had nothing to worry about. The situation in New York had been resolved, and I was back in good standing with the military. I hadn't known when I would be home, though. There were things I needed to take care of.

That was before I'd known seeing her as Jason was possible.

"I guess I wanted to surprise you," I said, setting her down and holding out the now-crushed flowers. "These are for you."

She laughed as she accepted them, petals spilling over her bare feet, and grasped my hand. There was something so amazing about seeing my hand—my *human* hand—enveloping hers. My thumb rubbed her fingers and touched the diamond engagement ring.

But when she pulled me toward the house, I couldn't follow.

"You *are* staying, right?" she joked. Seeing my grave eyes, she craned her neck toward the driveway. A black Escalade with tinted windows idled in front of the garage door. "What's going on?"

"My transfer orders came through," I said. "But my work out there isn't quite done. I've signed on for something else in the meantime. Something classified that requires a longish commitment. I'll take leaves as often as I can, but I have no way of knowing when that will be."

Watching the joy drain from Daniela's face was gutting.

"I am so sorry, Dani. But you deserved to be told in person."

"You can't stay for just one night, head out in the morning?"

"God, I would give anything for that," I breathed. "Believe me."

Her hand fell from mine and gripped her opposite arm above the elbow. "But you have to ship out," she said quietly.

"I do."

As she peered past my shoulder, I could see her steeling some inner part of herself as she'd no doubt had to do many times in the last two years. When her eyes returned to mine, they were glistening. "I'm sorry I doubted you in New York. That was wrong of me."

"Hey," I said, reaching toward her. But she held up a hand.

"No, it was selfish and ... and stupid. You told me there was something you needed to do, and that when you were finished you would report back to duty and come home. And look at you. You did exactly that. You're here." Smiling, she clasped the arms of my leather jacket and massaged her fingers into my triceps. "Maybe not for good, but you're here."

I enfolded Daniela in my arms, held her head to my chest, and rocked her gently. "I don't want to be anywhere else."

She nodded against me. "Our problem is that we were born to serve."

That was true of Dani. Whether it was still true of me, I didn't know.

"I'm sorry I yelled at you on the phone," I said. "You of all people didn't deserve that."

"Hush. The only thing I want to hear you say is that you're coming back."

"I'm coming back," I said. "And when I do we're getting married."

She leaned her head away to meet my eyes.

"I love you," I said, beating her to the punch.

She started to respond but then the skin between her eyebrows creased in question. "What's this?" she asked, her fingers tracing the faint scar on my right cheek—the mark of the wolf. A curse? An honor? I wasn't sure how to think about it anymore.

"A commitment," I said at last. "I'll tell you all about it one day."

"Call me when you get where you're going."

"Definitely."

When we kissed again, I felt the wolf stir inside me. It was time to go. At the back door of the idling Escalade, I raised a hand in farewell. Daniela's head tilted as she waved back. I climbed in and the vehicle backed down the driveway, Daniela watching until we were out of sight.

"I'm sorry we couldn't give you more time," Reginald Purdy said from beside me.

The drug had been a mild dose of what Centurion's bioengineering division was developing for me. I had been warned that it remained experimental, highly toxic, and that, at best, I could hope for a few minutes of normalcy. I could already feel my jaw beginning to jut and the itch of returning hair spreading over my back. But to be able to see and hold Daniela ... the risks were worth it.

"I'm just glad it worked," I replied. Besides being able to spend precious moments with her, it gave me hope that Centurion *would* find a cure—and that I would be able to keep the promises I'd just made.

Purdy shifted in the leather seat to face me. In the last week, I'd learned that the man wore nothing but pin-stripe suits. "Sure you want to chance a second dose?" he asked.

Though I could feel the drug's toxicity burning through my system, I nodded. I had one more stop to make, this one in Hawthorne, Florida. Parker's funeral was tomorrow, and his mother deserved a visit from her late son's commanding officer, someone who had considered him a brother and close friend.

And then it was on to Vegas to meet my new team.

"Very well," Purdy said, clapping my knee. "We're just glad to have you on board."

"One year," I reminded him, my voice starting to go wolfish again.

"One year," he assured me, and smiled.

AVAILABLE NOW!

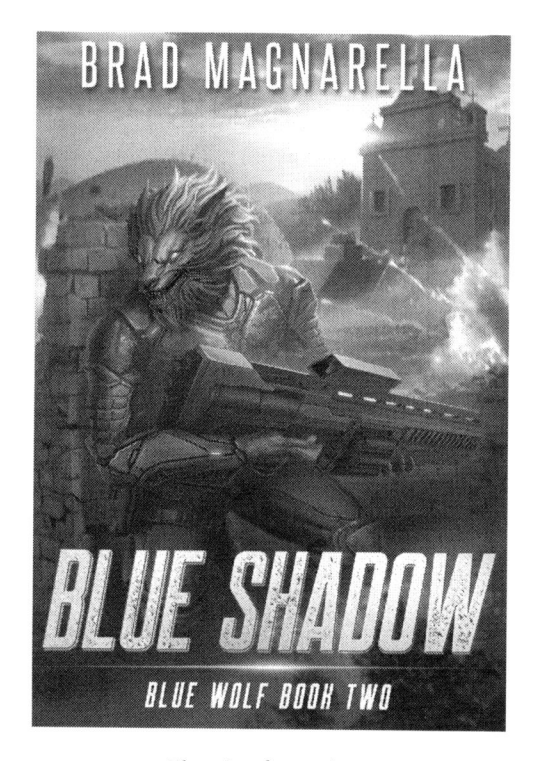

The price of normalcy...

**Blue Shadow
(Blue Wolf, Book 2)**

BONUS CONTENT
THE LAST TEAM TO ENCOUNTER THE KABADI PEOPLE

Waristan, 1985

Commander Bortsov shivered in the blast of wind even as his head felt like it was on the verge of exploding into flames. He took a final swallow of tea from his canteen, forcing it down his burning throat, then resumed pacing, the gravel crunching beneath his boots like old bones.

I'm going to die tonight.

The thought came in a voice that sounded hollowed out, not his own. He wasn't a fatalist. That wasn't the nature of a man who had earned the nickname *Kaban*, "the Boar," for his hard-charging style. In fact, when he had been ordered to this forgotten valley in a forgotten province—a spit in the face, if ever there was—he had rallied his men. "It is far from the fighting, yes," he told them, "but it may become an important conduit for supplies."

It was bullshit, much like the entire Waristan war. But necessary bullshit if he ever hoped to climb the ranks in the

Soviet Army, leaving these kinds of assignments to lesser men.

The assignment had started off well enough. After being dropped, he and his men had discovered a well-positioned hill up the valley and built a stone outpost on top. It was a sound structure, something they had put their healthy backs into and could be proud of. The first night after its completion they had stayed up late inside, drinking, laughing, and playing cards.

But barely three days later, the outpost now held the muffled moans of the dying. And the smells that leaked out? It was as though his men's insides were rotting to liquid and spilling from each end. Grimacing, the Boar turned from the bunker's horrid sounds and smells.

"The boulders," someone muttered. "The boulders are moving."

The Boar looked down to see Yugov, once his most capable marksman, sitting on the edge of the hilltop like a child, his rifle fallen between his splayed legs. Beside his left hip, a puddle of vomit soaked slowly into the rocky ground. The Boar followed Yugov's sweating eyes down into the valley. The quarter moon had cast everything in a deep blue shadow that was not quite black, and a mist drifted in on a chill breeze. A distant wolf's howl went up.

"See there?" Yugov said, raising a shaky finger. "They moved again."

"The boulders are not moving," the Boar replied sternly. "You are seeing things."

He was watching another of his men succumb to delirium. Soon Yugov would join the others inside the stone outpost, what the Boar had come to think of as *the Morgue*. They'd had to carry four men out already. Too weak to dig them graves, the Boar had his men pitch the bodies into a ravine.

"Here," he said, handing Yugov a cigarette. The marksman took it between his shaky lips and crossed his eyes as the Boar lit it for him. But after one puff, the cigarette fell between Yugov's legs in a splash of cinders, and he was back to shivering and babbling about moving boulders.

The Boar turned and called across the hill through the cold wind. "How are you faring, *tovarish*?"

"Freezing and burning," Franko answered.

The Boar arrived to find Franko's Kalashnikov tucked under an arm, hands and chin thrust deep in his coat, forehead shining with sweat. He was shaking, but other than the Boar himself, he was the only one on the team still standing.

"Some security perimeter, eh?" the Boar joked, which made Franko cough out a weak laugh.

Then Franko's mouth straightened. He turned to the Boar and looked at him gravely. The bruising that had begun under his eyes would soon consume his entire face. "We are all going to die, aren't we?"

"We will feel better in the morning."

"It's a curse, isn't it? For what we did to the boy?"

The Boar swallowed around the ragged knot in his throat. "I don't believe in curses."

"How else do you explain it? Right after we leave the village, the dysentery fell like an axe."

The Boar turned his face up the godforsaken valley and saw that morning's patrol in wavering snapshots. The walk through the village and compound, the silence of the strange villagers, the absence of men of fighting age. He'd posed question after question through his interpreter, the lack of responses making his face turn red and spittle fly from his lips.

But what had really set him off was the crazy old woman without eyes. Her twin sphincters of flesh had seemed to glare straight into his soul—stirring the anger he felt at being assigned out here, deepening his sense of impotence. It was as though she were stripping him bare before his men, even as some evil power in her shrieking voice drove him from the compound.

Leaving, the Boar spied a young shepherd bringing a herd of sheep down into the fields outside the village. The blue-haired boy looked back at him casually, without fear. That angered the Boar beyond all reason. He ordered his men to fire. The sight of the boy dropping amid his scattering sheep salved his frustration somewhat.

But Franko was right, the illness had started that afternoon. Not only that, their batteries had died, rendering their communication and night-vision equipment inoperable, stranding them. Yes, it felt very much like a curse. But admitting that would mean assuming responsibility for his dead and dying men.

"Those people must learn to respect our presence," he told Franko.

"The boulders," Yugov wailed behind them. "They're coming up the hill."

Franko fumbled for his Kalashnikov, but the Boar only shook his head. "He is not doing well."

Yugov unleashed a scream that could only come from pain. A wet rip of flesh sounded through the wind. Now the Boar wheeled too. He stared, but could see nothing through the shrouding darkness and mist.

"Stay here," he told Franko.

He led with his Kalashnikov, the crunching beneath his boots reminding him of bones again. Though he tried to steel his nerves, his head pounded with sickness and fear. And now shapes were moving beyond the mist. Was he becoming delusional too? He blinked the cold sweat from his eyes and stared around.

His right boot collided with something. He pitched over Yugov and into a small pond of blood. His marksman's body had been dismembered, ragged sockets for arms and legs, eyes gaping skyward. Behind him, Franko's Kalashnikov fired off a desperate burst, then went quiet.

"Franko?" he called hoarsely.

When the Boar stood, the wind made him stumble. Rubble scraped behind him. He spun and emptied his magazine into the night, the recoil driving him back on quavering legs until he landed against the Morgue.

And now he saw them too.

Yugov had been right, he decided dimly. The shapes did look vaguely like boulders. Three of them stalked toward him from the darkness, taking form as they broke through the mist.

But such things did not exist, the Boar thought in a final fit of reason. *Could not* exist.

A scream warbled from his mouth as he fumbled for his sheathed knife. The first wolfman struck, tearing into his throat with his teeth. The others followed, their savage weight and bloodied blue fur collapsing into him. Beneath the wet snarls, the Boar's hand fell from his knife's hilt.

Yes, I'm going to die tonight...

ACKNOWLEDGMENTS

I had the pleasure and good fortune to work with a solid group in transforming *Blue Curse* from concept to reality.

Big thanks go to my beta and advanced readers; to the talented Ivan Sevic for the cover design and Deranged Doctor Design for the cover titling; to Aaron Sikes for his stellar job editing; and to Sharlene Magnarella for final proofing. Naturally, any errors and/or inelegance that remain are this author's alone.

I also want to thank James Patrick Cronin for his excellent narration of the Prof Croft series and now the Blue Wolf audiobooks. Those books, including samples, can be found at Audible.com.

Last but not least, thanks to my readers for continuing to explore this world with me.

Till next time...

CROFTVERSE CATALOGUE

BLUE WOLF

Blue Curse

Blue Shadow

Blue Howl

Blue Venom

PROF CROFT

Book of Souls

Demon Moon

Blood Deal

Purge City

Death Mage

Black Luck

Power Game

Druid Bond

Night Rune

ABOUT THE AUTHOR

Brad Magnarella is an author of good-guy urban fantasy. His books include the popular Prof Croft novels and his newest series, Blue Wolf. Raised in Gainesville, Florida, he now calls various cities home. He currently lives and writes abroad.

www.bradmagnarella.com

Printed in Great Britain
by Amazon